"All the months are crude experiments out of which the perfect September is made."

Virginia Woolf

THE
September
STANDARD

REGENA BRYANT

WILLOW
BEND BOOKS

Ordering Information: Special discounts are available on quantity purchases for sales promotion premiums, fund-raising, and educational or institutional use. Special book excerpts or customized printing are also available. For details, contact the publisher at Regena@RegenaBryant.com.

ISBN-13: 978-0-9905780-8-6 (paperback)
ISBN-13: 978-09905780-7-9 (ebook)

Printed in the United States of America
First Printing, 2021
Contact us at www.RegenaBryant.com

Dedication

Blest be the ties that bind our hearts to Montgomery. The September Standard is dedicated to the memory of my beloved Sorors Lynn Hill McBroom and Virginia Wilson Steele.

Because of Lynn, we know, "… you can't hoot like an owl all night and expect to soar like an eagle the next day."

And at my son's wedding, I will heed Virginia's sage advice to "wear gray and keep my mouth shut."

From sorrow, toil, and pain, and sin, we shall be free, and perfect love and friendship reign through all eternity.

Bless Be the Ties that Bind
John Fawcett 1782

THE
September
STANDARD

Chapter One

Lord, help me hold my peace.

Regina Lawson repeated her prayer for patience as a snippy hotel clerk dragged out the check-in process. Coming off a relaxing, old-school gospel-fueled praise drive from Montgomery to Birmingham, she refused to let this clerk's bad attitude rile her up. Turning her head slightly to the left, she surveyed the lobby for her son Malik.

Bobbing her head to the music in her mind, Regina sang, "if I hold my peace," until a huff from the desk dragon drew her attention.

"Here go your ID."

She sucked in a woo-sigh breath. "Thank you. Can you ask a porter to assist with my luggage, please?"

The clerk with a long Beyoncé blond mane and multi-colored, striped, acrylic nails snorted. "Then you gonna hafta wait 'till J-Dawg come off his break."

How could anyone lucky enough to have a decent paying job in this economy display so much attitude toward a guest?

Her mother would say, "That gal ain't got the sense God gave a goose." The remembrance of her sainted mother settled Regina's spirit. To avoid snapping back, she bit her tongue. Her mother also taught her to be polite because you never know another person's struggles. An argument at the front desk would not set the right tone

1

for her keynote address at tomorrow's luncheon. She'd already hauled her luggage in from the last space in the parking lot.

I'll make it a few more steps.

"Here go your key." The desk dragon slid the key card across the desk and picked up a blinged-out personal cell phone.

Definitely not worth my peace.

After re-balancing her suitcase, purse, and box of swag, Regina moved away from the check-in desk. A nearby quilted sofa beckoned. She pushed forward, then plopped down on the sofa and whipped out her phone.

Still no text from Malik. No need to call and leave another message. Her youngest son didn't use his phone in the traditional way. When she called, he didn't answer. If she sent a text, he'd ignore it. Even though the only reason her less than reliable man-child was in Birmingham this weekend was to help her. Without his help, she faced a long, slow slog to her room.

Dr. Regina Lawson exhaled, stood and regathered her load. A little anger at her youngest son propelled her forward. As she pulled her things towards the elevators, her right arm throbbed in protest.

Why's Malik so unreliable? So unlike Mr. Smith.

While she rubbed her arm and waited for the elevator, a well-groomed, older man and three young women joined her at the steel-gray doors. The group spoke out of common courtesy. After saying hello, her eyes lingered on the man. He looked familiar. But she couldn't quite place him. Was he a church official? Someone's husband she should remember? Or one of her ex-husband's many associates?

She considered saying something, but the group seemed locked in an animated discussion. The kind where everyone had a point to make. Yet, they kept aware of their surroundings. All she overheard was a bunch of whispered slush.

The man noticed her gaze and nodded. Whatever the issue, he

didn't look like he was going to win, so she flashed him a sympathetic smile. The elevator doors finally opened, and the man offered to help with her luggage.

"What floor, please?" one of the young ladies asked.

"Sixteen, thank you," Regina said before realizing the number was already lit.

As soon as the elevator doors closed around them, she understood why they'd waited so long for the lift. This had to be the slowest elevator in the state of Alabama. The unspoken tension among her ride companions thickened the atmosphere in the small metal box. As the elevator crept past the seventh floor, Regina stifled a yawn and accepted her fatigue. It was way past time for her to lie down someplace.

After teaching this morning, she left her place in Mobile to attend a spiritually draining meeting at Earle Real Estate Holdings in Montgomery. Then spent too much of her evening in the beautician's chair—well at the beauty shop. The corners of her mouth tightened as the elevator inched past the fourteenth floor.

It shouldn't take three hours to get my hair done.

When the doors opened on sixteen, the man helped her out of the lift before heading down the hall with his companions. Her shoulders slumped as she stared at the hotel's directional signage. According to the placard, room sixteen thirty-four was at the end of a long, deserted hall. The last of her gospel glow dissipated as she contemplated the long trek to her room.

"May I assist you further with those bags?"

Regina turned to face the man who'd assisted her moments before. *Is he one of Vic's business contacts? Or fraternity brothers?*

"Have we met?" she asked.

The man extended his hand with a wide smile and said, "Not yet. Name's Dewey and I don't like the idea of a lady wandering these halls alone at this time of night."

Regina shrugged. "This is the Hilton."

"Even in the Hilton, sister. You never know."

She nodded. He seemed harmless. And he had escorted the young ladies to their room and promptly left.

But, surely, he knows them.

"Are you with hotel security?"

The man shifted his footing. "You want the help or not?"

Regina smiled. "I'm grateful for your assistance." She couldn't place him, but there was something familiar about this man. And he looked more like a pastor or politician than a villain. "It's down this hall. I think."

Without announcing her room number, she gripped the handle of her roller bag and allowed Dewey to carry her box. Short of door sixteen thirty-four, she hesitated.

"Tell you what," the kind stranger said. "I'll set your box down here and wait down the hall, at a safe distance, while you get into your room."

Regina Lawson peered into the man's face and read a bit of hurt in his expression. "I'm sorry. You've been very kind." She half-smiled. "Guess I watch too much TV."

Dewey shrugged his shoulders. "I ain't mad at you. With five daughters that travel, I'm always worried about something happening to one of them."

She nodded and softened her posture. "It's not only girls. I have two grown boys and I worry about them constantly. Thank you, again." She opened the door, pushed in her suitcase and dropped her purse. Then pulled back the door latch, so she wouldn't get locked out when she retrieved her box. When she stepped back into the hall, the man took two steps forward. She stepped back.

Dewey flashed a broad showman's smile. "You may know me as DW Thurman."

"Oh, my God. It's you." Her jaw flopped open in amazement. How could she not have recognized DW Thurman? The world-renowned gospel recording artist was her all-time favorite gospel singer. One of his classics kicked off the praise mix for her drive.

"Good." He exhaled. "Since you know who I am, have breakfast with me before I escort you to the opening session tomorrow, Dr. Regina Lawson."

Her eyes widened. "How do *you* know my name?"

DW grinned. "My girls. They got a big kick of out of my not recognizing you, but then again they had me distracted."

If she didn't recognize that she'd just shared an elevator with DW Thurman and The Sisters Fellowship, she must be tired. "I wish they would have said something."

DW Thurman shook his head no. "It's late. We understand that sometimes people don't want to be bothered. But, they did insist I help you with your luggage, and I never protest coming to the aid of a pretty lady."

A wave of excitement raced through her entire being. *DW Thurman knows my name, asked me to breakfast, and called me pretty.* After being married for so long, she wasn't quite sure if DW Thurman had just made a pass at her. *And at my age? I don't care how late it is. I'm calling Rena.* "Okay, but let me treat you to breakfast to thank you for helping me."

DW flashed his hands in surrender. "If that's what it takes. I'll pick you up here at eight-thirty?"

He picked up her box and brought it closer.

"Okay." She giggled like the fangirl she was and reached out to retrieve her box.

After handing over her property, DW Thurman *took* two giant steps backward. In person, he was shorter than she'd imagined and a little older than she remembered. She closed her door under the watchful eye of DW Thurman, dropped the box and screamed.

Dewey Wilson Thurman, the Crown Prince of Gospel Music stood outside of room sixteen thirty-four, at eight twenty-five am, contemplating. Talk about turnabout, women mostly uninvited, too often waited outside of his hotel rooms. He checked his watch, again. For some reason all five of his daughters were in awe of this Dr. Regina Lawson. The three with him last night insisted he help with her luggage and complained when he refused to include them for breakfast this morning.

Dr. Lawson was the hottest new voice on the women's empowerment speaking circuit. Last evening the buzz was all about her keynote speech for today's luncheon. Dr. Lawson struck a high note among the younger women, a demographic he found increasingly difficult to reach. From what he understood there wasn't much new in her message. Just a repackaging of the age-old *sisters live strong and get it done.*

The worth of Lawson's message didn't matter. At this point, he'd break bread with anyone who could get his girls to all agree on anything. And they were solid in their admiration for this Dr. Lawson. But, that wasn't the only reason he invited her to breakfast. Dewey extended his right leg and stretched his achy knee.

The girls had all missed something. How could they not see that Regina Lawson was just his type. Tall, brown skinned, still slim, fashionable chin-length bob of what looked like her real hair. He preferred natural or permed hair to weave. Another argument he wasn't winning with his daughters.

Dewey checked his Presidential Rolex again before knocking. Eight-thirty. On time, but not over eager early—even though he'd been waiting outside this door for ten minutes. Before he fully withdrew his hand, the door flew open and a tall, high-yellow, young man stood titan-like before him.

He stepped back and cleared his throat. "Umm, Dr. Lawson's room? Right?"

A flash of recognition erupted across the young man's face. "Yeah, DW Thurman?"

Dewey altered his stance. "Yes, I am."

"Hey, Mommy. DW Thurman is really here," He yelled back into the room. "I can't believe it. DW Thurman." The door swung open wide in welcome. "Go 'head on in." The younger man extended his hand for a hearty, hand-pumping, shake. "Right on time. She'll like that—real old skool playa."

He hesitated to enter. "Are you sure it's okay? Your mom doesn't know me that well."

"Oh, she knows *you*. It's okay. She told me about breakfast. But, I didn't believe her. I hung around to make sure it wasn't some old troll trying to run game on my Mommy-girl."

Dewey's lips turned down.

As he welcomed him into the suite, the young man continued. "I'm Malik, and it should be interesting. She's not a big, new music fan. But, she loves your old stuff. Hey, Mommy, I'm letting him in and I'm out."

A check in his spirit urged Dewey to stand in the open doorway. Dr. Lawson had been so cautious last night. He frowned for the son who had so casually let him in and left. Dewey's eyes swept the sitting room of the standard hotel suite. An unmade sofa-bed and the remnants of a fast food meal. Malik reminded him of a hundred young men he'd known at Morehouse College. Nice looking, seemingly well-educated, young man purposely speaking urban English to appear cool.

Regina Lawson rushed into the room, shoes in hand. "Um, hello." She scanned the room. "Malik?" she screeched.

"He's already gone."

She shook her head and hurriedly picked up a tossed aside sofa cushion and the greasy, paper food bag. "Excuse us. He doesn't pick up after himself like I ask." She paused for a second, then frowned. "Why would he let you in and leave?"

"It's okay. I'm harmless." He winked. "I see you're one of those St. John-wearing sisters. All right." He nodded in appreciation. "You look regal in deep purple. That knit complements your pretty figure. Why don't you put on those sexy slingback pumps, so we can get going? You can tell a lot about a person by looking at their shoes." Dewey grinned. "And, I'm interested in confirming my first impression of you. So far, I'd say you got a little flare."

She flushed and backed into the bedroom. "I'll be ready in a minute."

Dewey chuckled. She obviously wasn't comfortable bending forward or backward in front of him. Yet.

Chapter Two

"You're DW Thurman," Regina repeated as soon as they were seated in the hotel's restaurant. In person he was a good ten years older than the standard publicity picture floating around on the internet. This DW Thurman was bald with a well-groomed salt and pepper beard. His three-piece herringbone gray suit was expertly tailored and the yellow accents in his tie gave an understated clue to his style. She stared at him in open-mouthed awe. This man was older and even finer than the DW Thurman she'd always admired.

"Yes, and I'm relieved. I second-guessed myself last night because I knew someone as fine as you couldn't truly be on your own. Then I slept like a baby, because I trusted my instinct." He leaned back seemingly satisfied with himself. "I still googled you this morning after I prayed. I didn't want to catch a beatdown for trying to take some pastor's wife out for breakfast." Dewey raised his finger in thought. "No." He chuckled. "Not the pastor. Most of them brothers too holy to fight. But, the good sisters would beat me to death with their convention bags for trying to pick up their first lady."

She covered her nose and mouth with her hand to hide what was probably a teen-aged fangirl's grin. An awkward silence settled around the table as she searched for something to say. "I've always loved your music. And your daughters are The Sisters Fellowship." She gushed.

DW Thurman glanced away.

"Wait a minute," he said as the server poured coffee. "Your son said you weren't a music lover."

Regina shook her head. "Not true. We just disagree on what should be classified as music. I don't care for the negative images and suggestive lyrics in most of the hip hop and other popular songs. Even, I'm sad to say, in Christian music."

Dewey leaned forward. "I wholeheartedly agree. The girls are trying to sell me on a song concept they're calling hip hope. But, I'm not buying into it. And that's what I hoped to ask you about. How is it that you seem to get through to this younger generation?"

Regina froze. The man who wrote the most soul-touching, inspiring gospel songs of her lifetime just asked her how to touch a heart?

"Well…" He leaned forward to command her attention. "What's your secret?"

Startled by the insistence in his tone, she leaned back. "I wouldn't call it a secret. I'm simply telling my story. And trying to encourage young women not to wait to fulfill their dreams."

His left hand flew sideways and hung in the air. "That's it?"

Regina dropped her head and reconsidered the man across the table who she clearly wasn't impressing. "It may sound simplistic, but too often as women we put our dreams on the back burner. We think it's what's best for our families. But I've learned if you're willing to work at it, you can add your own dreams to the equation and still balance it all."

Dewey shook his head in incredulity. "What's this balance business?"

Her lips flattened. *Only a man would ask about balance.* "For many women, balance starts with adding themselves to the equation. It's so easy for women to get so wrapped up in caregiving, we fail to take care of our own needs."

Dewey pushed his back against his chair.

She mirrored his body language and crossed her arms across her chest. "It's not as selfish as it sounds."

Dewey leaned forward. "No, no. I get it. And I don't think it sounds selfish at all. I've matured enough to understand how men kind of let an unbalance occur. Especially, if there's a good woman taking care of him."

She exhaled and leaned in. "Don't get me wrong. I'm not advocating that we don't take care of our men and children…"

"Amen."

"I'm just trying to explain how we can do more through getting a better handle on our time. It starts with a focus on what is most important and establishing your priorities. It's amazing how many of our young people never learned to manage their priorities. Or were not taught the imperative of setting a standard for their lives. Once one is clear on their standard, achievement is just one long, hard, work-filled drive to success."

DW Thurman's head bobbled in agreement. "I love it. That's what I've been missing. The Sisters Fellowship hasn't set their standard." Dewey smacked himself upside the head and blurted, "I've been pushing my standards on them. That's what's not working."

Regina listened as he rattled on about how his girls were struggling to find their place in the gospel genre. A place that went beyond just establishing their public brand, but defined what the Fellowship would and would not do as artists.

"They've been searching to find a sound and message that's more modern than my eighties-era songs, but I'm not trying to go all—is this God or gangster-rap?"

She nodded. "I can hardly tell the gospel from secular music these days."

"It's clear now. I need to step back—a bit, and let the sisters define their sound. Set their standard. No wonder they are so sold on you. Brilliant."

The fangirl in her glowed. DW Thurman called her brilliant.

While he tucked into what could only be called a full breakfast—complete with biscuits and southern gravy, they talked more about modern and church music. Much of which, DW Thurman labeled profanely un-sacred.

DW leaned in and whispered, "Don't let this get out, but I've listened to Country music for years."

She raised an eyebrow at the Crown Prince of Gospel Music.

"It's the lyrics. You ought to try it."

Regina completely enjoyed having breakfast with the gospel great. And he seemed to enjoy her company, too. Well, after she toned down the fangirl stargazing. Their conversation was stimulating, he knew how to use a knife and a fork, and he'd made her laugh more than once with a frisky comment. She gave DW another assessment.

Refreshing and a bit racy.

Not the image of DW Thurman she carried in her mind, but a down to earth businessman and father. Dewey presented an interesting mix of old-fashioned charm with a touch of hip hop forwardness.

Regina set aside her empty oatmeal bowl, reached for her handbag, and stood. "Excuse me for a minute, please."

Dewey Thurman stood with her. "I like that. A real lady never powders her nose at the table. Go ahead, and when you come back, I want to know the color of that lipstick you put on."

She cocked her head to the side. "Why do you ask about my lipstick?"

"My dry cleaner likes to know what color he's scrubbing off my collar."

"And you think you'll have my lipstick on your collar?"

"Don't think." He winked. "I know."

⸎

As they lingered over a second and third cup of coffee they kept getting interrupted. Regina took mental notes at how gracefully he handled every admiring fan who approached the table to greet him. And how swiftly he dispatched them to refocus his attention on her. As his biggest fan, she thought she knew everything about DW. But her information was all public. He generously filled her in on the private details. All five of the girls in the Fellowship were his biological daughters. He'd been married and divorced twice.

"And," Dewey leaned back in his chair with a satisfied smirk on his face, "currently single and available. Dr. Lawson, while I appreciate your offer, I'm paying for breakfast. If this is all you eat, no wonder you keep your figure. And it feels like I owe you a meal. I'd like to fulfill my obligation by asking you to have dinner with me tonight."

Adorably fresh!

Regina picked up her coffee cup and held it aloft. She didn't quite know what to say. Being out in the dating world after so many years married, things had radically changed. Everything moved so fast now. They were still at breakfast, and he'd invited her to dinner. And expressed interest in having her lipstick on his collar.

"I take that back."

Regina's lips bent downward. She'd studied too long. Her sister, Rena, advised her last night that DW might be a fast worker and way out of her league.

"I can't. We've got the concert tonight."

Her shoulders slumped.

"Tell you what. Since you seem disappointed, come to the concert

13

as my guest, and I'll bring you an apple or something since you don't seem to eat much."

Dr. Regina Lawson set her cup down, smiled, and admitted she'd been charmed. She'd planned to hear The Sisters Fellowship perform, and seeing them as the guest of their father, would make the show extra special. "I'd love to."

As they lingered at the table, Dewey steered the conversation back to her career. "How'd you get started on the speaking circuit?"

"The First Lady at my church asked me to do a talk for the women's auxiliary and things kinda took off from there. And when someone suggested putting my workshops up on YouTube, Malik jumped at the chance to be my…," she lifted her fingers in air quotes, "producer."

"Well, he's getting it done. Half of all your hits may be from Thurmans. My girls have worn your channel out. Even made me watch a few." He grinned. "How else are you getting your message out? What other platforms?"

"Funny you should ask. I'm in negotiations right now with a book publisher."

He nodded. "Great, you'll do well with that."

Flattered, she felt an inner glow from his vote of confidence. "I only hope it will help others avoid winding up like me."

Dewey gave her a slow, appreciative assessment. "Looks like you're doing all right to me, St. John."

Regina pursed her lips and changed the subject. "How do you know so much about women's brands?"

"There are a lot of women in my family."

Two ex-wives and five daughters are a lot.

Dewey glanced at his watch, then abruptly stood and walked around to help her rise from her chair. "Time to get you to the ballroom."

She looked back at the handsome man gripping the back of the wooden chair. "How do you know my agenda?"

"I read my conference packet. You're the keynote speaker for the luncheon and doing an afternoon seminar. Dr. Lawson, I've been in this game long enough to figure you'll want to check out both spaces. Walk the rooms before you speak. Check in with your producer?"

How could he know my exact plans?

Chapter Three

A few hours later, Dr. Regina Pearl Lawson stood before a packed ballroom, surveying the crowd. Almost five hundred souls, mainly women, awaited her next words. Looking to her left, she smiled at the expectant faces seated at the table of *importants*: conference organizers and clergy. Glancing to her right, she made eye contact with Malik. He encouraged her with a silly face. Then her gaze shifted around the room until her eyes rested on DW Thurman.

He winked.

She flashed him her brightest smile. Crazy. She'd only spent a couple of hours with the man and was seriously considering sharing a little lipstick with him. Later.

❧

A respectable half hour after the luncheon's final prayer, Dewey appeared at Regina's side and whispered in her ear, "Well done, Dr. Lawson. Let's get you out of here."

She hadn't asked for his assistance, didn't think she needed a handler, but delighted in his help. Dewey's offer was a blessed relief from the overwhelming reception of well-wishers. In the past twenty minutes, the adulation and commentary about her speech had become more exhausting than exhilarating. How could she be tired after less than thirty minutes of actual work? And why was she so eager to hear Dewey Thurman's review?

She'd never delivered a message with as much passion and power as she had today. Her head spun from all the congratulations and compliments. It took several minutes for Dewey to guide her away from the dais and through the ballroom.

"I should have taken you through the kitchen. I don't know if I'll be able to get you through the lobby good." He wrapped his arm around her waist. "Allow me to use my years of experience dodging the people to get you upstairs," he whispered. "You have a powerful impact on our women. I want to explore that further. Your room or mine?"

Her eyes widened as a buzz raced up her spine. After a few moves forward, a skinny teenager stopped them.

"Excuse me, Dr. Lawson, I want to tell you how much I love your talks."

When she stopped to encourage the teen, a small crowd formed. And she felt compelled to thank, hug, and encourage each one.

"I can't thank you enough."

"I praise God for you."

"My daughter and I both look forward to your next video."

DW Thurman gently encouraged her congregants to speak quickly. Mid-lobby a young woman stepped into their path.

"Excuse me, Dr. Lawson." The young woman nervously blurted out. "I don't mean to take up too much of your time, but I came down from Huntsville just to hear you speak today."

Regina searched the young woman's face and planted her heels. "Not at all." She turned toward Dewey. "Can I catch up with you later?"

He dropped his hands to his sides, indicating that he'd wait.

Huntsville told a typical tale of a young girl who thought she knew more than her mother. And gave her innocence to the fantastic promises of a man-child.

A twenty-year-old man shouldn't be messing around with high school girls.

But, praise be to God. The mother's teachings came back to Huntsville through Regina's YouTube channel.

"I was so busy resisting my mother's standards that I failed to set a standard of my own," Huntsville confessed. Huntsville and her child were now back at home. She was finishing high school and focusing on setting a standard. "For myself and my son."

Praise Be to God!

Regina reached out and hugged the young woman. "If I've helped you, pass it along and help another sister. And don't forget you have power and potential."

After Huntsville promised, she gave way for another. A stunning, highly fashionable young woman reached for Regina's hand. As she spoke, Regina admired the woman's thousand-dollar-water-wave weave, Dolce and Gabbana sunglasses, and model-perfect makeup.

This young woman had "hung in there" with her football playing boyfriend. And even after he turned pro, the beatings didn't stop. Stunning thanked Regina for giving her the courage to end that abusive relationship.

Dr. Regina Lawson frowned in remembrance. Having *money to buy* was a poor substitute for real love. And there was no compensation for any type of abuse. She spoke again of power and potential and applauded the young woman's strength. Then nodded to Dewey that she was ready to move forward.

As Regina prepared to step away, Dewey reached out. "Dear sister, I implore you. Take the steps you need to get free before he kills you."

The woman's smile faded into a horrified scowl, and she rushed away.

Didn't he hear her say she'd ended the relationship? How could he speak with such surety, like she was still with him?

"Um, why did you say that?"

Dewey pulled her close and whispered, "That mask of heavy hair and makeup couldn't hide her wounds from me. Those transition sunglasses took in just enough light for me to see a freshly blackened eye. He probably hit her when she said she was coming here."

"I was taken in by the hair and makeup."

"Most people would be. I just pray she married that baller, so she can get half when she leaves. But pray she gets away from him soon."

Regina bowed her head. "I'm not ready for this."

"Yes, you are. It's your season. And I'm even more impressed with you. How graciously and without judgment you listen. I want to spend some more time talking with you about your message. There is something in there that motivates women, especially the younger ones."

Regina Lawson's heart fluttered for the first time in years. *DW Thurman is impressed with me?*

They arrived at the elevator bank and more fans joined them. The conversations shifted from her luncheon speech to tonight's concert. She understood why people wanted a moment with DW Thurman. But her? They took turns urging the other forward. Dewey managed deftly.

"Dewey, I'm not going to be late, am I," she asked in a clumsy attempt to reclaim his attention while they waited for the slow elevator. She was beyond ready to kick off her shoes.

"Why you asking me? I just met you," Dewey responded to entertain his fans.

"You're funny," she snapped.

Dewey winked. "Hope this elevator comes before more of your fans show up and you make us wait for the next one."

After an uncomfortable elevator ride and interesting encounter in the hallway, Dewey firmly shut the door to room sixteen thirty-four. "Whew."

"Oh, my God, I can't believe she asked me that," Regina complained as she moved to the sofa.

Two seasoned saints had taken notice as she and Dewey walked down the hall together. And one was bold enough to inquire about their relationship.

"That's nothing. You'll get used to it. What do they say? Inquiring minds want to know, and in today's world, they will either find an answer online or make one up." Dewey grinned. "Publicity-wise a rumored romance won't hurt me and may do you some good." He strolled over to the room's desk and grabbed two bottles of water.

Rumored romance? Whoa.

Dewey's fingers grazed her hand as he passed her a bottle. The simple, gentle contact sent a song through her nervous system. For the first time in years she reveled in the comfort of being cared for. The concern he'd demonstrated in escorting her from the ballroom reached a closed-off place in her heart. DW excited her in ways the retired Air Force colonel she'd dated off and on for the past two years hadn't approached. The Colonel was kind, but not particularly warm. Safe. But not fresh. Or funny.

I'm just star struck.

Dewey relaxed in the armchair and took a sip of water.

"You've been with me most of the day. I've enjoyed it and I appreciate your help, but I'm sure you have something better to do."

Dewey leaned forward. "No, and your seminar isn't until four. And you're not ready to get rid of me. I still have some fascinating things to tell you about myself."

DW Thurman had actually studied her published agenda for the day. "You sound like a used car salesman. And by the way," she smiled, "I'm already sold."

Dewey hopped up and parked himself beside her on the sofa. "Comfortable?"

"Very." She kicked off her shoes.

"You're comfortable enough to take off those sexy slingback pumps when not twenty-four hours ago you were afraid for me to come too close to your door?"

She flushed. "I know you now. A little. I think."

There was already something between them, and she planned to explore it after the concert this evening. Being married for so long, she'd almost forgotten the butterflies that came with an immediate attraction to a man. She closed her eyes for a second and tried to let the right side of her brain balance her thoughts. Left side was ready to offer him some lipstick. Right side presented seven reasons not to.

Dewey nudged her. "Are you comfortable enough to take this to the next level?"

Regina bolted to her feet. That surety in his tone. He sounded like he knew what she was thinking. "What! We just met."

Well, it's not like you're playing coy or hiding how much you're enjoying his company. Her mother consistently warned her and Rena against being "fass." *But, does that apply at fifty-seven?*

Dewey roared in laughter. "Put your feet back up. I'm joking. I wanted to see the toes on your pretty little feet curl up in those pantyhose. I like that. Women don't wear hosiery like they used to."

As she resettled closer to him on the sofa, she picked up the hints of bay rum, pepper, and something a little wicked in his cologne that reminded her of Jamaica.

DW stretched and asked a hundred questions she couldn't answer about the publication of her book.

What a total blessing to have met him. She'd gone back and forth for weeks over signing the publishing contract on her desk.

"I hope you don't mind. I've traveled this road many times over the years. But you never forget the feeling when the first contract comes."

Regina nodded. "No, I appreciate everything you're sharing with me." Her oldest son, an attorney, had advised against her signing. But… "I know it's Duck's deal, but the lure of being published is so strong."

Dewey's brow furrowed. "That's how they get you. But what's a Duck deal?"

"Oh, I'm surprised you didn't catch the reference. Remember the Five Heartbeats?"

"That Townsend flick, right?" He nodded slowly as he caught on. "Ah, yes. The first record deal they signed. Yeah, you're right. The first deal is usually Duck's deal. Not good for anyone but the record company. Or in your case, the book publisher."

Amazed at how easily she discussed her business with this almost perfect stranger, Regina continued. "But, you went through with your first deal."

"Yes, my first contract got me on the air, and I didn't make two dimes. But that's not the only pitfall in this business. Most people don't know that the record label makes all the real money in the music game."

"Really. I thought you got paid every time one of your songs is played on the radio?"

"Heck-y no, woman, I get paid when I perform. That's why I'm still working." Dewey turned sideways on the sofa. "By the time I bought out the DW Thurman Choir, I had enough experience and a lawyer to structure the recording deal. But with a fifty-member choir I wasn't ready for everyone, from the second soprano to the back-up pianist, expecting to make a million dollars off one single. Without investing a dime into studio time, I might add."

For the next half hour, Dewey explained what he perceived to be the similarities between the publishing and music industries. His experience validated the advice from Victor Earle, Jr., Esquire. Her son's legal advice was sound. Dewey's expertise and insight were a godsend. And she still couldn't decide.

"This is why I'm so careful with the girls. Since they are determined to do this thing, I'm going to make sure they don't repeat my mistakes. Right now, we're on a firm foundation. I just got to find a way to keep things under control as their star rises. And," he rubbed his bald head, "keep that baby girl from making me an old man."

After placing her hand on his knee, Regina peered into Dewey's rich, chestnut-brown eyes. "I never thought of you as a father."

He raised an eyebrow suggestively. "Or as a man?"

"You are so fresh." She snatched her hand away. "Why don't we continue getting to know each other?"

"Good enough for me."

When the door swooshed open, Malik sailed in and plopped down on the armchair.

"…sitting-up in a hotel room with your shoes off. And with this man you claim to have just met. And you…" he pointed at Dewey with a popular double finger salute, "with your jacket off getting comfortable with my mommy. I ain't having it. I'm calling Mr. Smith."

Dewey stood. "See here, young blood."

"He's fun, Mommy." Malik rose and laughed as he strolled into the bedroom.

"Funny, ha, ha. Who is this Mr. Smith? Is he the Colonel or someone else?" Dewey growled, then lowered his voice to a sexy mumble. "I need to know who I'm cutting in on."

It took two gulps of air before Regina could answer. "Mr. Smith is my oldest son, Victor, Jr. We call him Mr. Smith because he's a lot like that character from *Lost in Space*. Picky, crafty, edge of brilliant smart, and always up to something in an Eddie Haskell sneaky sort of way." She shook her head slightly in acceptance of her particular son. "And don't mind Malik, he's my joker."

"Good enough." Dewey grinned and drew two cards from his wallet. "Here's my card. Hand the black one to the usher at the door tonight. I'll arrange seating for you and Malik. Sorry, we can't have a nice dinner, but we'll catch a bite after the show."

"What's the second card for?"

"Woman, I just slid you all of my private information on the gold card. Phone, email, social media, slide into a brother's DMs. And please don't get the cards mixed up." Dewey moved towards the door and paused. "It seems like three dates in one day. So, I'll be wanting a goodnight kiss."

She chuckled. "That's some interesting accounting."

"It's entertainment industry math. I told you how it works. Now, I've got to go make sure the girls have a good rehearsal and find an apple. I can't wait to see you later."

Chapter Four

Hours later Regina Lawson presented DW Thurman's black card at the door of the hotel ballroom and received a raised eyebrow, followed by an escort to a reserved table. The room had changed two times since her midday presentation. This evening the ballroom was arranged theater style for the concert. Eight round tables lined the front of the stage—VIP seating. Beyond the tables, porters were still setting up rows of chairs for the other attendees. The usher led her to a front table already filled with the conference organizers.

A few minutes later Dewey slid into the chair next to her and presented her with an apple. "Where's my friend Malik?"

"He was invited to hangout backstage with the band."

"Cool, they caught up with him. I'll take his seat."

"Thank you, that's a very nice opportunity."

He nodded and engaged the lady to his right in conversation about a concert she'd attended in '83. While they waited for the show to begin, DW Thurman candidly answered the questions from their table-mates about his career and the Fellowship, while artfully dodging all inquiries about his date.

In the midst of chatting, Regina noticed Dewey glancing at his watch every few minutes and growing more impatient with each time check.

"Miss Regina, we do a lot of work on Sunday morning, and this isn't a good thing," he whispered. "If tonight's performance doesn't end before ten, it will impact tomorrow's schedule. I promised a friend that I'd bring the girls by his church for his eight o'clock service. At this rate, I don't think that can happen."

She nodded and uttered the same lame thing she'd said to her ex-husband for twenty years when he fretted over some event or meeting not starting on time. "I'm sure it will be fine."

DW Thurman rolled his eyes and excused himself.

In his wake, Regina let out a defeated air. Instead of engaging in the conversation going around the table about the success of the conference, she fretted. She mentally kicked herself for slipping back into the perfect corporate companion role and uttering the non-statement that made Dewey flee.

It was understandable why things were running late. The ballroom had to be cleared from the closing dinner, which was included in the conference price. Then re-set and reopened, for those who'd purchased a ticket for the concert. She'd skipped the closing chicken dinner in favor of a late nap. Rest, she hoped, would work in her favor after the show.

"Yes, thank you," she accepted another compliment from her earlier presentation and joined the general table conversation.

"Showtime, showtime," Dewey announced to the table when he returned a long ten minutes later.

As the ballroom lights dimmed, he scooted his chair closer to hers. She smiled, exhaled, and clapped joyfully, as The Sisters Fellowship took the stage.

Before the second song, the talented sisters had transformed the atmosphere of the hotel ballroom into that of a sanctuary. Their set continued with new classics from Yolanda Adams and Mary Mary before ending with a new arrangement of a gospel standard.

Those girls are anointed.

Following the spirit-rousing rendition of "Pass Me Not," the Fellowship paused for introductions. Regina relaxed in her chair with their father's arm resting comfortably around her shoulder.

"They're all beautiful."

"Yes, they are," the proud papa responded. He'd explained earlier how all of his girls came to have the same name. His first wife blessed their two daughters with names meaning beautiful; so, his second wife could do no less.

For their second set, the Fellowship presented a masterful mix of spiritually uplifting tunes. New songs, but nothing the most traditional among the chosen could object to.

"And now," Jolee, the glamorous spokesperson for the group, took center stage, "we'd like to bring our father and manager, gospel music icon, DW Thurman, to the stage." The room erupted in thunderous applause. "He doesn't do this often, and we didn't ask. But tonight, please help us welcome the Crown Prince of Gospel Music, DW Thurman!"

Excited whispers rippled through the ballroom, followed by a raucous round of applause. He wasn't scheduled to sing tonight.

"Help us encourage Daddy as he comes." Jolee cajoled to raise the applause.

Dewey rose slowly and feigned surprise while basking in the delight of those around him. When she raised an eyebrow at his phony acting, he winked and strode towards the stage.

Regina stood and joined the congregation in a standing ovation for the Crown Prince of Gospel Music.

The Thurmans were true professionals; they'd orchestrated just enough of a delay to have a white, baby-grand piano rolled onto the stage. Once DW moved into the spotlight, the room settled. When he took his position on the piano bench, the applause died down, and he struck a few tentative notes. Notes that did not approach the power with which he'd eventually play. The youngest, Tasnee, slid next to him on the piano bench and he hummed, "sing with me, baby." Then launched into his most famous song, "Everlasting."

Dewey's hands on the keyboard were matchless and his voice beyond compare. But when combined with Tasnee's vocals, the mood flowed into something next level. Ethereal. Their gifts ushered an air of peace and assurance into the space. All the Thurman girls were blessed with beautiful voices, but Regina experienced something more during the father-daughter duet. And she wasn't alone.

One of the ladies at the table got happy. Not in the loud, hollering-running-the-aisles way, but in the deeply-felt emotion of gratitude from a saint who knew the Lord. And as the spirit moved through the room, Regina reached into her purse for a tissue.

Only an everlasting faith carried her from the moment she decided to end her marriage until now. She focused on the back of Dewey's jacket as it ebbed and flowed with the passions expressed through his fingers and voice. Anticipation flooded her soul. *What might come from the time she'd spent with him?*

The warmth of their fellowship, the thrill of his touch, and the welcome weight of his hand on her waist as he guided her through the hotel lobby this afternoon had her nerves all jangled. Dewey's mix of old-fashioned charm and hip hop freshness enchanted her. She shined in remembrance of how many times he'd praised her in one day. Coming out of a long marriage where compliments were compulsory, she was charmed. But, what about the Colonel?

During the refrain of "Everlasting," Regina reflected on the everlasting faithfulness of her God. In the last five years, she'd transitioned from housewife and mother, to doctoral candidate and finally associate professor and seminar leader. As the song ended, she joined what seemed to be a collective exhale in the room.

After letting the final note resonate, DW Thurman's experience kicked in, and he musically bridged the mood in the space from spiritual to physical. With only his keyboard, he commanded everyone to clap and sway under a different spiritual expression. With only his keyboard, he led everyone to a different spiritual expression. The show ended on an upbeat note of praise.

During the extended ovation, Regina worked to engage the rational side of her brain. The surety when Dewey spoke comforted her soul, and his hip-hop-fresh attitude attracted her mind. She'd only met him last night and her body was hinting.

The man has five daughters and two ex-wives? What should that matter? I have no intention of becoming wife number three.

Rena's voice broke into her cautious self-talk. "Why not just enjoy yourself tonight?"

Immediately following the show, Dr. Lawson followed her table-mates to a private reception space. A small meeting room filled with the *importants*: pastors, first ladies, local missionaries, and conference organizers. All hoping to spend a few minutes appreciating the Thurman Family.

Regina pasted on her professional smile and spoke her way through the room. Accepting more compliments from her earlier presentations. Some attendees lauded the soundness of her message. Others hinted about additional invitations. Despite the positive comments and hugs, she couldn't settle. Something in DW's performance had both satisfied and disturbed her spirit.

Butterflies or bad tidings?

In the overcrowded uncomfortably tight room, she spied a quiet corner. Out of the way of the crowd, she watched the Thurman family manage the receiving line formed to greet them. Again, she marveled at DW's grace of putting everyone who shook his hand or gave him a Christian hug at ease. Like he had with her all day. Perhaps she'd read too much into his flirting. Maybe he was overly friendly with everyone. Or was she witnessing his true spiritual gift at work?

With so many people shifting around, she soon lost sight of the Thurmans and the disquiet in her spirit expanded.

What's my problem? Why is my spirit at such dis-ease?

She'd spent hundreds of hours in rooms like this. In the background. Waiting, while her ex-husband politicked his way up the corporate ladder. She shook her head, put her spirit in check, then chalked her complaints up to a long day.

Breakfast with Dewey, the conference keynote, their midday chat, her afternoon seminar, the concert, and she hoped—their dinner date. She prayed it wasn't over. But, the crowd didn't appear to be thinning. Unmovable, stalwart saints occupied the few chairs in the room. It was getting late, and they didn't seem inclined to go anywhere.

Her cautious inner voice suggested she go back to her room as she leaned against a wall for support. *Nope, I have a dinner date.*

Something about his music always renewed her. Even on her worst days when she turned to gospel music for solace, she'd found comfort in DW Thurman songs. Maybe that's the reason every moment with him ignited her spirit. And if nothing else, she wanted to share that insight with him.

As she contemplated, the room shifted. The crowd beyond the few chairs in front of her had thinned. She looked up to find DW Thurman moving in her direction. As he approached, Dewey tightened a white scarf wrapped around his neck. She smiled and took two steps forward. A moment later when he reached for her hand, she frowned. The twinkle she sought in his eyes had gone, replaced by what she interpreted as weariness.

"Hoped you enjoyed the show. I burned a lot of energy out there trying to impress you."

Her eyes widened with disbelief. No way was any of that about her, and he knew it. His performance was pure praise and worship.

Dewey slipped his arm around her waist and murmured, "Come meet my girls."

As he guided her towards his daughters, Regina let out a peaceful yawn.

Is Dewey Thurman the balm for my dis-ease?

Dewey's Daughters

Allegra, the oldest, was tall, practical, poised and grounded. A lawyer like her mother, she co-managed The Sisters Fellowship.

Bonita, his second born, seemed very thoughtful. A graduate of Moody Bible College, Rev. Bonita was on-staff at her stepfather's church in Chicago. "Grandma's going to love you."

The spokesperson and glamour girl of the group, Jolee, had inherited her father's fresh personality and stage presence. Jolee, was also in charge of fashion. South side of Chicago chic, she wore a tight, red knit dress and twice as many accessories as her sisters. The *brain* of the family, she was a second year medical student.

Calista, was Bonita's spiritual twin. There was something serene and almost ethereal about her. Dewey shared that soon they would all address Calista as reverend, too.

And the most gifted singer, the baby girl. Tasnee's duet with Dewey took the entire audience to a spiritual high. Eighteen-year-old Tasnee seemed impulsive, impatient and eager to prove her point. "Dr. Lawson, please tell Daddy how important it is for me to follow my own dreams."

Regina took a deep breath and sidestepped her request. "You are all so beautiful and talented. I was telling your father one of the reasons I agreed to speak at this conference was to attend tonight's concert. I am a huge fan of your family."

The sisters accepted her compliment, and they had a lovely chat before Dewey pulled her away.

After sweating so much on-stage, Dewey couldn't go out to dinner. But, insisted on having their third date. As they walked back to his hotel room, she sensed something different in his temperament. The frisky, fresh spirit she enjoyed earlier in the day was now a dark, sullen character. Since she didn't know the man well enough to say anything, she held her tongue.

But in the future.

If there was a future, she wouldn't hesitate to speak to the rather dramatic shift in his mood. She hadn't spoken up enough during her twenty-eight-year marriage. Not speaking to Victor's moods was a harbinger of their ultimate disconnection.

Now waiting in Dewey's suite, she checked the time again as she considered the view from the balcony window for the umpteenth time. Not much to see. The roof of the hotel's conference center, a series of HVAC pipes and a couple of crushed soda cans. Not even a decent glimpse of Birmingham's skyline. Why would anyone put a balcony with deck chairs in this suite? But a Styrofoam cup of ashes bore witness that somebody had recently sat out there. Inside the room there was much more to consider.

The shower had stopped twenty minutes ago and the melody of running water replaced by Dewey's rich tenor. Emotion in the muted tones of his voice reached her through the closed door connecting the living and sleeping spaces of the suite. Of course, DW Thurman's almost in-person voice would touch her spirit as it had for many years on cassette and CD. But, this expression was different. Dewey sang and-or-prayed, with an urgency and fervor, she'd never heard before. The spiritual outpouring sounded passionate, intense, and deeply personal.

"Maybe I should leave."

She'd met her gospel idol and spent a marvelous day in his company. Other than making sure to ask for an autographed photo, her encounter with the icon might soon be over. Regina turned at the swish of the outer door opening.

Chapter Five

He will keep you in perfect peace
As He perfects that which concerns you.
Beloved, be at peace in your journey, today.

"Sorry, I didn't expect you guys to still be here." Bonita Thurman stepped into the room, stopped and took in the song-prayer of her father. "Um. Good Lord. How long?"

"Almost an hour." Regina exhaled, thankful for the opportunity to ask. "Should I still be here? I mean I wouldn't want to be disrespectful of his personal worship or anything."

Bonita's lips turned up into an understanding smile. "No, not if he asked you to wait. And it's good that you did. He's been so excited all day. Talked about you nonstop and totally changed our set list tonight. Which he never does."

What a lovely compliment to pay her and the answer to her earlier question. His performance tonight wasn't planned. Regina's heart fluttered. DW Thurman was trying to impress her.

Rena's voice echoed in her ear. *Why wouldn't he?*

"I wonder?" Bonita grinned like she knew a secret. "Dr. Lawson, when he gets like this, we just wait and pray."

Why would his daughter let me in on such a private instruction?

34

Rev. Bonita tilted her head and listened again to her father's worship. "It won't be long now. Aren't you two supposed to have a late supper?"

"Yes, but—"

"He really is special, and I mean that beyond his being an awesome father. There's well... I'll let him explain it. And I pray you're open to hearing him out." Bonita moved to the desk and picked up the room service menu. "It's getting late. Why don't we order you guys some food? That's the best way to support him right now."

Support him?

After reviewing the menu, Bonita moved closer to the bedroom door and sniffed twice. "Daddy's not going to need more than a small sandwich tonight."

The sniffing was strange, but she didn't comment, since she wanted every moment she could have with DW Thurman. "A small house salad would be fine for me."

"Would you like apple pie or something like that? Daddy's been asking after apples today."

Regina grinned and declined. She'd eaten the apple Dewey gave her before the concert an hour ago to stave off her hunger. *Could his interest be genuine?*

After ordering, Bonita picked up a red leather book bag and swung it across her shoulder. "I'll be down in the lobby. I have a letter to finish." She cocked her head to the side and her face erupted in a big, happy grin. "Listen. Daddy's whistling. I'm so glad. Daddy whistles when he's happy. Something's been stirring in his spirit for a few days, but it sounds like he's made it to the other side." Bonita lifted her hands. "Praise God for the breakthrough." She smiled broadly and left just as Dewey entered from the bedroom.

"That was Bo?"

"Yes, she went to the lobby to write some letters."

He frowned.

"Everything okay," she said while wondering why Bonita wasn't going to hang out with her sisters.

"It will be and I'm sorry. There is something swirling and I can't... I must be obedient to the spirit. And I appreciate your patience. You just keep confirming what I already know." He grinned broadly. "But, we'll talk about that later."

What is this mystery they keep alluding to?

Casually dressed in slacks and a Cuban guayabera, Dewey looked and smelled refreshed. That impish twinkle had returned to his eyes, and he appeared much younger than sixty-two. "Now that I'm able, I'm shifting gears. We're supposed to have an intimate and romantic late supper."

Her internal warning bell sounded. "Wait!"

"Girl, I'm just messing with you. I find your alarm charming. And I can't wait until you stop taking me so seriously."

The way he talked about getting to know her both thrilled and frightened her. *I hope he's not toying with me.*

"Bonita ordered room service."

Dewey nodded his appreciation and asked a ton of questions about her afternoon seminar until their food arrived.

As they ate, Dewey told her more about the girls. Calista's ordination was scheduled for late fall, but he knew she wouldn't go through with it. Tasnee pushed back on starting college and was almost through her gap-year. Jolee struggled to manage medical school with the singing career. His strong, stable, and lonely Allegra was caught between her love for the Fellowship and the law. And finally, Bonita. Reverend Bonita was facing a major decision, but wouldn't share any details.

"Lately she's become uncharacteristically secretive, and that worries me. Can't explain it, but our Bo needs wisdom and clear vision right now. I'd hoped to figure out what was going on with Bonita Thurman on this trip."

As he spoke of making sure he had special time with each of his girls, Dewey Thurman the father, grew in her esteem. Gospel great as a good father, something she'd never considered. His handle on what was going on with each of his daughters kind of put her to shame. She'd just about quit nosing around in her sons' affairs. As long as they weren't making her a grandmother or in legal trouble, she wasn't asking.

They talked late into the night sharing their stories. Hers not particularly exciting. She'd married Victor Earle right out of college and taught high school while he went to law school.

"Yes, the stereotypical soap opera story. Husband becomes high-profile corporate executive and wife, a boring old mom."

"Nothing wrong about that."

"No, just boring."

"For your ex, maybe. Looking back, I was always better—married with children. And I hate I missed that everyday interaction with my girls. The weekend-holiday-dad role is a lonely thing."

Those words described her ex-husband perfectly; weekend-dad and part-time lover. For the years she was married, she'd kept up her figure because she wanted her husband to say "wow" when he looked at her. But that didn't stop him from straying.

"So, what happened?"

"We fell out of touch, and one day Victor said I bored him."

"Huh." He reached out and caressed her hand. "How can any sane man be bored with a woman as lovely and intelligent as you?"

Regina smiled and looked down at her feet. "For every woman, there's a man that's tired of getting it. Or at least tired of getting it from her. He said I didn't have anything interesting to talk about.

Like the active lives of our boys wasn't enough. I think I went for my master's degree to have something else to bring to our conversations. Then continued through my doctoral studies when I decided we were over. I stayed as long as I did to make sure all the tuitions were paid."

"Yours?"

"No, my boys. Smith was first-year law at the time and Malik a freshman at Alabama. I know a lot of corporate wives who got stuck with the education bills after a new wife entered the picture. So, I bit my tongue, cut back on the household expenses to pay my tuition, and the day after Victor Jr. graduated from law school, I filed for divorce."

"And what about Malik?"

"If I'da waited for him to graduate. I'd still be married."

Dewey went silent for a moment.

Regina fretted. *Do I sound mercenary for strategically plotting my divorce?* Rena warned her against over-sharing when they talked this afternoon.

"How long have you been divorced?"

"The decree was granted five years ago, but there are still a few things between us. Mainly my shares in Earle Holdings, our family's real estate business, and Malik's future. But enough about me. What about you?"

Dewey shrugged. He met his first wife, Myra, while working on his master's degree at the Interdenominational Theology Center in Atlanta. "We married Myra's senior year at Spelman. A few months later, Allegra was born."

While Myra went to law school, he kept the baby and played for the Georgia Mass Choir. "The Georgia Mass blew up right after Bo was born. And by then Myra had passed the bar. Something else we have in common," he chuckled, "lawyers."

His joke fell flat on her ears since her brain was now in full debate.

"Why did the marriage end?"

"Minnie Thurman's baby boy lost his mind. Too much time away from home doing too many things I had no business doing."

Maybe we'll just be friends.

"That was more than thirty years ago. And there's more to my story."

Regina shivered. For a brief second, it felt like he'd read her mind.

"After Myra put me out, I got saved and wrote "Everlasting." But it didn't take long for that success to fade, and I was another washed-up, one-hit wonder. And that's how I met Deborah. Dear Deborah coordinated what became my comeback concert at her father's church in Chicago, and we fell in love."

Then Dewey fell silent and it seemed like everything in the room stopped.

Does he still love her?

A moment later, Dewey took a big gulp of water and continued. "Deb had mercy on me, and I became the minister of music at her father's church. That music ministry was a huge draw and together we grew Family Fellowship Missionary Baptist into one of the first black megachurches. And then there were five little girls who I wanted so much for. And a church musician's salary wasn't getting it. So, I hit the road to sing for our supper."

She prayed he wouldn't say he repeated his mistakes before asking, "What happened?"

"While I was away, the devil seduced my good wife. A dirty-ole, low-down, ambitious dog preacher came in to take over after Deborah's father retired. Figured he should have the pastor's daughter too. Some writer called it the church scandal of the century. Just grateful this all played out before social media. It was such a big mess, and since I don't do drama, I chose not to fight. I gave Deborah custody of our girls and moved back to Georgia. Let Deborah heal and claim her place at Fellowship. She's his wife now."

Thank God, he hadn't repeated the same mistakes.

She'd experienced infidelity, too, and understood his description of Deborah's husband. "Would you think it rude if I said a perky, pink-toed, she-devil claims she took my husband?"

"Only if you're still bitter about it."

Regina stood and took a turn around the room. At first, she was angry. But, now it was all right. She'd made a comfortable life for herself. Lived by the ocean, taught English at Mobile Community College, and kept a townhouse in Montgomery. Thanks to her excellent divorce attorney, she had a share of Victor's success. Her future was secured with a portion of Vic's pension and a third of the family's real estate holdings. "I'm fine and I still let Mandy think she took Vic from me. How long have you been divorced?"

"About fifteen years now. And I'm not bitter anymore. It's the only bad thing Deb ever did in her entire life. But, I *do* hold it against him. He was supposed to be better. Know better. Do better." Dewey stopped again and when he spoke his voice was low and weary. "Deb's facing some tough choices right now."

Regina warmed at the notes of compassion in Dewey's voice. "I'm so sorry to hear that." She sat back down and took his hand. "Remind me which of the girls are hers, I'd like to pray for them?"

"Thank you. Jolee, Calista and Tasnee. But, pray for all of us. Deb's filing for divorce soon and things are extremely messy. But," he nodded his head and smiled, "she's going to come out of this stronger."

Her eyebrow lifted, something in his tone sounded like he knew how his ex-wife's divorce would turn out. *What kind of grace does he have to even care?*

"You have an extraordinary family. The love among the sisters is clear. I can tell there's not a step or half-sister among them. And from the short time I spent with them, I can tell they all adore you."

"I'm a great father." He chuckled.

She grinned at the puffed-up pride that rose in his chest.

"You looking for a sugar daddy, little girl?"

"Ha, ha." She shouted.

Dewey stretched out his legs and rubbed his right knee. "Why don't you tell me more about your children?"

"Um, well …." She smiled and shared her canned, glowing report on Victor Earle, Jr. Esq., perfect. "The only child to wear wing-tips in the third grade. Apple of his father's eye and the golden boy of the Alabama Real Estate Commission."

"Nickname Smith," he winked, "see, I listen carefully to everything you say."

"Thank you. Although I'm not sure what you find so interesting?"

"I'm fas-ci-nat-ed," he sang. "And I am also observant. That angel pendant you wear. It's beautiful. Any particular meaning?"

"Oh," she reached for her neck and turned the charm, "my boys gave this to me after my mother passed and I loved it so much—that an angel became the go-to gift for Mom. I have a collection of angel figurines from all over the world that I used to bring out during the holidays."

"Noted. Now finish telling me about your boys."

"Yes, there was no doubt Smith would become an attorney like his dad. We're very proud of him." She crowed on about Smith. His success in real estate law and the building he'd just purchased. Smith was following in his father's footsteps; keep a steady day job while building your own business at night.

"And Malik?"

"Well…" she hedged.

"Malik's your problem child?"

Regina yawned. It was late and the last thing she wanted to do was go through Malik's issues.

"I don't think you need to tell me," Dewey said. "I met him. I know."

Her eyes popped. She'd noticed earlier that he tended to speak with an unsettling surety. How could he profess to know Malik's story after two brief meetings? But, he'd pegged the football player's abused wife. After what? Thirty seconds?

"I encounter many young men like Malik at Morehouse. I call them the Peter Pan generation. They don't want to work, but dream of overnight success in the digital world. Is Malik a rapper, producer, or just make beats?"

She chortled. "According to him, all three. He does a great job with my videos and spends a lot of time and money producing local rappers. But he doesn't want to make the effort to earn a degree. I wouldn't care if he studied music or video. We only want him to learn *how* to run a business."

She didn't usually talk about her struggles with Malik or her divorce settlement outside of the family, but for some reason she felt comfortable talking with Dewey. "Malik does odd jobs for Smith and maintains the website for our real estate office. It's the only time he and his father can have a civil discussion. And because I took title to some property in the divorce, he lives rent-free, as the caretaker for my townhouse in Montgomery."

"Lady, it's an all too common story."

They talked for another hour about the Peter Pan generation and the impact to the greater community until Dewey yawned.

"Bo knows better," he muttered as he reached for his phone and shot off a text asking Bonita to wait in the lobby until after he escorted Regina to her room. "Can't have any of my girls walking these hallways alone at night."

Not being social media-crazed, Regina wasn't aware of the DW Thurman online, ministry-slash-fan-club. Too excited to sleep after Dewey walked her back to her room, she waited up for Malik to come in. And to keep her mind free from worry, she signed up for DW Thurman's morning praise song. After reading a few months of his daily affirmations, she added poet to her knowledge of the man. Then she fell into a deep, peaceful sleep. She didn't stir until Malik woke her up because Dewey Thurman was at her door. Again.

Chapter Six

Praise be to God, for the glory of the morning.
For the beauty of his kindness, and the mercy of his love.

At eight-thirty on Sunday morning Regina Lawson stood outside of room sixteen thirty-four, with Dewey Thurman's arms wrapped around her waist. Amazed, slightly sleepy, and thrilled.

DW Thurman come all the way down this long hallway, just to say good morning to me!

She wouldn't invite him into her room because Malik was sleeping on the sofa. Well, half asleep since he'd answered Dewey's knock.

Last night Dewey made it clear he intended to spend more time with her. But, she hadn't expected to see him again so soon.

"I sensed you needed to know I meant what I said. So, I came to greet you this morning with a kiss. Listen," he dropped his tone into a lower register, "when I call you tonight, I'm going to need to know where I'm going to sleep when I come to Mobile."

Her toes curled up in her slippers.

"Are you sure you can't stay and attend church with us this morning? If you come, I'll sing."

While the opportunity to hear DW Thurman and The Sister

44

Fellowship sing again was tempting, she had another task planned during today's church hour.

"No, I'm going to keep my previous commitment."

"Excellent, I like that in you." Dewey leaned in and planted a peck on her lips. He stepped back to bask in the radiance of her smile. "Glad that didn't alarm you."

Dewey Wilson Thurman, then turned Temptations style and strolled slowly, surely, seductively down the hall. He never looked back.

Because he knows I'm watching.

Ten hours later and still grinning like an idiot, Regina Pearl Lawson stretched out on her favorite lounger on her patio in Mobile. Since meeting Dewey, she'd grinned and giggled nonstop. The only break in her smile came when she broke it off with the Colonel. Just as she suspected, the man took the end of their relationship with a soldier's stoicism.

A few more conversations and she'd call it a Sunday. First, she needed to call her boys. Make sure Malik made it home safely and check in with Smith. Then return Rena's many calls before waiting for DW Thurman to call her. But, instead of picking up the phone, she settled deeper into the lounger. If she had her druthers, she'd spend a week out here on the sun porch, sleeping, reading, and talking to Dewey.

"But, I've got a book to write!"

It took longer than she anticipated to catch up with her sons. She was used to Malik not returning her calls. But today, she had to track down Smith. She was two breaths away from worry when he called. To gin up the pluck to call her sister, she listened again to The Sisters Fellowship's rendition of DW Thurman's classic "Favor Found Me."

"Siri, call Rena."

After a rushed hello, her older sister jumped right in. "When will you see him again?"

"In two weeks," she sang.

"DW Thurman. Regina, girl, I can't believe it! You are talking with DW Thurman?"

"It's so."

"Mama would say you caught yourself a big fish."

The sisters laughed in remembrance.

Then Rena rushed her with questions. "...and I googled him, because the man you're describing doesn't sound like who I remember. Hold on while I pull up these bookmarks. I've got questions."

While Rena clicked to her bookmarks, Regina rose from the lounger and surveyed the scenic greenery of the golf course bordering her property. Sometimes she felt a little sinful for loving this house so much. Losing this property in coastal Alabama seemed like the only tragedy her ex-husband suffered in the divorce.

"Girl, DW needs to update his publicity picture." Rena squealed. "He's much older than I'd realized. Nice-looking older gentleman. Um hmm, bald headed now. I like it."

"I'll be sure to tell John." Regina giggled.

Rena laughed off her threat. Funny, how things turned out. When Rena and John eloped right after high school forty years ago, everyone said it wouldn't work out.

"All five of these girls are his?" Rena continued the interrogation.

"Yes, The Sisters Fellowship. All his."

"DW Thurman of the Morehouse Ten, the Georgia Mass, and the DW Thurman Choir? Grammy Award-winning, gospel music icon, the Crown Prince of Gospel Music. DW Thurman—five grown daughters, two ex-wives, and you."

Dear Lord.

It was always wise to wait until she was home and rested before calling her sister.

"I don't know," Rena snarled. "He looks like a real player. There are plenty too many pictures on here of him; with all kinds of women. You weren't like a conference girl or something? A ship in every port, weekend kind-of-thing? You didn't do anything with him, did you?"

"No!"

"Just asking. I mean he is a major music star; you're his biggest fan. That star power might have done something to you."

Regina giggled. She hadn't done *that*, and she'd never tell Rena how much lipstick she'd shared with Dewey last night. Her spirit bubbled up with excitement at the very thought of his warm, amorous kisses.

"It's clear. He likes the ladies."

"Ugh."

"And you quit the Colonel?"

"Yes, stopped in Montgomery and had brunch with him. "He's a good man, but…"

"Mama would say you done throwed away a good man with a pension. Ump." Rena skillfully emitted their mother's disapproval grunt. "Because he doesn't do it for you like DW Thurman does. I understand why you're a little struck. Girl, you've been a fan since the Morehouse Ten. And if I recall," Rena teased, "the first time you got happy in church, the choir was singing something from the Georgia Mass featuring…"

"Oh, my God. I don't know how you remember these details. And you're right."

Rena went on to remind her of a few more things. Like how she owned all of his albums, and had paid Malik to convert them to digital. The time they drove to Atlanta on a lark for a DW Thurman

Choir reunion concert. Victor's complaints about her playing DW Thurman songs during corporate events she hosted. "And I got one more for you. If it wasn't for "Everlasting." I don't think you'd-a made it through the divorce and Vic's remarriage."

Regina dropped the phone. All true. She would have run off the road if she'd received her sister's remembrances while driving. Rena's memory proved a painful and powerful resource this evening. Dewey's music had ministered to her through her middling marriage and beyond. She picked up her phone and thanked God for the rigid protective case. "Wow, your memory is something. You're right."

"Um hum. I'm just glad you weren't acting all tight-lipped and Doctor Lawson on him. Cause from what I'm seeing, ole DW likes a good time. My Lord," Rena hollered. "A real good time. I'm in the *Gospel Gossip* archives now and um there are some pictures on here of ole boy looking tore up. And some more with your boy looking tore down. You need to get on Google and check this out."

Regina shook her head vigorously. "I'm not going to google DW Thurman anything. It just doesn't seem right for me to go online and find out things about him, which may or may not be true. But, he did google me." She giggled. "Can you believe it? DW Thurman wanted to confirm that I wasn't married or anything before we went to breakfast yesterday."

Rena laughed, too. "Al-righty, but be careful. Some of this stuff about women, drugs and alcohol, his celebrity lifestyle doesn't look like you at all. Eh…" Rena gasped. "Are you sure he only has five children? It says here there's a— what? Hold up, I need to check some dates."

Rena did some mental math, out loud, while Regina made faces at the phone.

"Six. Says here, he has a five-year-old son by a girl in Chicago who may be younger than two of his daughters. Ump…"

"Rena, we don't know that to be true. If there is anything to know about Dewey, I'll ask him."

"Just don't be a dolt," Rena said before switching topics to family business.

Knowing this topic would end up in a disagreement about Malik, Regina put her phone on mute and let Rena talk. The only common ground her big sister and ex-husband shared these days was their opinion on Malik. She stood alone in giving her baby-boy a few more years to grow up.

Rena prattled on for a few minutes before she interrupted. "Hey, Rena. I need to fix something for dinner. I'll call you tomorrow."

After she hung up, Regina fixed herself a light meal. After one bite, she smacked herself upside the head. Rena lived across the bay and always cooked a full Sunday dinner for her large family. She'd missed a delicious pot roast to sit by the phone and wait for a man to call. Rena was right, she was a dolt. Women didn't have to wait at home anymore for the phone to ring. "I have a cellphone."

After eating, she grabbed an academic journal and went back to the porch to read. What if she was a weekend chick—like Rena said—and he didn't call. She wanted to trust in what Dewey said last night and again this morning. The surety in his voice enticed her spirit to let its guard down. But, the caution she'd learned from her mother warned her to sit still.

She walked to the edge of her porch and gazed up at the reddish-orange remains of the day. The colors of the setting sun reminded her of the warmth of Dewey's hip-hop freshness and sexy-sweet kisses. Until her mother's voice creeped in. "Don't start being a fass-gal, like Rena."

As Sunday passed into dusk, Regina's eyes roamed the golf course behind her house. Twilight was always the best time of day for her family. For three hours every day, Victor Earle stopped working. He insisted they have family dinner every night when the boys were young. And after dinner, they'd walk the dog. Important conversations and family decisions were made on those walks. But that time had passed.

Ten minutes later, she picked up the journal. But, instead of reading, she stared at her silent phone. "What if he does call and Rena's right about his lifestyle? I can't get involved with a man like that."

She'd enjoyed every minute spent with Dewey. And it wasn't about his being famous. She sincerely liked the man. If the things Rena said about what went on behind the scenes, even at Christian concerts, were true? "Can I consider dating a man with five daughters, two ex- wives and the past Rena drudged up? Maybe I've been hasty in breaking up with the Colonel?"

It was unusual for her to be so discontent. Instead of being grateful for her dinner salad, she'd compared it to her sister's meal. She should be studying an article that might help her become a better professor instead of dwelling in the past. Or second guessing her decision to end a cold relationship. She opened the *Journal of African-American Student Studies* and finished the article she'd started reading at the beauty shop on Friday afternoon.

"What a difference a day makes."

She didn't know Dewey Thurman on Friday when she began reading the article on writing across the curriculum, and now she missed him.

It was fully dark when her phone finally rang. Before the end of the first ring cycle, she snatched up the device and mashed the green button.

"Thank you for answering so quickly. I was holding my breath, hoping you gave a brother the right number," Dewey blew out.

Thank you, God! Regina exhaled, before blurting out a breathy, "Are you really coming to see me?"

"Absolutely! I can't wait. I want to be with you again so badly, I spent money. Changed everyone's agenda. I'm going to step off a plane Friday next and board another for Mobile. Not even going to stop after three weeks on the road to sleep in my own bed. So, I'm going to need a comfortable place to lay my head when I get there."

Regina drew in an audibly sharp breath.

"Honey, I'm not coming to get in your bed. Not that I don't want to, but I don't think you'd let me. And I like that. What's the closest hotel to you?"

Regina pulled at her cheeks so she could speak. "I'll text you the address."

Resting in a hotel bed in Orlando, Dewey shared his schedule for the next two weeks. She'd never considered that DW Thurman did anything other than sing. The man ran quite a busy enterprise. His daughters, his agent, an accountant to keep the IRS in check, and a roster of musicians, roadies, and sound technicians. The daily online devotional ministry, a merchandise brand and was on faculty at Morehouse College.

Where did he find the time to teach?

"You're a busy man."

"Yes, and I am gonna make time to get to know ya," he sang in a resolute key. His tone echoed the persuasion of a country preacher's altar call.

She paused and tried to determine if that surety in his tone sounded prophetic or manipulative. "Not to sound coy, but why?"

Dewey chuckled in a slow, foxy key. "I can tell you are a woman of quality. You have a standard. You're going to make me work for it. I don't encounter that too often, and I want you to know I'm willing to do the work. I'm up for the challenge."

"Oh, my."

A shot of excitement raced through her body. She stood and

walked around the porch to settle her nerves. Thank God she refused to video chat with him. He didn't need to see her dancing around like an excited chicken.

"So, the next few days we will be in heavy rehearsal. Then on Wednesday, Allegra and I are flying to New York to give a deposition in a lawsuit. Have you heard of Young Iggy?"

She nodded. Malik was a fan of the rapper who had a gospel and R&B crossover hit a few years ago.

"I'm suing Iggy for sampling one of my songs without permission. Iggy thought because he lives in my building and we've had some deep conversations that I wouldn't mind. Young man has no understanding of the business, didn't know what he did was wrong. I'm sorry he has to learn the hard way. I wouldn't have sued him if he'd simply apologized. But instead he chose to act like he was the King of Spades with one hit record."

"I haven't heard that one in years." Regina laughed at the old Southern expression.

"Yes, it turns out to be a good case for Allegra. She's lead counsel on this and that's saving me a ton in legal fees. So, how 'bout I fly you out to Orlando for the weekend."

"No. Thank you."

"I'll ask again. Now, Dr. Lawson, after hearing you speak I'd like to present your name to a friend of mine in the Baptist Methodist Assembly. They have a women's conference coming up in early June, and I think you should be on their program."

"Well," she hedged. She was familiar with the BMA. The old, ultra-conservative denomination rarely sat non-members before their congregations.

"Don't say *no*. And I'd also like you to consider consulting with my girls this summer. They really need to spend some time defining their standard."

"Huh?"

"I think you are the perfect person to facilitate—maybe referee, as we discuss setting a standard for the Fellowship. No, let me re-phrase that. The girls will be setting their standard. I won't even be in the room," he paused, "unless you think I should."

For the first time he seemed unsure and she relaxed. Regina took in a cleansing breath and relaxed her assumption that he might be trying to manipulate her. DW Thurman wanted to visit her, present her credentials to the BMA, and lead a vital conversation with his children. Perhaps his intentions were as honorable as he'd described.

"I'm honored that you value my work enough to ask. So yes, if you think the BMA would have me. And I'll agree to facilitate for your girls, but refuse to charge for either opportunity."

"No, the BMA gots plenty-o money, they can afford to pay you. Ask for double. And I'll only accept your offer not to send me a bill if you add The Sisters Fellowship and DW Thurman to your client list and let me pick up all expenses. I'll just write it off on the taxes."

They bubbled at each other for a few minutes before Dewey interrupted their school-aged cooing.

"St. John, let me get your opinion on something, please? What did you think about the dress Jolee wore last night?"

Regina hesitated. She didn't have all the girls down. Who was who. But one dress did stick out in her mind. A curve-hugging, red knit that she thought a bit much for the occasion, but…"why do you ask?"

"Very nice, Dr. Lawson, and I already know. There's a body on Jolee and sometimes I struggle with her fashion choices."

"Young women embrace their curves more than we did in our generation."

"Yeah, I'm not questioning her style. It's her judgment. Social media is all abuzz about the Fellowship today and too much of it is about Jo's dress."

"I see."

For years Regina had relied heavily on noncommittal responses. One of the many ways she lost her voice in her marriage. But, there was no way she was going to make the mistake of saying anything against any of his girls.

"This is a busy, messy business. The critics don't stop and with all this Facebook, Insta-Snap-Twitter, it's fast and constant." Dewey went on to explain the social media spin following him and his girls.

Allegra, an alleged lesbian. "Not true. She's just wise and careful." Bonita and Calista, were tagged the saints of praise. Only positive spin followed them. "Appropriately so, since they're both truly good."

Jolee, the smart, sexpot; averaged two inappropriate propositions a week. "…they don't mess with Tasnee. Only because she wasn't of legal age. Now she's eighteen, I guess the gloves will come off. And, my dear there's sometimes gossip about me. Somebody even posted a picture of us from last night."

"Hold the line for a second." Regina picked up her iPad and found the newly posted item on *Gospel Gossip dot com*. Something Rena missed. A cozy side-by-side shot of her sitting next to Dewey during the concert last night. She didn't recall the sweet photo being taken. "My God, that's quick and the comments are kind of crazy."

Since she wasn't nationally known, speculation about her had run rampant. The blogger, PK1974 even wondered if she would be Mrs. DWT#3.

"It's okay with me," Dewey murmured in a low, confident, sexy tone. Then his voice switched octaves. "Now, are you ready to tell me about your decision?"

She took a deep breath. He sounded like he already knew. "I signed the publishing contract."

"Congratulations! I knew you would."

She bit her lower lip. How could he claim to know what she'd do? Was he always such a know-it-all? That could get annoying.

"Now, how best can I support your decision."

Her face broke out in a huge, glowing smile. Smith said she made the wrong decision when they talked. Malik asked how much money he could get from her advance. And Rena expressed a cautious pride. But, Dewey understood her decision from a different point of view. They spoke for over an hour about her plans before he yawned.

"Regina, let's say good night. I'm getting too comfortable, and I don't want to fall asleep on you. But, don't you forget to text me the hotel information. And for your edification, this is a real comfortable bed with plenty of room for two."

She stretched, yawned and giggled. *Lord, I like this fresh young man.*

Chapter Seven

Gentle healing in shades of Gray
As we struggle with all that comes with being human.
All forms of Iniquity.
All covered by God's grace.

Excitement and anticipation had her nerves spinning. Dreams, fantasies, and the possibility of seeing Dewey again didn't mix well with REM sleep. Neither did her mother's cautious voice advising her to settle down. When the alarm rang at seven a.m. on Monday morning, Regina dragged herself out of bed.

"Did I sleep? Or just doze off from time to time?"

No matter what happened with Dewey, she had a responsibility to her students and to herself. The independence she'd fought for in her divorce warned her to take one step at a time. "Don't count your chickens before they are hatched," she repeated her mother's well-worn mantra out loud as she prepared for the day.

∞

As usual, Dr. Lawson was in her classroom an hour before the start of her ten o'clock English class. As expected, not one of her students came in early for help to improve their papers.

"Going forward, I'll use this time to write."

Next week she planned to bring her personal computer and use the hour to work on her book. Warmth rushed to her cheeks. DW Thurman was coming to visit her, and she had a book to write. But most importantly, she sent up a prayer. *Lord, I hope someone I spoke to this weekend adopts the mantra. Keep your heels, head and standards high.*

Regina glanced at the wall clock. In a few minutes, her students would begin arriving. When she reached for her phone to place it on mute, she clicked on one notification. She'd forgotten to read DW Thurman's morning praise song.

"Good Morning, Doctor Lawson."

DW Thurman's morning message would have to wait. Regina lifted her head to greet one of her favorite students. "Good morning, DeAndre. How was your weekend?"

"The same, the same. A little work and a little play."

"I hope that work included getting your research paper outlined."

He shook his head and moved toward his favorite seat, in the back. "No, Ma'am. Worked a double shift at the security desk, because some folks don't like to come to work."

DeAndre had everything it took to be successful in college, if he could only get past his own limited thinking. A campus security desk job was perfect for studying. Few people visited campus on Saturday nights unless there was a function and there wasn't one this weekend.

Most of her students were working and parenting, while trying to get an education. For DeAndre and his classmates, she'd probably extend the due date.

"Good Morning." She made a point to greet and engage each of her students as they filed into the classroom. At the top of the hour, Dr. Regina Lawson began her class with only seventeen of twenty-five students present.

Twenty minutes into her lecture on MLA formatting, the door opened and a spray of purple flowers walked in.

Belinda, the college president's secretary, pushed a huge bouquet of mixed flowers toward her. "Dr. Lawson these just arrived for you."

"Whoo."

"Wow."

"Who they from?"

"Oh, my goodness." She beamed as she reached out for the bouquet. That Dewey Thurman was too much. He not only remembered where she worked, but her class hour.

Belinda passed her the bouquet, then waved a three-by-three card. "Don't you want to read the card?"

"Dr. Lawson got a man."

"I've never seen that many flowers except at a funeral."

"Maybe they're for her birthday," DeAndre yelled from the back.

Sonja shouted, "Those are from a man."

"How'd you know anything about getting flowers from a man?" LaTrella challenged.

"Thank you, Belinda, and you didn't have to bring these. You could have asked me to stop by your office after class."

Regina set the bouquet on the desk and turned back to her class. "Please settle down, and let's turn our attention back to our topic."

"See that smile," Sonja shouted. "That's a man."

The class erupted and Belinda clapped in support.

"You might as well open that card, although I already know," the campus gossip stated. "And I'm not going anywhere until you answer my questions."

"Miss Belinda, I'm in the middle of instruction."

Belinda leaned back on her heels. "Regina Lawson, don't act like we didn't go to high school together, and who do you think sent me down here with these flowers? Your college president. And she wants to see you after class." Belinda rolled her shoulders, then grinned. "Girl, you better dismiss these kids and tell me why DW Thurman is sending you flowers."

"DW Thurman? Who's that?" LaTrella shouted.

"Oh, my God." Belinda shook her head. "Whose raising you children?"

"Lord, today." Sonja started as she pulled out her cellphone. "DW Thurman, the Crown Prince of Gospel Music! Don't you go to church or to your grandma's house?"

LaTrella huffed.

Before the two high school rivals got into it again, Dr. Lawson stepped in. "Class is dismissed and those outlines are still due on Wednesday. And please do yourselves a favor and have something for me to review. Maybe use the rest of this hour to write?"

As the students left the room, most of them made comments about the size and beauty of the flowers. Sonja snapped a photo to show her grandmother, before Dr. Lawson could object.

That picture will be on the internet before I can call Dewey.

As DeAndre filed out with his classmates, he paused. "I hope this dude is a good guy."

Between Belinda and her network of campus security spies, there were so many people peering into her classroom, Regina dismissed her second class early and reported to the President's office. After she told the short story of how she'd met Dewey, Dr. Hardy and Belinda shared their speculations and a picture they downloaded from Gospel Gossip. Then leaned on the bonds of friendship to get DW or The Sisters Fellowship to sing at the next scholarship benefit.

An hour later as she walked to her car with an arm full of flowers, half the financial aid staff followed. News had spread quickly around the small, community college campus. Dewey was going to have writer's cramp, when he fulfilled the dozens of autograph requests she had for him.

Serves him right. Or maybe it's my fault for not giving him my home address?

Instead of going home, she had to go by Rena's house. Not only had big-mouthed Belinda spread her business across campus, she'd posted the bouquet on the college's Facebook page and called Rena.

At least she had a good lunch. Rena's Sunday leftovers served with a side of family gossip and a few more questions. If she hadn't claimed exhaustion, she'd still be at Rena's. Instead Regina now rested on her favorite chair in the den, enjoying her flowers.

The florist had outdone themselves. She couldn't remember ever seeing a floral arrangement with such variety. She recognized the lavender, roses, lilies, carnations, purple iris, greenery and even a few of the succulents. A couple of the flowers she had to Google image. The array of flowers blended perfectly. Regina took in a deep breath of the fragrance, and marveled at DW Thurman's attention. It couldn't be coincidental that the sweet violet and purple tones in the bouquet were among her favorites. Purple was her color and flowers were just the right thing to send.

"How did he know?"

The beauty of the flowers was only outshined by the fragrance of Dewey's morning praise song. As a poet, DW Thurman was insightful and inspiring. She'd picked that up from reviewing several months of his praise songs. Each one she read struck her as approachable. Comforting. Grounded. Not too heavenly-minded to be of any earthly good. As she looked back over the past few years of her life, she recognized how her healing had come gently and in shades of gray. Over time. And by the grace of God, a veil of grief had passed over her life.

Healing in shades of gray. Mama would love this expression. Healing in shades of gray perfectly expressed how time and grace healed the rift between Rena and Mama.

In so many ways, the wisdom she learned from her mother continued to shape and challenge her. And according to Rena, "still ruled her life." Their mother had been tough and focused. What many people in Mobile called high-minded. When their father proved to be the no-count gadfly, Gladys Lawson put him out and raised her girls alone. She was one of the first single mothers in their church. Everyone in the community knew not to bring any foolishness to Gladys Lawson. No man without purpose knocked on her door and the boys knew not to mess with her daughters. She called her mother's determination to make a better life a standard. For the most part, she followed her mother's every word and homespun expression. But Rena rebelled.

It took years for the rift between Rena and Gladys to dissipate and clear. It wasn't until they both became mothers that she and Rena fully came to understand their mother's sayings and fears.

After Mama's stroke, when there was too much tension in her surface-perfect household, Rena took Mama in. And the Lord graced them with three wonderful years.

"Geez." The notification mode on her cellphone chimed so much today it had become background noise. She reached for her phone and opened the Facebook app.

"Wow!"

There were over a hundred comments on a post about her flowers. Likes from people she'd never meet and a comment from her Cousin Barbara, who rarely posted. Dewey'd even posted a comment that opened up an entire thread.

'Looking forward to learning every individual flower that makes up the bouquet of you.'

"Oh, my God. That man is going to have my head totally turned. What an unbelievably sweet thing to say. But," she grimaced, "I wish he wouldn't have said it on Facebook."

Dewey's post generated hundreds of likes and she had some new friend requests. As she read deeper in that thread, she thought she noticed a post from one of the girls.

'Dr. Lawson is like a Rose of Sharon that blooms late in the season.'

"Lovely, I'll have to figure out if beautifulone3 is Bonita or Calista."

Reading further into the thread, she found seeds of ugly. BlessedAndHighlyFavored2 posted that the money Dewey spent on the flowers could have fed a hundred starving children.

"Why would someone post something like that? And more importantly, am I prepared to deal with this?"

The negative post got about fifteen likes, before Tasnee shut it down with a sharp retort.

'You have no right to comment on how my father spends his money, you ain't sang one note! And if you knew anything about DW Thurman, you'd know that his generosity is unmatched.'

"Whew." She set the phone aside and dozed off.

An hour later, as she contemplated moving: maybe going to the grocery store or taking a walk on the beach, the phone rang.

"Thank you, Dewey, the flowers are beautiful."

"You are welcome, and I got your text hours ago. But we're working hard today. I had to wait to call you real quick while we're on break. I've been longing to hear your sweet voice all day. It's a welcome reprieve from the cackling going on in the rehearsal room."

"Stop it." She giggled. "You know your girls sing like angels."

"Yeah, they can blow," he bragged. "But, I never tell them that during rehearsal. Can't have them thinking they don't need to practice. And don't you ever let on that I said so."

She shook her head and took a deep breath. That way he had of speaking into the future both fascinated and agitated her.

"Well, I guess I also have to thank you for blowing up my social media accounts. I've got more likes than I ever have, a dozen new friend requests, and somebody even attacked you for sending me flowers."

"You mean the note about feeding hungry children. I saw that."

"Yes. Tasnee jumped into that thread to defend you."

"Regina, don't pay it any mind. Some people are mean. You'll get used to it. Let it roll—"

"Like water off a duck's back." She added an expression she'd heard a million times from her mother.

"Yes. Just like that. Social media is full of sad, messy people and we've been trying to school Tasnee all afternoon about letting stuff like this slide. Think, I'll quote you when I go back in. See, how you keep teaching us, Dr. Lawson. And just so you know, teacher, I can't wait to study you."

That man can slip a fresh comment into any conversation.

"When I call you later, you can tell me which flower is your favorite."

Two weeks later, just like he said he would, Dewey arrived in Mobile. He actually came a day early. He drove in from Atlanta on Thursday evening, and they shared a romantic late night supper in his hotel suite. And when she chose not to spend the night, he drove her home, kissed her goodnight slowly and asked her to call him in the morning.

Regina Lawson woke up early Friday morning feeling like she'd slept on a bed of roses. She yawned and stretched. Then rolled over to gaze at the calla lilies on her bedside table. Last night Dewey Thurman confirmed her hopes. His interest was sincere.

DW Thurman left his daughters a day early to fly into Atlanta. Then drove straight to Mobile to surprise her. She inhaled. The remnants of the spice from his slightly, wicked cologne greeted the morning with her. Had he sprayed his cologne on the card he'd given her with the flowers?

Dewey's old school-charm would be her undoing. She reached over to pick up the card and inhaled hints of smoke and spice, "Um, sexy." Then read the card for the umpteenth time.

'Calla is Greek for beautiful. Blessed to have met such a beautiful woman. Looking forward to our time together—Dew.'

He knew just how to appeal to her mind, body and soul. Instead of hopping out of bed, she hugged his note to her chest and indulged in a daydream. With boyish charm and freshness, Dewey kissed and caressed her last night until she felt like a teenager. His touch needful, yet gentle. His lips soft, his tongue firm and he applied just enough pressure with his embrace to have her dreaming about saying *yes*.

"But," she said as she swung her feet out of bed. "We will see."

It would take more than a surprise arrival, wine and a perfectly seasoned grilled salmon dinner. As she prepared for the day she wondered how Dewey defined morning. After his long traveling day, she decided to wait until at least ten.

Around ten-ish, her first call went straight to voice mail. Maybe it was too early. She left a message and waited for his return call. An hour later, she checked her phone. No call, no message and no social media presence from DW Thurman today.

No matter, I'm sure he'll call when he can.

"But, what if he doesn't?" Regina shook her head and went to her study. She had research paper drafts to review, a speech to write, and a book to outline. "He'll call when he can."

Two hours later, she startled when the phone rang. "Dewey!"

No. "Hello, Rena."

"Are you ready for your weekend guest?" Rena reiterated the itinerary she'd mapped out for DW Thurman's visit. A list of expensive restaurants, jazz clubs, and of course a visit to her church on Sunday morning. "And remember, John and I are on standby. Any time you want us to come by the house or have us meet you somewhere, we're ready."

"Okay, okay. But, Dewey's already here. We had dinner last night."

"What? And you didn't call me?"

Regina rolled her eyes. "I recall being good and grown. And I don't have to tell you everything. But I will share that we had a lovely dinner in his suite, and he had me back home by eleven."

"You didn't spend the night?"

"Rena," she hooted. "You are a mess and of course not. That's not my style or speed."

"You know you wanted to. I think DW Thurman may have your number. Surprise visit, sending all those flowers and notes. That's just the Rom-Com movie kinda stuff that you like."

"Not so fast. I still haven't heard from him today. It's after one, and I called him at ten."

"Nothing since last night. Did you check social media?"

She shook her head sadly. "Nothing."

"Girl, you better call the hotel and request a wellness check on that old man."

Regina looked wistfully out the window. "I'm not doing anything. If he's changed his mind. Then that's that. I am not chasing after DW Thurman or any man. Just like I don't intend to get tangled up in any drama or nonsense."

"And you're not the least bit concerned."

"Umm, a little," she murmured.

"Well, I'm going to call around. Discreetly. Somebody's child works at the Hilton. It's not unheard of for a housekeeper to tap on the door at this hour. I'll text you if I find out anything."

"Ugh. I can't stop you. And I know you'll call me with what you find out." Regina hung up the phone and contemplated lunch. The idea Rena planted in her head pushed her from being annoyed to concerned. What if something had happened to Dewey? He had complained last night about something in the salmon sauce that didn't sit right with his palate.

At three fifteen, Dewey called and apologized. "It took longer to recover from my travels than I'd hoped. But I'm fit and ready to spend the remains of the day with you. Which means until at least midnight. But, instead of a walk through the Botanical Garden, can we go to a movie?"

Chapter Eight

Glory in the Morning
The freshness of the day.
And a new wash of his Mercy.

Dewey whistled a verse of "Tennessee Whiskey" before taking a deep draw on his pipe. On the exhale, he hummed. As he settled deeper into the wicker papasan chair on his balcony, he looked beyond the Atlanta skyline and imagined himself swinging on a backyard patio in Mobile.

Things were fresh with his new lady love. Regina was smooth, sweet, and warm just like the lyrics of Stapleton's song. And so totally unaware of the seductive power of her standard.

"I'm 'bout to fool around and fall in love."

In six short weeks, he'd been to New York, Florida, California, and Mobile, Alabama twice. He had no business traveling so much with his bad knees. But first thing in the morning, he was driving to Mobile, again.

This spring seemed greener, his steps lighter, and he'd almost convinced his daughters that the chronic pain in his knees had subsided. He could hardly wait to sit again with Regina on her porch. Swinging with her on that porch offered him a quiet reprieve from the hustle of his life. Perhaps, if he slowed down and spent more time on that swing, his knees would heal.

When he put off having surgery in February, he thought it was to avoid burdening his ageless, unstoppable mother with taking care of him. Now, he knew what moved him to change his agenda and attend that conference in Birmingham. Dr. Regina Lawson had lured him there, through her YouTube channel. He'd watched all of her videos trying to understand why his daughters were such fans. The woman he saw on YouTube was attractive, but came off as stuffy and unapproachable. But during that first encounter with her in the elevator, he saw through her well-crafted professional veneer. In that fleeting moment before she recognized him, he saw a hint of her character. And after she settled into their conversation during breakfast, he knew she would challenge him. His youthful spirit enjoyed teasing her. But, the compassion she showed towards the conference attendees pierced his heart. Dewey took another healing draw on his pipe and mellowed. Regina's attentions had renewed his drive and spirit.

Too bad she couldn't accompany him last week for his annual Easter concert at Harold's church. Now his best man wouldn't officially meet his next wife until she spoke at the BMA women's conference in June. But, that hadn't stopped him from introducing Rev. Mims to the lady virtually. Harold quickly became a standards fan via Regina's YouTube channel.

"Come Sunday, we'll be the grandest couple at the Shiloh Memorial Baptist Church," he sang. It was a big deal for a girl like Regina Lawson to invite a guy to church. And he couldn't wait to parade her around on his arm. He even had a new suit for the occasion.

Dewey reached for the paperwork in his lap. The offer from WSOL, the Soul Centered Network. A new Black-owned television network dedicated to ministering to the souls of Black people. The station's owners wanted "Everlasting" to serve as the opening image when the network premiered in the fall. They hoped to use the song as a prayer of faith that the network would endure. And beyond that, the station requested a clearance to create a network identity bumper using his song.

All that was left was his signature. If the network held true to its promise of integrity and positive programming, there could be multiple opportunities for his family. But, he hesitated to sign. This was the first time he'd ever agreed to sell any part of his redemption song.

Dewey placed the papers back in their envelope and set the agreement aside. Then, he flipped through the rest of the letters on his side table. Invitations for him or the girls to accept an award or sing at a fundraising event. Most of the invitations for him were from churches or charitable organizations. And too many for the girls were from secular organizations.

"I'll leave these for Allegra to decide." Dewey took a final deep draw from his pipe and set it in an ashtray.

He'd skip the annual homecoming service at Family Fellowship in Chicago this weekend to spend more time with Regina. If his mother wasn't already in Chicago, he'd take her to meet Regina this weekend. Allegra was more than capable; The Sisters Fellowship didn't need him to function. And Tasnee wouldn't give her any problems, not for a performance at her stepfather's church.

The girls and their mothers urged him to slow down. Minnie did too. They all thought that it was too soon to bring Regina into the circle of his confidence. Harold also counseled caution. Mims' challenge echoed in his mind. *"Is it vision or passion?"*

He'd consider Harold's advice. But he knew. It was time to share some truths about himself with Regina, and he prayed the spirit would reveal the right moment, this weekend.

On Sunday evening, Regina yawned and settled into Dewey's embrace as they rocked on her porch swing.

"I like it here," he said. "Swinging in the evening on this porch with you. I'm thrilled you finally thought enough of a brother to invite him to church. And I truly appreciate your pastor for not asking me to sing."

Regina nodded. "Thank his wife for pulling his collar."

"Ha-ha." Dewey laughed. "I haven't heard that one in a while."

"My mother used to say it every time the Mothers Board had to take hold of a preacher."

"Well, I thoroughly enjoyed my Sunday off. Excellent preaching, fellowship, and a terrific meal. And I'm glad you like your Easter gift enough to wear it for me today."

"Dewey, it's a beautiful piece. I absolutely love it and you spent too much." Rena had appraised the bronze and amber broach that arrived in a basket full of flowers for Easter at well over a thousand dollars.

Regina emitted a soft yawn and settled. It had been a minute since she'd opened her home to host a Sunday dinner, and she'd almost forgotten how much work it was. "I hadn't intended to have so much company. But, when one is dating a celebrity, a small family gathering morphs into a party for twenty. Thanks to church protocol and Rena's big mouth."

In addition to Malik, Smith, Rena, John and their five kids, she had to invite the Pastor's family and church elders to dinner.

Dewey grinned. "I enjoyed them all."

With all the attention her guests showered on Dewey, she felt like she hadn't talked to him all afternoon. Her guests completely monopolized the famous singer's time. Yet, observing Dewey's grace through all of their questions, remembrances and fan-gushing, had been her favorite part of the day. So far. She was glad they were all gone now, so he could sing to her.

Singing old torch songs was clearly his stock-in-trade. The way he planned to woo her into his bed. His singing was becoming her favorite part of their time together. As they planned for his third visit, she considered inviting Dewey to stay at her house. In the guest room. She decided against it since her boys were down for the weekend. Besides she didn't have the strength to resist him. Not when he sang.

"See how well I fit in?" Dewey teased as they rocked.

She let out a contented sigh. "It was a lovely Sunday."

"And you are perfect. Everything had your special touch. Very classy St. John. And if it comes with a pot of greens every Sunday, I'll marry you tomorrow."

She laughed. "You can get a pot of greens anytime you ask."

"Alright! But don't set a date until Rena agrees to make the wedding cake. Any more of her pound cake left?"

"Rena wrapped the last piece up and set it aside for you." She smirked at him. "Rena will bake you a cake any time you ask. Especially after you agreed to show up for her program next month."

Dewey's generous offer to perform as an unannounced, open secret, surprise guest for Rena's annual scholarship concert would triple the donations.

"I'm just trying to get next to you," he sang in a seductive key.

In addition to charming her, Dewey had made it his business to completely get into Rena's good graces. He'd also made fast friends with her brother-in-law, John. Those two were already planning to go deep-sea fishing as soon as Dewey could fit the trip into his schedule.

"So, when you coming to Atlanta to meet my mama?"

She shrugged.

He whistled.

On the backswing, Regina stretched her legs. A little release for her muscles after spending most of the afternoon on her feet.

"Dew, I've been meaning to ask you about the praise song from the other day. *A new wash of mercy.* Is that a line from a hymn?"

"No," he gently squeezed her shoulders. "But, hearing you say that…" He fell silent for a few minutes. "I'll dwell on that thought. Could be a song in there. A new wash of mercy sounds like a good country song. All I need is to find three chords for this truth." He chuckled. "DW Thurman pens a country cross-over hit. Wonder how my fans would react?"

"I'd hate to see us miss a blessing over a music genre."

"Yeah," he nodded, "not when a new wash of mercy is so needed for our people. Especially the young folk. Maybe I'll ask the girls to put some of that hip-hope spin on the phrase? Make it appealing to their demographic. I hesitate to say this, but maybe I should consult with Young Iggy. Cause, Lord knows I just don't understand this modern music. Songs aren't constructed anymore."

"That reminds me. Malik said he saw you on that Rappers of Atlanta TV show?"

"Yes, me and the girls are under contract to appear on the show from time to time. Little non-speaking cameos to keep our name in front of the younger generation. Because of the show and Young Iggy's criminal tendencies, celebrity photographers also skulk around the building—TMZ style. Sometimes they snap a photo or two of me. Since the gospel-gossip websites, and blogs also pay for celebrity photos. I've tried to work this connection to our advantage."

They swung in silence for a few minutes before Dewey began a now familiar refrain. "In R&B the woman who sang about heartache knows from experience. You can follow it in the lyrics and feel it in her voice. And when the soloist ministers about the goodness of the Lord; you know the singer understood from whence the song had come."

"Um," she hummed as the psalmist continued.

"I ain't saying nothing against any one of these other singers out here, but if you listen, there's no scriptural basis for most of those songs they're singing these days." Dewey shook his head in sorrow. "Lady, remember a few years ago when Young Iggy had a hit with just rapping through the books of the bible."

Regina chuckled in remembrance. "Sixty-Six Books" had a hot beat. But that was about it.

"Didn't take no discernment or anointing to put down a beat and spit out the books of the bible. I couldn't believe it when he previewed sixty-six for me. Even asked if I wanted to sing the hook. Pfft." Dewey blew out, before resuming. "But that's what counts for a song these days. How is that supposed to minister to a broken heart? Lead somebody to the Lord? Ain't nothing like a good-ole-been-through-something and came-out-on-the-other-end kind of praise song," Dewey clapped and shouted. "And that's what I want for the girls."

In the last month, Dewey had turned down a dozen offers that would move The Sisters Fellowship into secular music. Decisions that put him in the doghouse with both Tasnee and Bonita.

"Pop singers come and go. And, I don't want the girls to chance that fleeting fame. I want them to find the longevity I've had. If they keep it clean and scriptural, they will have long careers. But one misstep or scandal and the entire Fellowship could be over. I am struggling to help them recognize that any one of them can ruin it for all of them. That's why your work on setting a standard is so insightful. I can't wait for the blessings that will come from your work with the girls this summer."

As the sun faded into evening, her smile brightened. Dewey worked wonders for her ego.

When his phone chimed, Dewey smiled and opened a text from

Tasnee. "It went well today," he said before sharing a photo of Tasnee playfully posed with a little boy.

"That's a beautiful photo. Is he Deborah's grandson?"

"No Dewey stretched. "Beautiful picture and the pain behind Deb's smile. That's her husband's son and the reason she's divorcing him. She's tried, but can't reconcile the years of infidelity and living the reminder anymore."

"Oh my," Regina exclaimed, "I'm surprised the members didn't put him out."

"No, the newer members like having a pastor with real life struggles. But divorce might be the last straw for the deacon board."

She reached for Dewey's phone and looked at the photo again. "This is the boy the gossip columns said was yours?"

Dewey put his foot down and stopped the swing. "You know about him? Why didn't you say something?"

She frowned and shook her head. "I refuse to bring gossip to you. I decided to trust and wait—"

"Lady," he cut her off, "you don't have to wait for anything. Whatever you need to know," he pointed to his chest, "ask the source. And you understand that when Tasnee speaks about her little brother, it's often attributed to me. The public just knows me as her father. They don't care about our mixed-up, blended family." He shrugged, "I don't bother with the rumors, because they don't hurt me. At least not with anyone I care about. Tasnee adores her baby brother. But more than anything, I'm so glad you asked me instead of believing the gossip." Dewey lifted her hand to his face and kissed her palm. "You just keep affirming what I knew from the moment I met you." He held her hand for a moment and turned it over in his. "There is more I want to share with you. And I believe the time is right."

"I'm here."

Dewey drew in a deep breath and stood. "Lady, I feel blessed beyond measure to have found such a jewel at this point in my life. And I don't want there to be any secrets or misunderstandings between us. If we are going to continue, I need you to know that there will be times when I won't be present."

She planted her feet on the stone patio floor. *I've already lived this story. Maybe, this fantasy is about to end?*

"Regina, my spiritual gifts require that I spend time alone. Significant time to dwell in the spirit. To listen, play, sing, and write. Time when I will not be available for you." He ended with a sad tone.

Regina closed her eyes. "I understand. Sometimes people need their own space. I've come to cherish mine."

"No, ma'am, it runs a little deeper than that. I can spend hours, sometimes days, waiting for a Word from the Lord. And even then, if He gives me a message or revelation, it might take days to process and come back from a time of communion. Lady, I hold the spiritual office of Prophet and it holds prominence in my life."

While he spoke, the light seemed to shift in on the patio. Regina shivered and one of her mother's adages crossed her mind. She wrapped her arms around her body until the chill that supposedly comes over the body when someone walks over your grave subsided. Her eyes twitched as she tried to grasp what Dewey was telling her. She hugged herself tighter as a need for light and warmth rushed into her spirit. She hopped up and headed towards the back door. "Let's go in the den and talk."

Chapter Nine

What have we lost because we cannot stand still?
Take a moment today to stand still and find sweet solace in silence.

A dozen thoughts raced through Regina's head as she rushed to the den. Once in her favorite room, she focused on the décor to settle her nerves. When she moved to Mobile full-time, she immediately took all of the sports-themed memorabilia, and teen-aged-boy strong furniture from the room and redecorated with overstuffed sofas and soft, floral prints. The first time she'd ever set up a room solely for her own comfort.

After plopping onto a chair, she repositioned herself twice. Dewey's revelation had her spirit jangled and her nerves dancing. Uncomfortable in her own home and unable to settle in her favorite chair. She squirmed as her right brain tried to find a word for how she felt. It wasn't anything sinister. Or fear. Just dis-ease. She took several deep breaths before admitting Dewey's announcement had totally-kinda-freaked her out.

"Regina, what are you thinking? Want to say? Ask me?"

She sank further into her reading chair, took several deep, cleansing breaths, willed her mind to settle and her chills to subside. Then clarity struck.

That's why his songs are so timeless.

As she thought about the prophetic message in all his songs, it dawned on her that Dewey told her something she already knew. There was always something special about his music. His admonition on the destructive force in music that would unleash on to the black community in the late '80s was chilling. And the refrain from "Everlasting" prophesied a happy ending for the lives of the faithful. That song was almost forty years old and it still spoke volumes. Regina shook her head in affirmation and warmth slowly returned to her fingers. "Nothing. This might sound strange, but I think I already knew."

Dewey exhaled. "I'm so glad to get that off my chest. Everyone said it was too soon to bring this to you. But, I knew you'd respond well. Bo shared with me how patiently you waited in Birmingham. Listen, Lady, I wanted to tell you this so you'll understand. There are times when I need to be alone to dwell in the spirit; wait and listen. It happened the first time I visited. I'd planned to take you out to breakfast. In fact, I was so excited for the day I woke up too early to call. Then I lost track of time while praying. I'd been seeking a word about that hip-hope thing the girls are talking about. I'm still not clear on why I'm so reluctant. I should have shared this with you then. But, I wasn't sure of you. But I am now. Lady, I don't want you to ever feel neglected. Or think you can't trust me when—."

"Dewey," she interrupted. "I think I get it."

He raised his hands in praise. "I know you are a Godly woman because of how you responded to the shepherd's crook before I ever met you. Your every action confirms it." He spread out his arms and motioned for her to come to him.

They sat in the solace of silence for a long while. Sitting next to Dewey fully restored her warmth. Her pulse returned to normal and a few coherent questions formed in her mind.

"Dewey, I did wonder about something. Can I ask?"

"Anything. Any time."

"I still marvel and don't understand how you gave that word of wisdom to the football player's wife in Birmingham? Did you receive a revelation in that moment?"

"No." He shook his head. "That was more about my observation skills. It wasn't difficult to see into that situation. I always look twice at anyone wearing sunglasses inside. And when a little light got behind those sunglasses…" He shrugged. "But, I understand your question. The two graces are often confused. Too often we fail to recognize or simply miss what's right under our noses. These days people shy away from really, looking at others because we're trying to be polite. In some ways, we are being conditioned not to pay attention and speak out. In most families, you dare not say anything about somebody's child. Find something you object to in the so-called entertainment they are pushing these days. Question something on social media and see what happens. We are missing so much. How'd the old folks used to say? 'If it was a snake it would have bit ya.'"

Regina nodded. "Pick it up and brush it off."

"Yes." His face softened in a brief smile. "My mama says that too. We also miss too much because we're so inwardly focused we can't see what's clearly in front of our faces. It's not so much a spiritual gift, but an awareness I've developed over the years. Remember how the elders always seemed to know when a child was going astray? It's because they were observant. Some things are just common sense. Anyone who's paying attention can see when a young person is doing things that will lead to success or destruction. But, it's more than just observing. Everybody in the family knows which teenage girl is going to pop up pregnant next. But do they sit and gossip among themselves? Or share a word of wisdom to try to redirect the child.

Our families are in ruin because our elders are sitting on their standard and not speaking that wisdom."

Regina's brain tried for several minutes to reconcile the difference between prophesy and observation. Her great aunt Pearl had what they called second sight. Aunt Pearl seemed to see everything anyone in the family was doing wrong and never had a positive word for anyone.

Rena still teased her about how she got the middle name, Pearl. Family legend held that shortly after birth, Aunt Pearl came to write her name in the family bible. Like she did with every member of the family. Aunt Pearl blessed her and wrote Regina Pearl instead of Regina Elizabeth. Growing up, she feared she'd eventually turn into her great aunt. At every family gathering, the creepy old woman would sit quietly at the table nodding or frowning. Observing. She steered clear of Aunt Pearl. In the eighties, there was a huge rift in the family because of one of Aunt Pearl's observations.

"Dewey, a prophetic word isn't always something bad, is it?"

Dewey rubbed his head. "It might seem that way. But, in my experience, it's conditional. A prophetic word is a blessing if the hearer is obedient."

"Aunt Pearl always said a word to the wise is sufficient."

"Truth."

"And can I ask if Bonita and Calista are spiritually gifted, too?"

"Yes." He smiled. "It seems you're observant, too, Regina Pearl."

Regina groaned. They sat in silence for a while longer while she processed. As she pondered, Regina crossed her arms over her chest and shifted her body. This was too much. Prophecy, second sight and observational spiritual gifts. She was purposefully practical and always steered clear of the metaphysical. Dating a man with spiritual gifts. Dating a prophet? Could one even do that?

"Regina," he nudged her, "I'm just a man."

Regina blew out the breath she didn't realize she'd been holding. "Do your powers include mind reading, too?"

"No. I'm just picking up on your facial expressions and body language."

"You're not just a man, Dewey. You are extraordinary, and it goes beyond your fame. There is something in your daily praise songs that lifts and inspires. There's this uncommon grace about you when you are engaging with people. You can feel it from the stage. The way you've fashioned your family is extraordinary. I can't imagine having lunch with Mandy, much less banding together with her for the sake of the boys." She placed her hand on his arm. "Thank you for sharing more of yourself with me tonight. It does or will help me reconcile the mystery of you. But I do have to admit, it kind of freaks me out that you always seem to know what I'm thinking."

"I assure you, I'm just guessing or," he winked, "trying to be suggestive."

She tensed. "And that's it. How do you move so effortlessly between your roles of being this gospel music icon and father? Business man and beau? The way you switch from a frisky almost teenage-like boy to stately gentleman. It's charming and confusing. And now between prophet and observant." She twisted her lips. "It's a lot to take in."

"I know. And that's just a guess, based on the look on your face."

They allowed for more silence as she worked to pull it all together. Dewey was an enigma and it was increasingly difficult for her to figure out if she could see herself in a long-term relationship with him. And this was *not* something she'd planned to figure out after a month or so of long-distance dating. Dewey tended to speak in the future tense, while she was still trying to reconcile her past.

"Regina, I need you to know, I never use my prophetic gift for personal gain. And I cannot. Will not, use it to manipulate or force my way. I know too many who use God's gifts to take advantage of the people, especially women. The gift is to guide the people to the Lord, not myself. And I need for you to understand that as you seek to understand me. The Lord is the shepherd. I am simply the crook used to pull the sheep back into the fold."

Regina let out a contented yawn and shifted in the warmth of his embrace. Over the years, too many people had approached her with a "God told me to tell you" message that almost always ended up in a request for money. In the month or so they'd been getting to know each other, Dewey hadn't asked her for anything. Not even to stay at her house when he visited.

She rested in the assurance of his fidelity, not to her, but to the Lord. The knowledge of Dewey's spiritual gift gave her new insight into the man sitting patiently with her. There was definitely a chasm between the fresh young man she was halfway in love with and the profound, know-it-all prophet.

Regina shook her head *no* to push back the questions that raced through her brain. This was not how she planned to spend the balance of this evening. All she wanted was to sit back and let Dewey charm her with classic R&B loves songs. They only had one more day before Dewey started a three-week tour with Morehouse.

Instead Dewey forced her to deal with transcendent questions. He also challenged her to deal with a reality about herself. She wanted to believe her work was about giving good advice. But he saw more in her message. His revelation combined with the weariness of a long day re-set her nerves. She closed her eyes and prayed for a few minutes to settle the battle between the left and right sides of her brain.

"Regina."

She startled at his gentle nudge. Then glanced at the wall clock. Half past ten. He'd let her take a nice little snooze.

"Lady, I'm sure you're tired. Why don't you turn in. I'm going back to the hotel and I'll call you in the morning. I've got an itch to play and since you don't have a piano," he nudged her, "I think I'll make use of the instrument in the lobby. Some poor night clerk's going be annoyed or blessed."

A slow smile covered her face. He'd threatened to bring a keyboard with him this weekend when the hotel couldn't accommodate his request for a piano in his suite. "No, I'm still a little freaked out, and I don't know if I'll be able to rest." She shuddered. After their conversation, she needed comfort. "Will you stay with me tonight?"

"Come on." He helped her up from the sofa. "You go ahead and do what you need to and get ready for bed. I'll get you a glass of water and make sure your house is secure."

She yawned again, comforted by his care.

Regina spent more time in her en-suite bathroom than usual. Apprehensive, after inviting Dewey into her bed because she didn't want to be alone tonight. Not after feeling the chill and the spooky vibes she experienced on the porch. Oddly, she'd disassociated those feeling from her need for human contact tonight. Not just human contact. Dewey. *But what if he's the type of man that confused comfort and consolation with sex?*

Regina took a deep breath and reached for the doorknob.

"Girl, do you always take so long in the bathroom?" Dewey growled, as soon as she walked into her bedroom.

He had the cutest way of modulating his voice to express his moods, and she beamed. "You always got jokes." She exhaled. "I recall waiting over an hour for you to come out of the bathroom that night in Birmingham."

Sharing a laugh eased the tension.

Regina yawned. Dewey's fresh-boy spirit replaced the haunting mood of their discussion in the den. As she focused on the shadowy figure sitting across the room, she rejoiced in knowing that for once her bedroom chair wasn't covered with a stack of laundry. She turned her head slightly towards the bed. He'd only turned down one side.

"How did you know what side I sleep on?" she asked.

"I keep telling you I'm observant. And, Regina, if you'll allow it, I'll sleep on top of the covers tonight. I brought myself a throw from the den. Or I can sleep in this chair?"

She stretched out her hand. "I'd like you closer."

Dewey slowly ambled over to join her in bed.

"Listen," he began in a muted tone after they settled, "we can talk more if you like, or if you're comfortable, it will be my pleasure to hold you until you fall asleep."

Chapter Ten

Beloved, face the world—
With equal parts of grace, strength, and steel.

Hours after waking up in Dewey's arms, Regina drove to the Mobile Hilton to pick him up for lunch. She worried about how effective she'd been in the classroom this morning. Since her mind wasn't on teaching. She would have rather stayed in bed all day, but Dewey insisted she get up and go to work.

As she waited for him in the lobby, she mentally re-sang this morning's praise song. Her sorry rendition of "Grace and Strength" didn't compare to the Crown Prince of Gospel's singing the morning praise in her ear earlier. And, before he left this afternoon— she hoped he'd sing the torch song he owed her. Their weighty conversation last night left no room for love songs. Or anything else. Last night he'd only held her close and gently caressed her forearm until she fell asleep.

Every time the elevator chimed, she looked up. No Dewey. She shrugged off her disappointment and hummed the song that soothed her soul.

"Grace, strength, and steel." *He really ought to write a country song.*

Lost in thought, she'd tuned out the lobby sounds. She looked up several minutes later to see Dewey approaching. The smile that spread across her lips drooped as he moved closer. From the pace of his steps, she knew something was wrong. Maybe she was observant?

Did he know something was coming? Is that why he told me about his spiritual gift last night?

After all of his honest talk, this seemed a little too coincidental. As he approached, she braced for that proverbial other shoe to drop.

"Lady, it's not spiritual."

She scowled. *Why did he always speak as if he could read my mind?*

"I've finally found out what's going on with Bonita."

She reached for his hand. Her heart skipped a beat at the deep sadness in his eyes. "Is it something you care to share?"

Together they moved to a sofa a few feet away.

Without an ounce of his usual vigor, he laid out his pain. "My Bo claims to be in love with an inmate at the Illinois State Penitentiary. Someone she met while doing prison ministry. The hip-hope music pressure is coming from him. This inmate is trying to enter the Christian rap game with Bonita Thurman as his vehicle." Dewey rubbed his bald head. "She claims it's real. I know it's not."

"Oh, my God. That's the last thing I thought you were going to say."

As a father, this couldn't be what he wanted for Bonita. For any of the girls and it's certainly not something she'd want for her sons. But how could he be so sure Bonita hadn't found true love?

Bonita got caught up after the Reverend Banks of the Family Fellowship Missionary Baptist Church couldn't inspire any volunteers from his congregation to support his new prison ministry.

Dewey explained. "As part of her training, her stepfather asked her to join. I called Banks this morning."

Rev. Banks shared Omni's background. Initially, Rev. Omni's assistance during the bible study visits by Family Fellowship was welcomed and appreciated. Until an observant guard discovered that Omni was grooming Rev. Bonita. The guard explained the psychological con-game to Rev. Banks and pointed out that Bonita had already brought the inmate a telephone calling card and put money on his books. Money Bonita claimed was for Rev. Omni to bless the other inmates.

"Banks stopped taking her on the prison visits. But the die was cast. Bonita continued corresponding with inmate Omni. We need to pray she sees the light. There is nothing an association with some prisoner can add to her life."

Of the dozen or so thoughts that ran through her mind, one rose to the top. "This isn't public knowledge, is it? I mean we're not going to see this on Gospel Gossip, are we?"

"Don't know," he shook his head, "It hasn't gotten out yet. But, that's one more thing to worry about. No, right now and as of this morning, it's just known within the family. Bo let something slip when she and Tasnee were talking about that hip-hope music concept last night. Tas called me this morning. I have mixed emotions about Tas. I'm glad she alerted me, but," he frowned, "she also had three other choices on how to handle Bo's revelation."

"Good Lord, Bonita seems so level-headed. How's the rest of the family taking this news?"

"Not well. Mama's staying in Chicago for a few more days to try to talk some sense into Bo. Deb's upset and feeling guilty. Four years ago, she paved the way for Bo to move to Chicago and train under her husband. Myra is so furious I can't even talk with her. It took me a couple of hours to settle Bo from the tongue-lashing her mother gave her. I had just gotten her settled when you called. I should have asked you to come up and help. Sorry I kept you waiting."

"No, no. I'm just floored." As her mother would say "that's life. In the blink of an eye it all changes."

She nodded. "I'll understand if you want to catch the next flight to Chicago."

"No." He looked into her eyes and pushed out a weak smile. "I am here with you. And you promised me some good gumbo. I've been holding on to that all morning. Please, let's salvage something of our day. I had to cancel on John without sharing any details. Will you let him know I want a rain check on our golf game, if I don't get a chance to call him later."

"Sure." She grasped his hand.

As sorry as she felt for the trouble in Dewey's extended family, she prayed it was still possible to enjoy what was left of their last day together for almost a month.

⁓

"Are you sure this is the place?" Dewey turned up his nose twenty minutes later when Regina pulled onto a gravel lot in back of a small, seafood shack.

"I'll ask you not to judge this book by its cover." She shot him a little side-eye. "I agree it doesn't look like much, but I promise you the freshest, tastiest, most authentic, and best gumbo in Alabama. And," she pointed her index finger, "put on that showman's smile because the owner is a high school classmate."

Of course, the best table in the small eatery was reserved and waiting for DW Thurman. His mood lifted a bit as the chef and restaurant staff showered him with attention and fan-memories. But, as they feasted on gumbo, red beans, and sweet tea, Dewey's phone repeatedly buzzed. Between bites, he shot off quick texts to most of the notifications. Halfway through the meal, he answered one particular ring.

"Baby, I am not in a place to talk right now." Dewey spent almost five minutes before ending the call with his youngest and placing his phone on Do not Disturb. "Sorry, but she won't hold that for long. Tasnee is upset about the dragging her stepfather is getting today, and she's trying to bring me into that drama long distance. I can't bite on that. But, this gumbo?"

"Hmm," she murmured.

"I'll stick to the tune of today for only a minute longer. Even with the evidence of the man's infidelity and Deb's suffering, Tas loves her stepfather. I can't argue or be bitter about that. Banks has been kind to my daughters, and I am grateful for that. But, Tas is struggling with her own questions of loyalty to her stepfather. There's a lot of emotion in that house today."

Regina empathized with the stress at Deborah's house and worried about Dewey's youngest. She'd noticed when she met the girls that Tasnee could be dramatic and a tad too much. A tendency that seemed to play out well for her on stage. She sent up a quick prayer that Tasnee would settle down and give her father some rest. It seemed awfully selfish of Tasnee to call Dewey with her stuff. Especially after dropping the Bonita situation on him.

Regina sighed, and switched to a new tune. "What stop are you most looking forward to on your tour?"

"The one you're going to join me on." He winked.

Regina smirked. He'd asked and she'd declined a dozen times. Last week she shut the door on riding with Rena and John to meet the Morehouse tour in Nashville. For the next few weeks she planned to glue her butt to a chair and write. She intended to meet her publisher's deadline. Now that he'd switched to his playful nature, she'd continue with her plans for their day. They only had a few more hours before he'd get on the road, and she wanted to part on a high note. "Up for a walk on the beach?"

Dewey raised his hand to signal the chef. "Come on, let's take those pictures. And make sure y'all tag me on social media when you post."

"I love it out here." Regina breathed out as they strolled along the boardwalk outside of the restaurant. She glanced across the waters at the multimillion-dollar houses she dreamed about in her youth. "When we were girls, Rena and I would come out here and dream about the houses on the other side of the bay."

"And look at God. You live two blocks from the beach now," he said before reaching down to rub his right knee.

She smiled and nodded. "You're right. I got really close. See the black and white one with the wrap around windows. It's a newer house and my current favorite."

"If that's the one you want, it's yours."

"Yeah, right." She laughed.

Dewey reached for her hand. "I'll sing a thousand songs to get it for you. You know I'm out here trying to be your cake daddy."

She hooted and stepped off the boardwalk to plant her feet in the sand. They didn't move a hundred feet before Dewey's phone vibrated.

"Bonita," he mouthed and motioned towards a bench on the boardwalk.

She shrugged and waved him off. Walking on the beach always energized her as a girl, and in recent years, she'd found her peace again by walking on the beach. Regina removed her shoes and moved towards the shoreline. Something about the way sun, sand, and surf worked together helped her organize the world. Each element fulfilled its own function, but in unity. She turned her back on the water for a moment to wave at Dewey as he sat on a public bench talking to Bonita.

His devotion to his daughters kinda put her to shame. While she understood dating such a doting father would mean sharing some part of her life with his girls, she didn't think she'd mind. Not at this stage in the relationship. But, today's drama brought new questions.

If she continued dating Dewey, what role would she play in his daughters' lives?

The way Dewey and his ex-wives had banded together for the girls was nothing short of miraculous. She couldn't imagine working with Mandy for the good of her sons. "But, when the day comes," she turned and spoke to the water. When the boys married or had children, she hoped for the grace to work with the Step-Grandma Mandy.

As she made footprints in the wet sand, Regina celebrated the current peace she enjoyed by not being caught up in her sons' business. "But, day coming." She spoke the old-fashioned phrase out loud to the wind.

It was time to ask some long overdue questions to Malik. Victor sent several terse emails last month asking when she planned to stop financing Malik's Peter Pan lifestyle. Her ex-husband suggested she cut their son off— financially. Because he had. And recommended she check in with Smith, too. Victor worried Smith was stressing too much about the opening of his business. But she had a sneaking suspicion something beyond the opening his business was bothering their oldest.

Regina moved away from the water's edge to bury her wet feet in warm, dry sand. A free spa treatment she'd enjoyed since childhood. As she drank in the sea air and sun, her mother's wisdom reminded her "not to get gray hairs over other folks worries."

"Regina, Regina," Dewey yelled and waved as he wobbled toward her. His steps uneven as he crossed the sand.

"You get Bonita settled?" she asked when he came within earshot.

"No. There's more to share."

She took a deep breath and prepared for the second wave.

"When we talked last night, you picked up on Bonita and Calista being spiritually gifted?"

Her toes curled up in the sand.

"When Tasnee couldn't get a word out of me, she started in on Calista. She pressed Calista for a prophetic word all afternoon and then started in on Bo."

Regina gasped.

"I know Tas is wrong. She's desperate to know if things in her life will settle. She's fearful that she'll lose the relationships she has with her stepfather, little brother and at the church. Tasnee loves the spotlight of being in the first family."

"What more can her sisters say that you haven't. And I hope she's not worrying Deborah?"

"No, Miss Minnie's got that. Bo called because Tasnee got to her. She's got Bo questioning her gift. And speaking with Bo put something new on my mind."

"Do you want to talk and walk?"

Dewey shook his head *no* and massaged his right knee. "Regina, can we start back. I'm afraid I didn't bring the right shoes to walk on this much sand."

"Sure." She frowned. Taking long walks on the beach was one of her favorite pastimes. She'd hoped he'd enjoy a relaxing walk this afternoon. The trouble with his knees today was the first sign of any age in his fresh, playful soul. If he didn't enjoy walks on the beach, or couldn't, she'd continue to walk alone.

As they moved back toward the boardwalk, Dewey poured out his latest trouble. "It's not that I'm snobby or think we're better than anyone else. But, Bo has a bright future in the ministry, and there is nothing an association with some prisoner can add to her life. And, what kind of life is she going to have running down to a prison. I've seen that show where the women spend hours waiting in line for a brief visit. If she stays in this relationship, it will rob her of her youth and any possibility of ever having children."

Regina scratched her head as they settled on a boardwalk bench. This was far deeper than anything she'd hoped to discuss today. She was still processing last night's conversation. Now, a dozen new questions swirled around in her mind. *Why was he worried about Bo having children?* The *boyfriend* was locked up. "Dew, why are you dwelling on grandchildren?"

He rubbed his hands together. "It's a dream that I've carried for a few years now. A vision of large family gatherings with the girls and their children. And, of course, husbands. But, I'd settle for decent significant life partners at this point. But," he held up his index finger, "that's not what I wanted to ask you about. Lady, Bo's in crisis over her gift. She claims she's led to be in this relationship—but her story sounds more to me like a bad man manipulating a soft-hearted woman. Her vision is not clear, and she's suffering. Bo knows God's blessing doesn't bring this level of confusion. And the tone in her voice when she admitted that the months of secrecy were wrong, near about broke my heart. She's struggling, and I'm at a loss for how to help her. I'm hoping there is something in your book of standards that might minister to my Bo."

Yikes! This is not mud I want to step in.

From the little she knew about Dewey's ex-wives; the girls didn't need any more advice or input. And she hadn't planned to offer any. *But the only reason I met him was because of his daughters.*

"I'm not sure I should add anything beyond what you and her mothers have said. But," she paused as Dewey's deep frown melted a bit of her resolve. "Would it help if you listened to my YouTube channel while you drive home, and we can discuss any thoughts or insights you have. Then you could share those insights with Bo?"

"Yes, of course. Thank you." He nodded. "You are wise and beautiful. And rightly cautious. I understand you don't want to step on any toes here. But I'm convinced there's something in your work that will help us." He shook his head, sadly. "I can't understand why Bonita would even consider this relationship."

"You know I totally agree with you all about Bonita's choice." She frowned. "My mother used to say it's just as easy to fall in love with a rich man as a poor one, and to avoid any confusion, don't talk to the garbageman."

Dewey winced.

"Yeah, I know it sounds harsh. But, I don't think she meant garbageman in a literal sense."

Dewey shook his head *no*. "From what you and Rena have told me about your mother, I think she meant what she said." He reached for her hand. "Back in the day, I wouldn't have stood a chance with you. Skinny, funny-looking kid that only wanted to sing and play the piano. Always looking to lean on good church folk for a room and a meal. You know that's how me and Minnie lived for years. We'd take the Greyhound bus from city to city during the summer looking for folks to take us in for a few nights. And I would sing for our supper."

"You're probably right," Regina admitted. Happy that a little of his snappy attitude broke through his troubles.

"Ask Rena. I know I'm right."

Regina pulled in her lip, "I would have rebelled for you."

"Ha, ha. No, you wouldn't have. You're still a Miss Goody-Two-Shoes. That standard of yours didn't just show up last night. You're not the jump into the deep end of the pool girl. And I know I'm not your usual safe, steady type. I think you're just playing with me, anyway. Got me on my toes trying to figure out what I need to do, to convince you to take me seriously." Dewey flashed his best stage smile. "When are you going to take a chance on me?"

Her eyes widened. His words came as a bit of a shock and it took her a beat to respond. Prophecy, observation or perception, he'd figured her out. "I'll admit that I'm still processing it all. You are DW Thurman."

"Woman, I know who I am. And who I'm trying to be."

What was she going to do with such a frisky boy? He was right. She wouldn't have known what to do with Dewey in her youth and could barely handle him now. "Dew, I just don't want to make another mistake."

"It's okay. I know where we're headed, and I'm patient."

Regina looked out at the water and contemplated. He'd pegged her right. Now she was stuck between being annoyed that he was right again and amazed that Dewey was prepared to be patient with her. In the past twenty-four hours, he'd shared a startling truth about himself and confronted her with a spot-on assessment of who she was.

Dewey wanted more than the laughter of a summer romance. While she enjoyed his playfulness and cherished every minute spent with him. She was holding back. Her plan was to date for companionship, but never fully engage or give her heart to another man. She didn't plan to go through any trauma or drama of any kind with a man again.

After her divorce, Regina Lawson declared herself a no-drama-mama. Stepped away from all gossip and everyone else's business, even stopped meddling in her son's affairs. When Rena came with family gossip, she only wanted to know if the trouble required prayer or money. When it was money she gave without asking too many questions. Maybe she'd been hasty in dumping the Colonel. There was no chance for drama in that relationship. And there was also no possibility of a love that could rejuvenate and energize. With Dewey, she felt young again. Opening her life to a full relationship with him wouldn't be all rainbows and sunshine. What more would Dewey ask of her? And what else would he bring to her life? Mysticism? Drama? Joy?

Dewey nudged her to break into her thoughts. "Thank you for a wonderful lunch, Lady. But, would you mind taking me back to the hotel? I'm sorry, but I need to take my medicine and get my knees together before I get on the road."

Walking back to the car she remembered her manners. Out of courtesy she asked, "Dewey, is there anything I can get for you?"

She'd purposely stopped short of asking any questions about his medical needs.

Not wanting to engage in or understand his medical needs was emblematic of the distance she'd placed in all of her post-divorce relationships.

This is just what Dewey just challenged me about.

Rena had challenged her to just let go and fall in love. But, by nature she was cautious.

"No," Dewey said and squeezed her hand. "Thanks for offering. I've got everything I need to pull this pain down before I get on the road."

"Dew, do you have any idea of how this will end for Bo?"

He shook his head slowly. "You asking the father or the prophet? It's important for you to know that we cannot see to the end of a personal matter."

Hours later Regina hesitated before picking up Dewey's call. She'd pondered since they parted over his charge that she was toying with him. Most days she wasn't sure if he was toying with her. For the first month they were together, she'd held her breath. And she'd definitely held onto her virtue. Not because she didn't want him. But, because she knew it wouldn't sit well with her soul if Dewey played love 'em and leave 'em with her. And didn't she have a right to protect her soul?

"Hello."

"I was just about to leave you a message. Is this a good time to talk?"

"Yes, of course. I hope you've had some rest from your drive." He'd texted earlier that he'd made it home safely and was taking a nap. She steadied herself for the conversation she didn't want to have about his daughter.

"I gained so much insight during my drive home by listening to your work. And I want to talk to you about Bo. But, if we continue to see each other, it's got to be me and you first. Let's talk about us first."

Regina's eyes widened. How was it that he seemed to see through her so clearly? Was it his spiritual gift?

Or maybe I'm just that transparent.

"Regina," he called to her. "I hope you know I don't say these things to you lightly. I want you in my life."

She exhaled, "I really want to believe you. My time with you has been amazing. And, I am still not sure what the attraction is?"

"Lady, you don't know how rare you are? You are an absolute treasure. Quick-witted and can take a joke without offense. Smart enough to remain open to learning. Not overbearing with your wisdom. Your presence and sweet spirit drew me from the moment we met. It's a pleasure to just be with you. I could sit on your porch swinging with you for days. And don't get mad, but I find that you're still sexually a little shy and you have no idea how that thrills me."

Regina covered her face with her hands, thankful he couldn't see her. Dewey was right. If she wanted to continue seeing him, she'd have to accept that his intentions were pure. Being with Dewey was truly like having her cake and eating it too. He delighted her soul in a way she'd never experienced. Victor gave her security. The Colonel, companionship. Dewey gave her joy.

"Regina, I'm not saying we're at happily ever after, but I'm ready to see where this thing goes."

Regina closed her eyes and sent up several prayers of thanksgiving. "Me, too, Dewey. How's your knee?"

"Fine, thank you," Dewey answered before launching into an old man's recitation about his arthritis.

She listened intently as her sweet old man complained about his knees and scalpel-happy doctor. Then the conversation turned to today's pain, Bonita's relationship.

Dewey reviewed the insights he'd gleaned on how best to help Bonita from her teachings. He'd actually spent time beyond his drive home meditating on her words and went on for twenty minutes. "If we can get Bo to focus on the high mark that she's always set for herself. That should work. She's always been one that wanted to get everything right. Kinda like your Smith. Bo's the neatest of the girls, and she has the most perfect penmanship. I know it's old-fashioned, but Bo really takes pride in her handwriting. If you ever get a handwritten note from her, it's something to cherish."

"And how would it look to get Bo to refocus?" Regina knew it was a consultant's question, but she was still a little hesitant.

"Um, I hadn't gotten that far. But you're right. I need to think about that. Thank you for a challenging question."

"Well, you're welcome. I'm sorry that you are going through this."

"A pain shared is a pain halved."

Chapter Eleven

Praise the Lord for the promise that comes with ordinary days.
To rise and work, then fall back asleep, and rise to another ordinary day.

The inspiration and peace Regina found in Dewey's daily reminders of God's goodness softened her heart and altered her morning regimen. First, she read his praise song and meditated on the inspiration words. Then she prayed and called Dewey before her feet hit the floor. In four months together, they'd established a routine. She started their days. He sang her to sleep. Every night.

To her delight, Dewey worked hard to nurture their long-distance relationship. Old-fashioned and charming, he courted her with chocolates, flowers and sweet little gifts. The angel broach he gave her for Easter was already her favorite.

Fresh and forward, Dewey communicated with her throughout the day with direct messages. Mostly tender sentiments. Sometimes racy *suggestions*. He'd slipped some things into her DMs that curled her toes.

So much to accomplish for an ordinary day.

With a busy Thursday ahead of her, Regina spent more time meditating on the morning's praise song than she'd intended. First, she needed to finish her grade reports, then drive to Montgomery for an Earle Holdings meeting. With any luck, this month's meeting would be an uneventful reading of the minutes and financial reports with a total run-time of one hour. Which would put her at Sheer Elegance Hair Salon on time for her four o'clock appointment.

"But tomorrow." She grinned and reached for her phone. Most mornings she felt a little selfish for calling Dewey so early. Their schedules were completely upside down. She had a traditional nine-to-five work life, while he mainly worked nights and weekends.

"Good morning," she whispered when he answered.

"Always," he groaned, "how is it that you always call right when my dreams are getting hot."

Dewey liked to hint that she woke him from erotic dreams starring her. In her opinion, things were progressing rather quickly. Dewey claimed age as his motivator and joked about the double-edged sword of their September romance. He suggested they get it together before "it's everlasting too late."

The weariness she detected in his voice whispered that rehearsal had lasted long after they'd hung up last night. He often cheated and called her while the musicians worked without him. "Dew, what time did you really finish last night?"

"This morning," he moaned. "I put the band out at eleven, so the fellas can get up and go to class. Then, stayed on the keyboard until about three." He yawned. "Made some videos."

An alarm went off in her mind. As heat rose in her cheeks, Regina swung her feet to the floor. The last video he sent had her ready to share his bed.

"I went all the way back to "Lift Him Up." Iggy, probably doesn't know the song, but that fourth verse speaks the truth."

Regina stepped onto the floor without her slippers to cool her wanton lust.

For the past few days he'd worked on a response for his neighbor,

Young Iggy. The rapper-singer had dissed The Sisters Fellowship on last week's episode of the *Rappers of Atlanta.*

"Umm, I still don't think you should dignify that dig with a response."

This modern game of hit me and I'll hit you back seemed beneath the dignity of the Crown Prince of Gospel Music.

"I agree with you about not posting a response in anger and maintaining my standard." Dewey yawned. "I'll pray about this some before I release anything. But, I won't let an insult involving my girls go unaddressed. You'd think that little boy would have learned by now not to mess with me."

Regina shrugged, switched to speakerphone and began to move around the house. Her student's research papers weren't going to grade themselves. In addition to turning in her grade reports, she had a few stops to make in Mobile before driving to Montgomery.

"Lady, are you sure I can't convince you to skip that meeting and come on home to me."

Her morning glow expanded. "As tempting as that sounds, *no*. I'll be there tomorrow. You know I don't like to miss business meetings. The boys need my vote to block any nonsense from Mandy. And, I still have to get my hair and nails done, and finish my speech."

Dewey yawned again. "Then I've got some more dreaming to do."

An hour later as she evaluated the final essays of her first-year English students, Dr. Regina Lawson couldn't keep still. "Ugh."

With the marks on these essays, she'd have to fail Sonja. While she worked hard to inspire and retain her students, she had to stand firm on basic academic standards. After making the mark, she took a quick break. To soothe her restless spirit, she pulled up Dewey's RSS feed and checked in on the commentary from today's praise song.

PK1974 wrote, 'grateful for that word to start my extra-ordinary day.'

KTHIG88, chimed in with a daily thank you.

SavedandSanctified must have been a biblical scholar because they regularly added a scriptural reference. Today's was Psalm 143:8. And Dewey's best friend, RevMims@aol.com posted "the ordinary word" has refreshed my soul.

She scrolled through the comments to read the responses from the girls; a requirement from their father. Allegra, Jolee and Bonita posted simple a-mens. Calista expounded on the praise song with a current feel-good news story about how a stranger's ordinary act of kindness blessed a Chicago family. And Tasnee shared a too-personal note about her mother. Deborah Banks was Not having an ordinary day. This morning Deborah was served notice to vacate the house she'd lived in for over thirty years. The house was church property and the board wanted her out.

Thinking about Deborah's decision to finally separate from an unfaithful husband took her back a few years. Things were tough for Deb, but Dewey held onto his prediction that she'd come out alright. When she questioned him about how he could be so sure, Dewey urged her not to confuse his prophetic gift with good old-fashioned common sense. Of course, Deb would get through this. So, many women did. She had.

Dr. Lawson resettled at her desk to finish her work. Rena would not forgive her if she missed their planned coffee chat. There was fresh family and church gossip to catch up on. She'd sit and listen to her sister for only an hour. Victor Earle, Sr. would gladly start the business meeting without her.

As she packed up the car, her phone pinged. Of course, Malik needed money today.

When Malik first built her website, he added it to the server at the real estate office. Now she was using more bandwidth, Mrs. Mandy Earle had made a fuss. To keep his wife happy, Victor Sr. demanded that Malik move her URL—or something like that—to another host. Today.

Just the kind of mess Mandy liked to stir up before a family business meeting, because she didn't have a vote. Regina frowned and took a minute to figure things out. Her web address was on the printed materials for her speaking engagement on Saturday. So, she needed to act. But, Malik had messed up with her credit card too many times. He didn't have her new card number. Since this issue was best resolved before the meeting, she sent Smith a text. Then responded to Malik.

'Go see Smith to use my credit card.'

Six hours later, as she sweated under a too-hot hair dryer, DW Thurman's smile flashed across her phone screen. She hadn't expected to hear from him until much later.

"Lady. What else do you need to do to get ready?"

She grinned and lifted the dryer bonnet to talk. Free from the heat of the dryer, she experienced a different kind of heat. A hot flash of desire. He'd have the pants charmed off of her in no time; this weekend, if he wanted. She ran down her list of errands: nail appointment, drug store, then back to the townhouse to finish her speech.

"Okay, but don't stay up too late. I'll be by to get you early."

She screamed, "You're coming to Montgomery" and drew the attention of every woman in the small shop. Sometimes, she couldn't believe how hard Dewey worked to be with her. The plan was for her to make the two-hour drive to Atlanta.

"I hadn't planned to, but when I woke up this afternoon

something in my spirit said to come get you. Didn't you watch the video I sent?"

"Yeah, I saw that video," she replied flatly. While she was having coffee with Rena, Dewey's response to Young Iggy hit the airwaves. She'd watched the video a second time before the family business meeting. It already had two thousand views. As with everything DW Thurman posted, the video was well done.

"I thought you were going to think on that some more—"

"Not that video, woman." He let out a low, slow whistle. "The one I slid into your DMs. Watch that. Now listen, I know you aren't just getting yourself together for me. Your work with the BMA on Saturday is going to lead to bigger things. And beside that, I want you looking your best if you expect me to introduce you to my friends."

She clicked off the call and immediately opened the direct message he'd sent. "Oh, my God," she shrieked. Then fanned herself with the back of her hand as she viewed Dewey's sultry rendition of The O'Jays classic, "I Want You Here With Me."

"Shh," the patron under the dryer on her left hissed.

The lady on her right nudged her. "Vernice is calling you."

She slid the hot phone in her bag and quick-time marched to the stylist's chair. Per the rules of the beauty shop, your stylist could make you sit and wait for hours. But you'd better rush to the chair when she called you.

"Ohh wee, tell me what you thought of DW's post. Cause I know you didn't like it." Vernice babbled as the black styling cape settled around Regina's shoulders. "And I'm-ma get you out of here soon. 'Cause, DW Thurman is not going to blast me on social media. Have you looked at the numbers? Viral and trending. That old man is on top of this social media game," the master-stylist hooted before shoving an iPad into Regina's hands.

For all his old-fashioned ways, Dewey Thurman was sharp in the ways of the new media world. Everyday, his morning praise song appeared on Facebook, Twitter, Instagram and a dozen other social media platforms she'd never heard of.

In a three-minute video Dewey totally burned Young Iggy, while setting forth a powerful lesson. The little sung fourth verse of "Lift Him Up" had power, just like he said. Dewey had struggled for days over the insult to his girls. Far longer than he should have in the present quick-hit age.

Dew must believe this video would bring somebody, maybe even Iggy, to redemption.

Although she was a little upset with him, the hint of sadness she detected around his eyes when she watched the video for the third time, led her to trust his vision and grant him a little grace.

"And, Lord, the comments," Vernice hollered.

She lowered her head and watched the active feed. The comments were running about three to one in Dewey's favor. Sadly, the ones that opposed him were vulgar and ugly. Why couldn't people simply disagree without being disagreeable?

"Ouch!"

"Hold your head up, please." The master-stylist commanded as she pulled the flat iron through Regina's hair. "Lort! I'm-ma talk to my choir director about singing that from the hymnal this Sunday. We need to sing the whole song, like they do in the AME church. People need to hear all of that, get it all up in their spirits."

The woman in the next chair shouted. "Glory! Glory!"

Vernice shook, shimmied and belted out the refrain from the gospel standard, off key. "Y'all know that's going to be the sermon text in many-a church across the nation this weekend." The stylist kept up a running commentary about Dr. Regina's man and city gossip until she spun the chair around. "Alrighty, Dr. Regina, I'm done."

The client in the chair on Regina's left cried out, "Your bob is fierce. Ver-girl, you need to stop lying and tell us what kind of hair you put in Dr. Regina's head."

The master-stylist laughed. "I keep telling y'all if you take care of your hair and come see me on a regular, your hair will grow out pretty like Dr. Regina's."

The ladies chopped it up about Vernice's overt attempt to hustle them into making more hair appointments, while she settled her bill. Vernice was too slow, but also too good. Which is why she kept coming back.

◈

Regina left the salon and rushed through her errands. Only slowing her roll at the nail shop. There was no way she wanted to detract from her presentation on Saturday with botched-up nails. As she sat under the hand dryer, she tried to keep still and think about her speech. But, the personal video Dewey sent had all of her senses hopping.

Dating Dewey was nothing like she expected. When he visited, they enjoyed ball games, the botanical gardens, and quiet nights sitting on her moon-lit porch. Activities he couldn't enjoy much as a teenager, because his mother was dragging him to every church in Georgia to sing. Although he was grateful for Ms. Minnie's vision, he'd missed a lot of his youth.

They even went roller skating one Saturday night. Well, tried. Dewey only made it around the rink once before his knees gave out. They laughed so much that night she went to bed with a bellyache.

DW Thurman loved to stop by a small church's fundraiser just to bless God's people. Last month they drove a country mile to attend a pastor's appreciation dinner at a small BMA church. There couldn't have been fifty people at the event, but Dewey performed that evening like he was in a sold-out stadium. As word spread that DW Thurman had interest in Mobile, every church, sorority, and civic group in town sent her their invitations. The appearance he made at Rena's annual scholarship concert, set an attendance record and blew the financial goal out of the water.

As a father, Dewey was determined that his girls had great childhoods. And he'd spoiled them all. Now that Tasnee was eighteen, he declared this his season.

Above all, Dewey supported and encouraged her. Treated her like she mattered. Saw success in everything she touched. Especially her book, if she'd buckle down and get it written. He'd recommended and pushed for her to speak at the Baptist Methodist Assembly's regional women's conference. An engagement she could only dream about securing.

At eight-thirty she opened the door to what she hoped would be an empty house. Instead she found Malik hard at work on her website.

"Smith said you didn't ask for my credit card to pay for the website."

Malik looked up from his computer. "No, couldn't find him before the meeting. But, I got it done."

Her lip twitched. Over the past few months, catching up with Smith had become increasingly difficult. They all figured he was working on his event center business. She'd prayed he had sense enough not to conduct his personal business on the Alabama Real Estate Commission's time. And she'd began to suspect Smith might be seeing someone. She hoped he was seeing someone. Her oldest son worked too hard. "How?"

"Daddy."

After getting over the shock that her ex-husband paid to repair some Mandy damage, she went upstairs to put pen to paper. Dewey was coming first thing to pick her up and she wanted to be rested and ready. Instead of polishing her speech, she worried about Smith.

Chapter Twelve

I see the light of Christ in you.
I see His love in all you do.
Love to each and every one of you.

As Regina stood in Dewey's condo on Friday evening admiring the bejeweled Atlanta skyline, she wondered. How could she be in love when she hadn't even spent a full week with this man. She inhaled, then sniffed again. Dewey's home had a sensual, earthy essence. She couldn't quite place the fragrance; sage or musk. But it was relaxing. Enticing. Seductive? Was old-fashioned Dewey still burning incense?

Turning from the window, she admired his tastefully decorated, all-white living room. A design choice she'd never make, but she liked the room. How can a creative and a conservative make love work when their basic daily lives seemed so out of sync? She took another deep inhale and began to pull apart the notes of the room's fragrance. She inhaled the essence of his home in the same way she drank in the notes of bay rum and pepper in his cologne.

Her smile broadened when Dewey waltzed into his white living room and took a seat behind the antique grand piano. The accent of those black keys added a base and balance to the room. Without one word, he began to meet out a familiar tune.

"Everlasting." She sighed. "You won't believe how many weddings I've been to where the bride walked down the aisle to your song."

He charmed, teased and tantalized her by singing the often quoted first verse.

"Ohh." She swooned and glowed as DW Thurman sang just for her.

"That's not what this song's about," he lamented before belting out the chorus.

"It's still one of the most beautiful love songs ever."

Before he sang the lesser referenced second verse of the song that made him famous, Dewey stopped playing. "The song that almost ruined my life."

After moving to the piano bench, she nestled in beside him. "Wasn't this your biggest hit?"

Dewey stopped playing. "Yes, and the biggest challenge to my faith. A cross over gospel hit comes with a rock-star lifestyle. Post-concert after parties complete with drugs, sex, and rock-n-roll with a faux praise twist." Dewey shook his head. "You think the adoration women give the preachers is something. What they give a minister of music will curl you hair." Dewey playfully nudged her with his shoulder.

She closed her eyes; he'd shared all of this before. And every time her left brain urged her to end the relationship.

"But, the biggest devil was the record executives. Blood-sucking, vampire-devils. I still haven't made a dime off of "Everlasting.""

"Huh?"

Dewey played softly and re-explained the ninety-nine points on the album. "I earned less than a quarter-point on this. I didn't know any better, and, of course, I couldn't listen to anyone. I wanted it so bad. Wanted the world, and they gave it to me. Clothes, cars, cash, booze, drugs, and the people. I don't know where all those people come from, but somehow, they find you. Men and women that keep you geeked up. Inflate your ego till you forget that it's God's grace, not your voice. I thought everything was free because they loved me." He played a couple of solemn strains on the keyboard. "I got lost and God's favor found me."

"Favor" was one of his lesser-known tunes that she knew all too well. The slow-moving melody of the worship song always gave her hope. Sinking into the richness of the lyrics, Regina let the Crown Prince of Gospel Music minster to her. Next, he flowed into a softer-sweeter melody.

"Lady, do you know this tune?"

"I don't recognize it."

"Bet you know this." He upped the tempo, switched keys and played the same notes with a driving up-tempo beat.

Jarred from the pleasant space he'd created with his music, she shook. "Yeah, I know that. The kids like it. State's marching band played it a few years ago. I didn't care for the words, well the ones I could decipher. You wrote that?"

"No, I wrote this," he replayed the melody, softly and sang a simple praise song.

"Ah, that's lovely." She melted back into the peaceful place. "But how…?"

"Does this," he slammed out the hip-hop tune, "become this?" He toned the music down. "I sold it. It's how I make a living. There's still tuition to pay, people to support, so I sell songs. I don't exactly sell what the Lord gives me. It's not what they want anyway. The good Lord gives me inspiration and from that— comes this."

Dewey played another song made famous by a R&B artist. She never knew he wrote. Over the years, he'd become a highly sought-after songwriter and had penned award-winning songs for all genres. All the while refusing to become a cross-over recording artist.

Regina glanced at his shelves of awards glistening in the soft lighting of the living room. Grammy, Stellar, Dove, and American music awards, all testified to Dewey's great talent. Trophies, plaques and certificates from world famous organizations to local service clubs testified to his charity toward his global community.

"Dewey, I don't understand. Why don't you perform the songs you've written?"

"Because, I've sold the rights. And I can't play them like this in public." He shifted keys to change the tone of the song he played. "This is why I'm asking you to be careful as you move forward with your book. You don't want to wind up with the regrets I have."

As he continued playing a slow, soul-moving hymn, his words resonated in her spirit. They spoke often about the pitfalls in the entertainment industry, his struggles guiding the girls and the threats he saw on the horizon. He offered her sage guidance for her journey.

"This is from the movie *Black Church* and the second Grammy winner."

His version sounded nothing like the hard-sung song that played in heavy rotation on R&B stations ten years ago. While the words were familiar, the feeling coming from his heart left her breathless. The sincerity in his song went straight to her soul. His songs always moved her and tonight she wasn't sure if he was singing to her or unto the Lord. As with much of modern gospel music, one could hardly tell. She moved to the sofa to enjoy his gift of a private concert.

As he played though some of his unpublished charts, all of her stress and worry melted away. Restful, peaceful songs that would surely bless the hearts of God's people. If he'd release them.

The rich, soulfulness of his voice and the comfort of his presence, helped her release all apprehension about tomorrow. She still couldn't believe he drove to Montgomery to pick her up this morning. Falling in deeper, she took a deep breath and let the rest of her worries go.

After a while, Dewey stepped away from the piano and reached out for her. She stood in his arms for a few minutes, to enjoy the now familiar essence of him.

"Made dinner reservation at Sweet Auburn's. Do you want to get ready to go?"

She inhaled and sank deeper into his warmth.

"What is it that you really want," he hummed in her ear. "We're at the age when we can do whatever we want, when we want." He nuzzled and nipped at her neck.

"To be with you," she purred.

Dewey released her and hopped like a teenager. "Dinner can wait."

Regina shrugged as he retook her in his arms and kissed her with the caution and grace of an older gentleman.

"If," he gazed into her eyes, "…if you're sure this is what you want and you're ready."

She responded with the quiet melody of her kiss.

⚬⚬⚬

Hours later the smell of bacon roused Regina from a deeply, satisfying sleep. She rolled over and stretched as her stomach rumbled. Famished, yet surprisingly mellow with a tinge of misgiving for having given it up so easily. "I'm not that girl. Maybe I am." She giggled. She rose, pulled on a black silk robe she found lying at the foot of the bed and followed her nose to the kitchen.

"I'm impressed," she said as she accepted a ready plate of bacon and eggs. "Good to know a man will cook."

"Your man is doing his best to please you." He kissed her gently on the cheek before moving back to the stove to fix his plate.

Regina polished off her plate quickly, but wasn't satisfied. Her eyes searched the kitchen counter, passing over a bowl of apples and bananas, to settle on a plate of brownies on the counter. "I'd like one of those, please."

"Uh, no. If you've got a sweet tooth, I think I have some candy."

"No," she shook her head as the brownies called to her in all their chocolatey goodness. "I don't know why I'm so hungry tonight."

"I'd like to call it good loving. Well that," his face scrunched up, "and the munchies."

Regina shifted in the chair so swiftly she almost fell over as hot angry tears welled up in her eyes. "What do you mean the munchies?"

Dewey winced. "Let me explain. Please? I forgot I was burning when you came in earlier."

Her eyes widened in shock. She understood Dewey was a musician, an artist. But sex, drugs and rock-n-roll wasn't her lifestyle. Tears of disappointment and regret escaped. She was a dolt. A drugged dolt.

He reached across the table for her hand. "It's medicinal. I have a prescription."

When she should have withdrawn her hand, she couldn't.

"Lady," he continued. "I'm sixty-two years old and have chronic arthritis in both my knees."

As he spoke, she listened intently for something to make this right in her head. She looked up when Dewey squeezed her hand.

"The life of a performing artist is about as hard on a body as that of a pro-athlete. All that praise-dancing, stage climbing, and running."

"Running, Dewey?"

"Yeah, from all those women." He grinned.

She snatched her hand back and bowed her head. Her mind raced with second thoughts. *Not funny. He drugged me.*

This all was very different for her. She'd always been the classic American good girl. She'd never been fast, wild, or interested in bad boys. My God, she'd married the first man she ever did it with and would have stayed married, even though Victor hadn't been faithful. She raised her tear-filled eyes to take a long, hard, last look at Dewey Thurman.

As she stared at Dewey through tear-heated eyes, the man seemed to glow under the recessed lighting of his kitchen. Was this what being high did to one's vison? Shiny. Rock-star shiny, with a glowing bald head, sparkly diamond ear stud and glossy, black silk pajamas.

This isn't for me. She lowered her eyes in regret and shame. *How could I even consider continuing a relationship with him?*

"Before you tell me how you feel about it, I need you to know it's the only thing that truly relieves my pain. I tried every conventional treatment available. Nothing works and leaves me with the ability to function. Lady, I'm sorry. I wasn't thinking when you came in. That drive took something out of me. That's why I called Allegra to take you shopping this afternoon. I spent most of the time you were gone trying to get myself together. And by the time you got back, well, my knees weren't hurting, my fingers were loose and I was feeling good. You seemed to be feeling good. It didn't dawn on me until I woke up hungry as heck." Dewey stood and opened all of his cabinets. "If you're craving sweets, I can make you... pancakes?"

Pancakes?

A slow steady smile crept across her face. It wasn't his offer to make her pancakes, but his active search for something to make her happy, that softened her heart. Regina stepped over to Dewey and wrapped her arms around his waist and leaned into his body. Shiny, sixty, pot-smoker, with arthritic knees, and yet still so darn sexy. What she craved was some more of his good loving.

Am I still under the influence?

"Dewey, how about you mash up three of those bananas and I'll use that pancake mix to make a banana skillet cake." Regina went through the cabinets he'd left open in search of a few more ingredients. "You keep a well-stocked kitchen for a person that's rarely home. Good, you have vanilla. I'm impressed."

Dewey grinned. "The girls like to make cookies when they're here."

While the skillet cake cooked, he washed the dishes. They sat at Dewey's kitchen table for hours discussing everything from his health, to world events and their children. Long after midnight they shared a laugh about something else they had in common. Their youngest had issues.

Tasnee still wasn't handling her mother's separation well. The stress of the first family breaking up, combined with the attention of being Dewey Thurman's daughter proved a huge challenge for Tas. Young, gifted and feeling herself. Tasnee had resisted every bribe and reason to start college. This put her in the dog house with the whole family. When Tas turned to her social media family for support, they returned her need with another level of drama.

He ran his hands across his bald head. "Tas is going to grow-up and be alright. So is Malik."

Regina leaned back in her chair and frowned. "Malik has his problems and I'm just about ready to turn it all over to his father. Let Vic try and talk some sense into him. But, it's Smith that's worrying me now. This disappearing act is so unlike him."

"You sure it's not a woman?"

"I don't know. He's usually open about the women he dates. High achievers, like himself. Until now he's been proud to have me meet them."

"You know I think the world of both your young men. I pray Smith will bring his mystery lady into the light soon? And if she's not someone to bring home, I hope he gets it out of his system quick. I'd like to think on Malik for a while, see if there's anything I can do to encourage him. We've got to keep on praying the same for Bonita. Nothing good will come out of this prison relationship that she will not end. We got to stay before the Lord for all of them." Dewey yawned, took a deep breath and rose. "Now," he said as he refreshed their coffees, "let's move on to the future. When your book is successful and your speaking career blows up, I have one request. Reserve one day a week for me."

Again, she wondered how he knew the book she hadn't finished writing would be successful. And why she wanted to believe him. What sane woman wouldn't stay with a man who expressed such unwavering faith in her?

As the early light of dawn peaked through the kitchen window, Dewey asked if her head was clear before leading her back to his bedroom.

Chapter Thirteen

For a heart left ajar; Love is well come.
Beloved, open your heart and welcome, HIS Love.

Nerves usually buffeted Regina before a major speaking engagement, but today she was a study in calm. Early this morning hours, Dewey solidified their relationship and alleviated all her fears about his past. And in that know-it-all way of his, he spoke about their future. That was a bit much to take in. Would Dewey's surety and assurance always clash with her cautious inner voice?

As she dressed, Regina meditated on Dewey's morning praise song. Another beautiful verse that he claimed to have scheduled months ago. How could he have known today was the perfect time to release that verse. Love in any form is always welcome. Regina prayed that HIS love would shine through the message she'd deliver this afternoon.

With barely enough time to make it to the Atlanta University Center, Regina and Dewey stepped from the sanctuary of his home. A sense of well-being and security washed over her as she floated beside him as to board the elevator to the underground parking garage.

As soon as they stepped off the lift, a stark white flash shocked, then blinded her. She stumbled and Dewey pulled her close as repeated blasts of stark, bright light washed over her.

"Ah, man. This ain't necessary," Dewey barked as he attempted to shield her from the blasts.

"You know the score, DW. Welcome, Dr. Lawson."

Regina straightened to see who'd addressed her by name. Her movement gave the photographer a clear shot. During the third wave of blinding flashes, she turned and burrowed her face into Dewey's shoulder.

"Please, don't sell these pictures. Regina's a classy lady, and she doesn't deserve to have her business paraded out before the public. She's not a media figure."

Her happiness deflated, Regina Lawson righted herself to get an understanding of the situation. Had she gotten caught in what her students called the *slut walk?*

The photographer lowered his camera as Dewey pleaded for their privacy. The cocky disrespectful, dreadlocked young man dressed in combat fatigues, black bandana and a traditional photographer's vest standing before her reminded her of Smith's fraternity brothers.

"Not yet, DW. But, it was a long night and thanks to Wi-Fi, I had time to do my research. Your lady, Dr. Regina Lawson, 'bout to burst out big on the church scene. She's even speaking for the highfalutin BMA this afternoon." The young man tossed his locks and nodded slyly at her. "Wonder if these photos will meet their standards? And by the way, DW, your morning praise song was real, inspiring this morning. Well come."

Regina blinked rapidly as her eyes struggled to recover from the assault of flashes. Worry flooded in and burst her happy bubble. The BMA were a very particular denomination. She frowned. For this to happen after Dewey pulled strings to get her this engagement? It wouldn't look good for the girls to see their father's private life in the gossip section of the next gospel music blog. What about her boys? Yes, they were grown men. But this wasn't how she wanted them to see her.

Dewey bristled and stepped closer to the young man. "Shouldn't you be somewhere lying in wait for Young Iggy to roll in?"

"Yeah, and thanks to you, I'll get two for one night's work."

Dewey let out a deep, exasperated breath. "I'm sorry, Lady. I should have seen this coming."

She turned to him. "Don't I get a say so in this?"

Dewey frowned. "I'm sorry, but no."

"You don't look bad, Dr. Lawson." The photographer glanced up from scanning photographs on his viewer. "Tell you what, since this is your first time and you're about to be big in the God world," he winked, "I'll hold on to the pictures I took when you came in yesterday. And you can tell people this was a breakfast meeting."

The photographer turned as the garage door rattled to announce its opening. "DW, you need to school ole girl and don't forget to explain to her why she owes me a favor."

As a Hummer H-1 urban assault vehicle roared into the garage, the photographer ran off to position himself to no doubt violate someone else's privacy. She prayed he'd keep his promise and not sell a portion of hers.

✑

"We glory in our freedom, but have no standard. We've forgotten the distinction between the two. And we are no longer teaching to a standard at home or in the church. Freedom says yes, if you are able to do it, go ahead. Your standard asks if it's wise. Freedom says if he's fine and you want him, go for it. Standards ask if he's a ninja. You know who a ninja is, ladies. No income. No job. And no accountability in his life. Ladies, pass on him. I don't get it, he already has three kids, no car and lives with his grandmother. How can you even consider binding yourself to him as baby-mama-drama number four?"

Laughter and shouts of "teach" and "tell it," filled the ballroom at the Atlanta University Conference Center as Dr. Regina Lawson began to close out her talk to the Baptist Methodist Assembly's Southern Regional Young Women's Conference.

"Freedom says if you got the money and you like it, buy it. Standards pause," she stopped speaking long enough to regain everyone's attention, "your standard makes you pause and ask if, you've paid the rent and the power bill. Your standard asks if the garment is appropriate? For you. Does it fit and cover? Does it even look good on me? Some of these clothes and makeup are not for daily wear. The music stars and celebrities that you are trying to emulate, are not walking around all day in their stage makeup!"

"Yes!" an older women in the back yelled and an amen corner erupted around her. While Regina waited for the applause to settle, she noticed a few of the younger women checking in with their friends.

"By the way your hair is pretty, doesn't mean that the hair looks good on You. This thigh-long, bone-straight hair doesn't flatter everyone's face or figure. Why do you hide your beauty under these hair capes? Let us see you. Your beauty. Your pretty face. Let us see you as God sees you. You are beautiful. And They don't want you to know this—you do not have to go along with everything the world is serving. You are free to set a standard!"

Although she thought her speech was a little tough, Regina felt confident in her words today. Too bad the BMA did not allow videotaping. This would be a good one for the channel. From her survey of the younger attendees, she understood that her words would need some time to sink in. She took a deep breath and rested in the knowledge that someone in the audience would hear and do.

"Let me close with this. There is a distinction between freedom and freewill. It seems we've lost the distinction between these concepts. Just because it's a hit song and your favorite performer is singing it. And," she paused for effect, "it's got a kickin' beat doesn't mean you're supposed to act out the lyrics. Freedom to listen to the hot-one-hundred hip-hop-drill murder music. A standard changes the station. Especially when there are small children in the car. The doors of the church are open, and you are free to wear what you choose—but a standard dictates that you respect the house of the Lord and not come to church looking like you are on your way to a dance hall. And please don't go to work or school wearing that half-naked stuff. Sometimes I can't tell if my students are early for the club or stopping by class after a night out."

As Regina began her closing prayer, an unexpected and sweet, gentle, melody accompanied her. Without opening her eyes, she knew. Dewey was playing and his anointed music co-mingled with her spirit as their prayer ascended. The completeness of the moment both surprised and overwhelmed her. She was soon moved beyond speech and stopped. She lifted her hands, lost and caught up— all she could do was join in the praise.

No. She shook her head after the last note was struck. *Dewey's gift ushered in the spirit. Not my carefully planned words.*

Only a couple on one accord could have flowed with this kind of unplanned, symphonic praise. Thank God an observant usher guided her to her seat when DW Thurman began to sing. His soulful rendition of the "Gloria Patri," soothed her and the audience. DW let the ladies linger in the glow of grace just long enough, before upping the tempo. With his skills on the instrument, DW Thurman shifted the flow and led the group in a joyous sing along of "Favor Found Me."

The man was a master at bridging an audience from a spiritual to a physical space. The whole room was now standing and clapping—giving up a mighty hand praise. Dewey delighted the audience long enough for Regina to compose herself for the post luncheon meet and greet.

How could he have known how much time I needed?

"Dr. Lawson," one of the leading ladies of the Assembly gently urged her to attend to the present. "The receiving line is forming?"

Regina stood and moved to the line forming to the right of the platform. To her surprise, the presiding Bishop was first in line to shake her hand. She pasted on a bright smile, even though she wasn't ready to deal with the memory the Bishop evoked.

Bishop Eddie Johnson would never know that something he said to her ten years ago triggered the most difficult period of her life, and lead to her divorce. Regina quick scanned the room for Dewey. She caught only a glimpse of him, surrounded by fans, most likely turning on that very effective DW Thurman charm. What she wouldn't give to go into a private space with him right now and just be. But—

Regina drew a cleansing breath. She was here to work and part of her role was to set aside her personal desires and greet the people waiting to shake her hand. She reinforced her smile and extended her right hand in fellowship to Bishop Johnson.

"Dr. Lawson," the Bishop started with a huge toothy grin, "your speech was outstanding, but the ending. That, that was an unexpected grace, great pleasure, and God's own doing. The way Thurman blended with your flow. My Lord, you two need to connect, do some work together."

She glanced down at the floor. Bishop Johnson had no clue how she'd connected with Dewey a few hours ago. She accepted the compliment and many more during the next hour of meeting and greeting. All the while worrying if the pictures the Pappi took had already hit the internet. Those photos could do real damage to her ministry.

Drat.

She'd left the book pluggers she intended to pass out today in the holding room. The promotional team of Malik and Dewey had really stepped up her social media game. She now had a blog, Twitter handle, and a Facebook group. This was the perfect audience for her book. Her PR team would not be pleased that she'd fumbled this opportunity.

Thirty minutes later, with the end of the receiving line in sight, Regina adjusted her stance. A few more words of encouragement and affirmations on setting a standard with young mothers and their mothers and she'd be free.

No wonder Dewey has bad knees.

She lifted her left foot, then her right, for a bit of respite. If she was going to continue standing through events like this, she'd need support hose. Or wear more supportive shoes and abandon the sexy slingback pumps Dewey liked.

Why is Bishop Johnson in this line again? Is it BMA protocol? One of those first shall be the last things the traditional denomination's so proud of.

Before greeting the elder again, Regina scanned the room. The porters were busy breaking down tables and across the room Dewey sat on a bench talking with Harold Mims.

"Dr. Lawson," Bishop Johnson started, "I've asked the staff to bring a fresh pitcher of water. You must be parched. Unless, of course, you prefer something else?" The cleric raised his arm to beckon a staff member.

"No, no, that's very nice. Thank you."

"Why don't we sit down over there for a minute." Johnson gestured towards a bank of cushioned benches placed along the walls of the AU Center ballroom.

"Yes."

After they settled, Johnson joined her in an ice-cold glass of lemon water.

"Thank you so much. I really needed that bit of refreshment."

The Bishop complimented her again on the usefulness of her message before inviting her to give the same presentation during the BMA national convention this summer.

"I'd be honored," she gushed. Things were falling in line like Dewey predicted. And she couldn't wait to share this news. "Isn't the program already set."

"Yes, and I'm a sitting Bishop." Johnson grinned. "You have a great future as a speaker. I'd like to support you, and I'd be delighted if you remember when we last met."

As if I'd ever forget.

Bishop Johnson had officiated when Victor, Sr. was inducted into the Amaranthine Order, the highest honor bestowed by their fraternity. The ceremony was the first public event Johnson celebrated after burying his wife.

"I recall your being the perfect hostess. That barbeque at your house was wonderful." He clapped his hands in joyous remembrance. "And," he focused his eyes on her, "I enjoyed your good company, too. It was kind of you to sit and listen to me that evening."

Regina lowered her head. During the hour she listened to Johnson speak so lovingly about his sainted wife, she wondered if Victor would mourn her death for more than a minute. In the days that followed, she'd realized Victor would only miss the tending, mending, and the household administrative tasks she provided, that made his life run smoothly. Knowing everything she did for her husband could easily be replaced cut her deeply.

"Do you remember?"

She nodded and recalled a few more things about that night. "Yes, it wasn't often that police and fire were called to my home."

Bishop Johnson shook with laughter.

After the official celebration ended, things got way out of hand. It seemed like every fraternity member in middle Alabama got the word to drop by. Victor failed to tell her about the late night feast he ordered. After she went to bed, the fraternity took over the backyard; eating, drinking, stepping, and marching. Sometime after midnight, somebody threw moonshine into the fire pit.

"Yeah, that was one heck of a good party." He chuckled with that faraway look of fond remembrance in his eyes. Regina smiled at the distinguished clergyman, who was still a frater at heart.

"I'm glad you stayed and were able to enjoy yourself."

Months after that party she walked around in a shroud of sorrow.

Chapter Fourteen

Let the praise song fill your heart and calm your mind.
When the edge of the present is sharp. Reach beyond the break.

Dewey watched Regina from across the ballroom as he enjoyed a much needed, in person, catch-up with his best friend.

"Man, don't think for one minute that Regina will miss what we just pulled." Dewey grinned.

He'd conspired with Horace weeks ago to position a piano in the room, so he could support her ministry today. And turns out today was an appropriate time for them to begin working together. He couldn't remember being with a woman who rejoiced in his celebrity, but didn't try to profit from it. Regina hadn't asked him for anything beyond his attendance this afternoon.

"Dr. Lawson?" Horace scoffed. "To me, that prayer and praise flowed too well, not to have been coordinated and choreographed."

A beam of satisfaction coursed through Dewey's spirit. Horace was right. He and Regina were in sync, physically too. "That's how it is between a man and his wife."

"Ha, ha," Horace burst out. "We both know there don't need to be no-mo Mrs. Thurmans."

Dewey nudged his faithful friend. Horace had been there for him for over forty years. Horace walked with him through the heartbreak and overwhelming sense of failure that blocked his spiritual gift after both his marriages ended. Few people knew it was Rev. Horace Mims who prayed him out of that dark place where he thought he'd lost the anointing. Three years after his second divorce when he was in the wilderness of lonely popularity, Horace helped him hear God's voice again.

"I didn't believe I'd meet a woman like Regina."

"You've also said that you aren't able to see to the end of a personal matter," Horace countered. "Why are you claiming to see the end of this so clearly?"

Dewey swatted at Horace with a rolled-up event program. "And that blows the stereotype that black preachers don't listen. I told you I had a vision that I'd be happy again. I am. And I've only shared with you the prophecy of sons."

Horace turned his head in Regina's direction. "I see what you like. If Myra and Deb had a middle sister she'd be it." Horace rubbed his jaw. "You might need to talk to somebody about that."

"Ha!"

"Brother, I'm delighted that you have someone special in your life. Dr. Lawson's still got it. I'll give you that. But, I don't think you're getting any *sons* from her. Dew, you definitely have some sons-in-law coming. Possibly grandsons—"

"Horace," Dewey spoke in his authoritative don't-question-the-prophet tone, "that woman is my wife and her sons are my sons."

"I hear you and always accept your word. But," Mims pointed to the other side of the room, "you best get over there. You don't know everything if you think for a minute Bishop's over there waiting on me."

"Dewey." Bishop Johnson rose as he approached. "It is always a blessing to hear you sing. I had no idea the AU Center would bring out its finest for us. But then again," the Bishop chuckled, "we are the BMA."

As the men exchanged greetings, Regina stood. She was more than ready to go. Sitting with Johnson stirred up too many unpleasant memories. She had a feeling this would happen when she saw Johnson today.

"Thurman, I'm actually glad you happened by. I was just saying to Regina here that the two of you should try to come up with some sort of collaboration. You were correct. Her message is essential for our young people. Standards. I think there's a song in there for you or your girls."

"Whoa, stop right there." Dewey threw his hands in the air. "I can't receive that word from you. Next thing you know, you're trying to claim my next hit record."

Dewey winked at her. "You see, *Regina*, Eddie Johnson has been accusing me of turning his revelation into song for many years."

Johnson folded his arms across his chest and stomped his foot. "You, did! You know you did. And I'll always believe you did."

Dewey gave Johnson a good-natured swat with the event program in his hand. "Bishop, I'll tell you for the umpteenth time. I am not a mind reader. How could I have stolen your song?"

Johnson's lips twisted. "You wrote the song that was waiting in my spirit."

"My learned brother, how do you continue to figure that the Almighty's going to wait almost forty years for you to write and produce the music HE intends to bless his people with. You can hum a few bars in the pulpit, but you can't really sing." Dewey reared back on his heels. "But, you a bold fellow though. Bold enough to make the Almighty wait. And still keeping him waiting," he added in his authoritative tone. "When are you going to be *truly* bold and release that which the Lord has given you. Why do you wait? Or are you holding out 'till *you* get ready to bless God's people?"

The Bishop responded with the good-natured grace of one defeated in a verbal battle. "Well, you're right again, and I receive the wisdom in your words. And you are so right about my being bold. Of late. Nice to see you, Dewey." He waved him off. "If you'll excuse me, I'd like to return to the delightful conversation I'm having with Dr. Lawson."

Dewey planted his heels, folded his arms across his chest as his face exploded in a huge Cheshire cat-like grin.

"Well, you can stand there." Eddie Johnson turned his head. "Regina, I was hoping you'd be free to join me for dinner this evening?"

Dewey rocked back on his heels. "After you feed 'er, bring her home."

Eddie Johnson's head spun around. "Huh?"

"Catch up, man. Are you the only person here that doesn't know Regina's my lady?"

"What," Bishop Johnson turned to take in Regina's quick smile. He nodded and stood to shake Dewey's hand, again. "I should have put two and two together when you called and asked me to book her. Ah, when the prophet is involved, I'm too slow, again. She's far too good for you."

Dewey nodded his agreement. "Truth."

"Then, in that case, why don't the two of you come to the Mount as my guests in the morning? And you can sing my song."

"Regina?" Dewey extended his arm. "Eddie, I'll call you next time I'm home. You can buy me dinner. Someplace expensive. I got something to tell you."

During the quick, quiet ride back to his condo, Dewey suggested twice that she lie down for a while. When he joked about wanting her well rested, she snarled at him. Although, in truth she longed for some time alone to reset her mood. The past Bishop Johnson dug up threatened to disrupt her good present.

⚬∞⚬

For the next three hours, Regina flipped over in Dewey's bed. From her left side, then back to the right. She rubbed her forearms. Then opened and closed her eyes. One of her mother's favorite old adages about letting sleeping dogs lie just wasn't working. Her thoughts of the past refused to rest. She sat up in the bed, walked around the room. Unable to move beyond what happened the week after she first met Bishop Johnson, she returned to the bed.

On a Sunday evening long ago, when Victor tapped her shoulder for the weekly maintenance bump, she'd cried inconsolably. She wept so hard, Victor had to stop and attend to her tears. That night they had the last honest conversation of their marriage.

Victor said he loved her and only made love to her. Which he did. He made love to her, weekly. Faithfully, like he walked their dog and took out the trash. His explanation of his infidelity—his final insult—sent her over the edge.

"My being with other women doesn't have anything to do with how much I value you." Victor assured her he wasn't bringing anything home. She knew there was no need to worry about any outside babies. But life-threatening disease? He asked her not to worry, because he was careful.

Careful?

She'd asked why he did it? He couldn't explain. But said it wasn't for any lack in her. Victor complimented her on how good she still looked and how proud he was to call her his wife. Said, she was his greatest asset.

"A utility," she spit out.

Nothing more to Victor Earle than electricity, water, or gas for his car. Nothing more than his other essential household services like cleaning and childcare. When Victor Earle, Sr. flipped the switch for her to host a dinner or sit in a designated chair as his perfect spouse, she was there. Her reliability was even assured for his weekly *need to make love,* not just have sex.

Awful thoughts about utility and Victor not mourning her death bound her for several weeks, before they evolved.

What if Vic died?

No, it would be a long time before Victor Earle expired. He was in excellent health. She knew because watching over his health was one of her maintenance tasks. After a full month of deliberating, agonizing, and second-guessing she arrived at the unthinkable. She was gonna have to kill him.

Wasn't this how it started on those *Lifetime* movies—where women killed their husbands? Or how people snapped? Guilt over her plots to kill Victor used their potential to try and drive her mad.

In the end she decided it was better to end a dead marriage than kill her unfaithful husband. As soon as she resolved to let Victor live, unforgiveness took the place of guilt. It took months for her to forgive herself for even considering damaging her sons by hurting their father.

For the remainder of that year, she moved around in a deep funk. Publicly, she kept up the proper social appearances. Made sure the boys had everything they needed. And continued all—except one—of her maintenance tasks for Victor.

Her husband had given her everything: a new car every three years, a yearly family vacation, and he'd never missed an anniversary or birthday. He'd been a good provider and had never abused her in any way the public would understand. And he'd been discreet. No one ever reported seeing Victor Earle out in public with another woman. Montgomery was shocked when their surface-perfect marriage ended.

"That's it!"

With the resolve it took to end her marriage, Regina rose, freshened her hair and makeup, packed her bags, and went to find Dewey.

⚬∞⚬

For twenty minutes, Regina Lawson stood in the doorway of Dewey's study and watched him sorting mail and whistling. He knew she was there. But never looked up. Another reason she fell, so hard for Dewey. He always let her move in her own time.

In her wildest dreams, she'd never imagined a relationship like this. Not because he was famous. Or for his sexy, hip-hop ways. Or the mental and physical excitement. That whistling old man placed a real value on her as a person. He listened to her and affirmed her aspirations. With him, she was ecstatically happy and totally unsafe. Like her mother would say, "out on a wire, without a net."

And I love it.

The old Regina would have never interrupted her man at work. And especially after he'd complained about needing to attend to his mail.

What I need to say is important.

She moved into the room. "We need to talk."

He glanced up and slowly set aside a stack of envelopes. "I know."

Regina twisted her lips and took a deep breath. His knowing everything was freaking annoying. "Then you know if you plan to have other women while you're with me. I'll go home now."

"Whoa. No!" He stood and stretched. "Lady, where's this coming from?"

She sighed and plopped down on an over-stuffed armchair. For the next hour Dewey listened without interruption as she shared the profound impact Bishop Johnson had on her life. "Everything in my life turned on that meeting."

Dewey nodded. "Yeah, in a way that is Johnson's gift. You're not the only one who's had that experience with him. He's a revelator."

"A what?"

"A revealer of truth. Johnson's gift is to reveal those hidden truths within each person that will lead to their salvation."

"Um." She paused to reflect. A revelator? Who knew there was such a gift? Johnson had helped her recognize a truth that she'd denied for years. Her life wasn't perfect, and she deserved more. And now it was time for her to live in the blessings that came from that truth. "Dewey, my truth is that I don't...I won't ever be in a relationship again where I allow a man to say he loves me, but sleeps with other women."

"I understand that's what your husband told you. But hear me. I only want you."

Her eyes rolled upward.

Dewey's faced twisted and his lips formed a deep scowl. "That doesn't mean I didn't take what was offered to me in my younger days. My immoralities are past crimes. And that's not what you need to hear, either." Dewey joined her in the chair and secured her on his lap. "You need to know that I'm not interested in any foolishness. I'm far too old for any nonsense. I've been up front with you since the day we met. You know my children, most of my business, and I want you to meet the rest of the family, soon. Lady, I have fallen completely in love. And don't you dare say it's too soon. It's only you, if you'll have me. From let's say "Everlasting" to ever-lasting.

Regina sighed and settled her head on his chest. How could she love him so much after only a few months? It didn't make any logical sense, but her heart wanted this fairy tale. *But?*

"I don't want to have to kill you."

"Whew!" He gently squeezed her. "You got me with that. I'm so glad you didn't kill your ex. I wouldn't have met you, yet. I never even considered prison ministry until this thing with Bo." He paused. "I'm sorry to bring Bo up. This is about us. There is a gravity to the discussion we're having, and we need to remain on this note for another measure or two. There are some things I need to say to you."

She lifted her head from his chest. "You listened to me."

Dewey nudged her to indicate his need to stand. Then, took an uncharacteristic turn around the small room.

She sat up straight to give Dewey her full attention.

Does he always pace or create physical distance when he needs to discuss something serious? I can't claim to know all his ways. Which is why I need to let my brain rule instead of my emotions.

"Regina, we've spoken about my spiritual gifts...I think you've seen and heard enough to know that my gifts are used solely for the encouragement and redemption of God's people. I've never used it for personal gain, and the Lord has blessed my obedience." He stopped dead and stared directly at her, then began to shift from one foot to the other.

For the first time since she met him, Dewey seemed unsure. He was also repeating himself. He'd told her all of this before.

"What I need to know. What I want to ask is—can you accept, work with, deal with, live with a prophet?"

They'd talked extensively about his gift, but more from the standpoint of her understanding. Acknowledging his prophetic gift helped her appreciate why his music had such an impact on people. Personally, she struggled for the grace to accept his lifestyle. The late hours, travel, fame, and drugs were all too high-speed for the simple September season of life she'd planned.

Dewey stood before her with arms outstretched. "What I want is to settle into some ordinary days with you. It's time for me to downshift. I've been thinking about what the next season of my life would look like for a while." He gave her a shy smile. "Now, I see myself on a patio with a porch swing, near a beach…"

Regina shivered. Sometimes his insight was Halloween night spooky. This was exactly how she spent her time when she wasn't teaching or in Montgomery with her boys.

"And anyone who's ever been in love can see that I adore you." He reached down, helped her to her feet and wrapped her in his arms. "What are you thinking?"

Her arms encircled his waist. It would be her biggest challenge to understand when he was operating out of his prophetic anointing and when he was speaking out of his personal insight as a compassionate man. She had no doubt in her love for him, but they were nowhere near ready to talk about a lifelong commitment.

"It is a lot to consider." She smiled softly. "What do you think I'm going to say?"

"Woman, I can't see to the end of a personal matter. My gift, as with all spiritual gifts does not interfere in any way with another person's freewill. You need to know that." He rocked them slowly. "But, I'll do whatever it takes to try and influence you to stay with me."

Regina lay her head on his shoulder. "Um, like that influence you had me under last night?"

Dewey took her by the shoulders and moved them apart as a storm brewed in his eyes. "I'm so sorry about that. It won't happen again."

Regina smiled and reclosed the distance. "That was a joke, Dew. I was only under the influence of some good loving."

"Be serious, woman. Walk the last mile of the road with me?"

Regina exhaled. "Oh, let's slow down. Keep moving forward and see what happens. There's much to consider, but I do love you and want some more of you after you feed me."

Chapter Fifteen

What have we lost because we cannot stand still?
Take a moment today to stand still.
Stand still and find sweet solace in silence.
Still enough to pray. Quiet enough to hear the answers.

Summer didn't start as she'd planned. Instead of going home after the BMA event, Regina flew to New York with Dewey. While he testified in his copyright infringement case against Young Iggy, she lounged and recharged at the spa. At night they took huge bites out of the Big Apple. Sightseeing, jazz clubs, working overtime to spoil each other. Dewey actually seemed to enjoy shopping with her or, rather, buying everything she'd expressed any interest in. They had a long, lovely week in New York before boarding a flight to Texas.

Over the next three days, Regina would facilitate the standard setting workshop for The Sisters Fellowship. In the short time they'd been together, she'd come to respect Dewey's business acumen. He'd strategically scheduled the family retreat in Houston, so the SOL network would pick up the expenses. After all of Dewey's support and encouragement, she was determined not to let him down. Self-doubt plagued her as the plane taxied down the runway.

What if things don't go well? What if his girls rejected the process and I lose his favor?

"Hey," Dewey leaned over, "I have that stack of invitations I want you to look at in my bag? Want to do that now? Or are you going to catch up on your sleep?" he teased with an impish grin.

"I'm going to sleep, if you let me. I'll look at them later." She yawned.

Regina closed her tired eyes, but couldn't rest. They'd pushed the limits last night. Dewey sat in with the house band at Birdland and after the last set they went to breakfast with the percussion section. Since they were out, he insisted they stay up and watch the sun rise over the Hudson. They overslept and had to rush to LaGuardia for their three o'clock flight.

With the busy week ahead of them, she prayed everything in Texas would mix and blend like a good pot of gumbo. She started the week working with the girls. On Wednesday afternoon, she'd accompany Dewey to WSOL for the taping of the station's opening image. Then the entire family would return to the station to tape the Thurman Family Christmas Sing-A-Long. A holiday special that would air on Christmas Day. Dewey asked that she sit on the piano bench with him during the finale. A brief appearance designed to drive people to look her up, increase her media standing, and boost her speaking engagements.

As they jetted towards Texas, Regina worried about how the girls would respond to her? As an instructor? And as their father's...what? Woman, Lady-friend, Boo-thing, Bird? She still hadn't found a good word to describe their relationship. Dewey called it September love. She prayed for God's grace to help the girls set a standard for their lives and group.

The Sisters Fellowship with their mix of modern R&B and traditional gospel was on the rise in the industry. Their music and message was now reaching young people worldwide. But Dewey saw threats on the horizon. And he only wanted The Sisters Fellowship to sing songs he thought would endure and bless God's people for generations.

But, Bonita and Tasnee were forcefully pushing for the hip-hope concept. Calista and Allegra agreed with the longer arc their father saw. Struggling in med school left Jolee without an opinion. Regina prayed the individual personal issues the girls faced wouldn't interfere with her workshop. Beyond Bonita's relationship and Jolee's struggle, there were other issues lurking beneath the surface. She prayed the time spent together in retreat would provide a positive launch to their summer tour.

Since summer was the only time the group could do more than weekend or holiday events, this week was work, some rest, and intense rehearsal to kick off an aggressive summer schedule. Thirty venues and twenty states in under two months. She couldn't imagine embarking on such a hectic adventure with Rena.

The quiet summer of writing she'd planned wasn't going to happen. Dewey wanted her to attend a month's worth of awards ceremonies, galas, gospel music workshops, and testimonial events. She opened her eyes at the sound of Dewey's light snoring, then took in a deep cleansing breath. That man never seemed to worry. But why should he? He claimed to know everything and said the busy summer ahead would be filled with good times and celebration.

Smith's place was set to open at the end of June, she had a second engagement with the Baptist Methodist Assembly in July, and a few weddings to attend. And if things worked out like Dewey planned, she'd help Malik enroll at Morehouse in the fall.

"Hey, Lady." Dewey nudged her. "We're about to land."

Regina stretched and frowned as she up righted herself in the airplane seat. "What if—"

"Hey, remember it was the girls who brought you to my attention."
His all-knowing is annoying!

"Don't worry. They are super excited to spend time with you. Actually, they're hoping that you can get me sorted out." He took her hand and squeezed. "Hey, you'll get a chance to catch up on your sleep." He winked. "I'm sharing a room with Tasnee this week."

His old-fashioned gesture of respect for his daughters touched her.

"I got you directly across the hall from us. Don't want you wandering the halls at night. If I can't have you in my bed, I want to keep you as close as possible."

The first hour of the standard setting seminar hadn't gone well. Calista and Allegra were the only ones fully focused on the work. Carrying the conversations frustrated Allegra. Dear Calista upheld her sisters with a certainty, surety, and grace that echoed her father's. Bonita couldn't stay in the room for an entire hour, and Jolee was just too tired to focus. And that youngest was more than a notion.

Young and hurting about her mother's divorce and without the vocabulary to properly speak to it, Tasnee gifted Regina with the brunt of her emotional immaturity. Tas challenged every concept she presented.

"How is that supposed to help us? I mean everybody's free. I don't get it."

"Tas, I don't think Dr. Lawson is talking about freedom in a literal sense." Calista cut in. "It's more like the freedom she has to speak her truth without worry. Some of the things Dr. Lawson says are not popular, like when she talks about how some people wear stage makeup every day. I mean we don't walk around every day in the clothes and makeup we perform in."

"Speak for yourself," Jolee playfully interjected.

Everyone laughed.

"Yes, glamour queen. That's you. Fabulous every day. You can carry it off and you are free to do that. Me, I'm free to rock this ponytail." Calista tossed her ponytail and winked. "Because it's the best I can do without you to beat my face and dress my hair."

After the sisters stopped laughing, Bonita looked up from her iPad. "Tas, freedom is a state of mind, not just a physical truth. Dr. Regina is trying to get us to think beyond what we are today and set a standard to guide us into tomorrow. Like Daddy says it's about having our music stay around."

"Then let's close the door on that hip-hope hype." Allegra sighed.

While the sisters chopped up the pros and cons of the hip-hope concept, Regina stepped aside. Beneath the surface was an unspoken tension among the sisters about Bonita's relationship. As the facilitator, she gave the sisters some time to talk off topic before pulling them back.

§

After almost five hours of pull and tug with The Sisters Fellowship all Regina wanted to do was go somewhere and lie in Dewey's arms. But he was still at the television station.

Regina turned off the PowerPoint presentation at three o'clock to end the session. They hadn't made much progress today, and she hoped to end on a good note by asking a deceptively simple question.

"If you could find one word to describe my ministry, what would it be?"

Jolee answered first. "Standards, that's too easy."

"True." Allegra agreed.

"Right." Bonita concluded.

Regina shook her head. "No. It's freedom. A standard gives one freedom to create and become what they desire to be—to accomplish. What I do now is possible because of freedom. Ladies, let's call it a day. Take some time to rest and reflect. And I'll see you at dinner."

Thurman family tradition included at least one fancy, dress-up dinner every trip. Tonight's dinner would be courtesy of the SOL Network. Instead of returning to her empty room to change, Regina remained in the conference room to catch up on her work. Last week she'd purposefully neglected work and focused on her relationship with Dewey. She hadn't written a word in two weeks. After wasting five minutes deciding which chapter to work on, she pulled out her phone to check in with her boys.

After two attempts, she caught up with Malik in the *studio* producing a local rapper's mix tape. It was clear from the screed of profanity she overhead while chatting with Malik that it was time for her youngest to make some changes. She couldn't see a future in Malik's efforts. And she knew without asking, he didn't have a proper contract in place for his current product.

Smith didn't call her back. So, she tried to write.

Another hour of no progress on her manuscript and wondering why Smith didn't return her calls. It just wasn't like him. He used to tell her everything. She'd been his secret-keeper and the only one who knew his deepest fears. What secret could Smith have that he felt was beyond her capacity to love him through?

Seated in a private dining room in Houston's swankiest restaurant, every member of the Thurman family seemed to be on their last nerve. To bless the restaurant owner for hosting his family, Dewey added his personal promise to post an online review of the food and singing service. Regina looked forward to the entertainment from the singing waitstaff almost as much as the meal.

"After dinner, let's take a tour of the city," Calista suggested to cut a little of the tension.

"I'm going to bed early. So no for me," Jolee grumbled. She'd complained all day about not being able to rest. Not with Bonita staying up all hours recording video voice mail messages for her boyfriend.

Dewey also complained, "think I'll turn in early, too. I didn't sleep well last night either with Tasnee hee-hawing at all hours over social media posts."

"I offered to go to the lobby." Tasnee defended herself.

Allegra, Calista and Jolee all shot back. "You know better than that."

Tasnee huffed. "Can I ask you a question, Dr. Regina?"

"Of course."

"Daddy is trying to make me start college in the fall, but I don't see any reason to sit in a classroom all day when I already have a career."

Regina swallowed hard and almost choked on a sip of water she'd just taken. *Best sidestep this.*

Tasnee continued, "You talk a lot about women not waiting—"

"Baby girl," Dewey shot Tas a warning look, "we'll talk about this later. Back in the room."

Tasnee shook her head no. "Dr. Regina won't be there. So, I'm asking her now."

"I don't think Dr. Regina means—"Allegra started.

"I wasn't asking you," Tasnee snapped.

Allegra reared back in her seat and took a deep breath. Before she could speak, Dewey intervened. "Stop it! Everyone, let's just stop. I brought my ladies here tonight to relax and enjoy a fine meal. I am sure we can find something to discuss that won't end up on Gospel Gossip's front page. I can see the headlines now." He moved his right hand from left to right high in the air. "Thurman Family Food Fight."

A little bit of laughter lifted the mood and everyone took a few minutes to study the menu. As if on cue, the waiter arrived and sang the dinner menu and specials.

"Bravo."

"Yeah."

"Well done!"

The entire party lauded the young man with a rich baritone voice. Dewey stood to shake his hand. "Young man, you have a wonderful instrument. Stick with that training."

The waiter beamed. "Thank you, sir."

As soon as the waiter stepped away to give them time to study the menu, Tasnee piped up again. "I was just making dinner conversation, trying to get to know Dr. Regina better."

Regina placed her hand over Dewey's. "I don't mind answering Tasnee's question."

Dewey cut his eyes at her so sharply, Regina drew back her hand and placed it on her neck.

First, he wants my input with the girls, then he shuts me down. Fine.

She cast a side-eye at Dewey. She could more than handle Tasnee's question, without overstepping. She wasn't going to tell Tas anything new or different.

"Tasnee," Calista stepped in to diffuse the situation, "why don't you finish telling us about your adventures, doing a sing-a-long with the pre-schoolers."

It hadn't taken long to discover that Calista was a sweetheart, peacemaker and an artful dodger. More than once today, Calista had intervened or redirected a discussion. Regina scowled as the singing server placed a mixed greens salad in front of her.

"Excuse me." Bonita popped up when her phone rang.

Eyes rolled around the table as Bonita excused herself. The first course conversation continued with general complaints. Tasnee and Calista whined about not having time to go shopping this afternoon. When Bonita returned, she challenged the summer schedule and Allegra grumbled about doing all the real work for the Fellowship.

"Listen," Jolee interrupted. "If I knew dinner was going to be a bunch of complaining, I would have stayed at the hotel."

Dewey turned a concerned eye towards Jolee. "Jo, what's going on. Your sisters said you took a long nap this afternoon. Which is why I didn't bother you to rehearse."

"Thank you, Daddy. It's...," Jolee paused, "Bo, stayed up half the night singing and making videos, and I couldn't rest knowing she was making videos for that inmate."

Bonita jerked her head and turned toward Jolee. "His name is Omni and the videos are for worship since I can't be there this summer. If I was bothering you, you should have said something. I would have gone down to the lobby. And we all know how tired you are because you keep telling us."

Calista reached out and touched Bo's hand. "You know better than that. I'll sit in the lobby with you tonight so we can support Jo."

"Thank you."

"Bo, why don't you call it an early night and get your rest. That man's not going anywhere." Allegra issued a rare shady word.

"Snap, snap." Tasnee popped her fingers.

Allegra leveled a nasty gaze at her baby sister. "You should be the one offering to sit in the lobby with Bo, so Daddy can get his rest."

With that comment the family broke out in general and specific arguments. Each one voiced their complaints against the others. Regina sat quietly by as the girls bickered and Dewey seethed in anger. His family dinner was in shambles. When she reached out to him, he covered her hand with his for a moment. She wasn't happy with him either, but they'd get to that later. When the meals were served the family ate in silence and no one ordered dessert.

While they waited for the post meal check-in from the restaurant owner, Tasnee re-lit the fire. "I called Uncle Harold last week."

Dewey stood and clapped two times.

The Sisters Fellowship came to attention and Daddy Dewey re-took his seat. "Lil' girl, I've 'bout done had it with you. Why do you keep fishing in a dry hole? I know you called Harold. And I know he told you to start school in the fall."

Tasnee looked a little embarrassed after being called out. Then shot back, "Dr. Regina's son didn't finish college."

"We don't bring other people into our family debates."

Regina leaned back in her seat. *So, I'm other people, now?*

"Tas, it's true you have a special anointing, but you still need training. You can sing and play, and you've mastered neither craft. Won't even try. Haven't taken a lesson all year. You always got some lame excuse when it comes time to learn something. You are lucky to be my child, because you couldn't make it in anyone else's choir because you won't listen. Or train. College will teach you that and some discipline. Your biggest problem is you think you don't have anything to learn."

Dewey took a deep breath and lowered his voice. "I'm not having this conversation with you, again. Come to my house and you're enrolling at Spelman. And I know you asked Uncle Harold for a job, but what can you do? You can't even work for me because you've got no qualifications. Can't send you to warm up a choir or do a workshop in my stead, because you don't know enough music theory. There is more to this than looking and singing pretty. After sitting in church all your life, you haven't even studied enough scripture to lead a decent bible study." Dewey paused and closed his eyes.

Regina reached out and tugged at his pant leg. "Dew?"

His eyes popped open. "Daughter, stop trying my patience. We have a standard of education in this family set by Grandma Minnie. And there is no way you are going to find any agreement with the nonsense you're talking amongst any of us and that includes Dr. Regina." He drew in a deep cleansing breath. "Okay, I'm sorry. I'm finished. But," he pointed at Tasnee, "I'm not through with you, little girl."

The room went quiet until the owner came in to take a photo with Dewey and their waiter. Then several with The Sisters Fellowship. The little photo shoot seemed to improve Dewey's mood a bit. Or rather DW Thurman put on his stage persona to charm and compliment the restauranteur and waiter.

"Young man, continue with your studies, but don't let them train the Dr. Watts out of you."

The girls all laughed since they'd heard this advice before.

"Sir, my grandmother won't let that happen." The singing waiter took a deep breath and belted out. "Heeey-aaa, chile-eee."

"Umm hmmm. Umm hmmm." The Sisters Fellowship hummed in unison and everyone shared a good laugh as the waiter completed a stanza of the old devotional.

As the family prepared to leave the general manager rushed in. "Mr. Thurman, I'm so sorry but a bit of a crowd has gathered outside. I don't know how they found out you and your family were here. It certainly wasn't from any member of our staff."

The family turned in unison towards the youngest. "Tasnee?"

Tasnee's full head of fresh weave shook like a strong wind had blown her way. "No, I swear. I only post after I leave a place."

"Um hm."

"Yeah, right."

"Sir, we're happy to ask your car driver to pull around back, so you and your family can exit through the kitchen," the worried manager offered.

Dewey rolled his eyes and clapped twice. "That won't be necessary. Okay, everybody, put on those smiles. Let's greet the people. And," he reached into his pocket and drew out his hotel room key and passed it to Bonita, "when we get back to the hotel, pack up your things and move into the suite with Tasnee. Jolee, get yourself a good rest tonight."

Jolee tilted her head to one side. "Daddy, are you sharing with me? You snore."

"No." Dewey reached for Regina's hand and whispered in her ear. "We're all grown. They know we're together."

Chapter Sixteen

When darkness covers surround us
And the storms of life beat round us
The Lord is our shelter.

Still a little frosty, Regina held her tongue an hour later as Dewey moved his things into *their* room. There was no way she was going to support Tasnee's immature manipulation of her message. But, when he called her "other people." She folded and unfolded her arms. Then looked forward and caught her reflection in the mirror across from the bed. Her expression revealed her entire mood.

"If you want to revisit the Tasnee argument we can?" he said after setting his toiletries up in the bathroom.

"No, let's not. I hadn't planned to say anything other than what you and Deborah, and probably Myra and Minnie have already said. Lord knows the girls have enough voices in their ears."

"It wasn't your lovely voice or good counsel that was going to ruin our meal. I cut you off because Allegra and Jo are about sick of Tas, and I didn't want them to get started."

Regina nodded.

"I'm still angry with Tas, but she's forgiven. I had a long talk with Deb this morning and I'm sorry to say she's wavering. But, I'm going to try again this week to encourage Tas to come to Atlanta and enroll at Spelman. But, after that. I think it's done. Deb and Tasnee will decide this one. Which is another reason I didn't want you drawn into it."

"You asked me here to work with your daughters. You've asked in general for me to find a place in their lives. And the first time one of the girls reaches out to me, you shut it down. I wasn't going to support her. You know I've struggled with the idea of offering any advice to your daughters. But, I've grown to admire them all so much that I feel like a hypocrite. I'm running around sharing my insights with anyone who will listen, but for your children, I come up empty. And I don't even want to talk about my boys."

"You're tired. Let's go to bed. I've missed you."

"Really?" She huffed and folded her arms across her body. "No wonder the girls were so difficult to work with, today. Why should they listen to me? You're not."

"Listening to you is why you're here," he hummed. "We didn't have a chance to talk about how it went, today. Tell me what happened." He plopped down beside her on the bed and attempted to nuzzle at her neck.

Regina hopped up and moved to a chair on the other side of the room. Then gave him the Readers Digest version of today's disaster.

"Lady, you can't see the end of this work. It's a process, and you will make it through the messy middle to a victorious end. I know it."

Regina shrieked, "You don't know everything. You weren't in the room while I had to pull out every response while working double time to keep Bo in the room and Tasnee off of Snapchat."

"Just let it go." He yawned. "Let's watch a movie or something."

She shook her head. "No, it's a mess. And before you invited yourself over here, I'd planned to work on tomorrow's exercises." She threw up her hands. "Because what I did today… Didn't work."

With all the surety of his spiritual office, Dewey proclaimed, "The truth doesn't require your belief."

"Sometimes your creepy, all-knowing attitude is too much to take," Regina yelled before storming out of their room.

An hour later Dewey found his lady-love sitting in the hotel lobby. He tread lightly as he moved toward her and pointed to a seating group a few feet away.

"I can't have any of my ladies walking around unescorted at this time of night. I'll sit right over there until you're ready to go back to the room. If you need space to work, I'm happy to walk you back to the room, then come back out here to sit for a while." He offered with a tentative smile.

"No, I've had a chance to cool down." She motioned for him to sit next to her. "I don't need to change anything for tomorrow except my expectations and attitude. I wrongly assumed I could skip some of the initial trust building exercises I do because the participants are sisters. I'm going to backtrack and start there in the morning. Get us on a firm footing."

Dewey nodded. "That sounds like a plan. Set your course and if I may request one alteration. I'd like to join you for the afternoon session. Just to support you. Lady, I see the successful ending of your work with the girls because I have faith in your process. I've heard you speak. Watched all of your videos and I've read the outline of your book. Your message is anointed and appointed for this generation; the girls will respond. I offer this observation up as a prayer of affirmation."

"Amen," she said. "Now, let's go back to our room."

Halfway into the second day of the retreat for The Sisters Fellowship things were worse. Tasnee completely missed the point of the trust building exercise and started acting out. It took a half hour unplanned break for Calista to minister to her baby sister's imagined offense. After the break, Bonita came back late. A well-rested Jolee seemed annoyed by the wasted time. Allegra and Calista grew weary of carrying the conversation and trying to encourage their sisters to participate more. By noon, the girls were at odds with her and each other. Totally aggravated, Regina broke for lunch early.

When Dewey came in after lunch, the mood in the room was still funky. Ever optimistic, he stepped to the front of the room and clapped twice. The well-trained chorus rose and waited for their choir master's direction.

"Let's begin this afternoon with a verse of "I Love to Tell the Story.""

Although she was still a little salty, Regina smiled and stood with the girls and as a family, they sang the old hymn. As they sang the second verse, the mood in the room shifted. The simple act of harmonizing also settled Regina's rattled nerves.

"That was lovely. Bet y'all didn't know your esteemed seminar leader could sing, too." Dewey said as he moved to an empty seat next to Bonita. "I'm going to stay and work through the exercise you all attempted this morning. So, Dr. Lawson," he winked, "I am your humble student."

As Dewey settled into his seat, Regina returned to the front of the room. It took about an hour for Dewey to work through the exercise to find his theme. His one word. Praise. With the purpose behind the praise—redemption. Every song he ever wrote was about redemption. So, moved by the process, Dewey shared his testimony on how "Everlasting" brought him back to the cross.

"You know why we always spend Easter with Uncle Harold?"

They all nodded in acknowledgment of Dewey's old, old story. He'd shared his redemption story with her months ago, and it still had the power to bring her to tears. In the early eighties, Dewey hit rock bottom. The Morehouse Ten were scattered across the country. The DW Thurman Choir had disbanded and the Georgia Mass wouldn't have him back. All the people who'd flocked to him disappeared along with the money and celebrity.

"I'd lost my family. Myra wouldn't let me near her house. Me and Mama were arguing because she agreed with Myra. I wouldn't admit that I was out of control. Confused and lonely. I lost what I thought was God's favor. No church would hire me as a pianist, let alone a minister of music. No gigs. Not even a children's birthday party. And everybody was sick of hearing about my visions. Except Harold." Dewey spent the next hour detailing how Harold Mims stood by him, ministered to him, believed in him and introduced him to a revelator.

"Yes, Bishop Eddie Johnson, well then just Rev. Eddie. But always wise beyond his years. The year I spent in the BMA church under Eddie and Harold brought me to the place where I acknowledged my spiritual gifts, got a true and unvarnished education about the spiritual offices, which led me to an understanding of my assignment. I am to advise, encourage, comfort and praise. But, at the end of the day, it all leads to the cross. The longevity I've been granted is only because I changed my ways and have tried to be obedient."

"So, Daddy every song is really about redemption?" Bonita asked.

"Ultimately, if you really think about it."

"Even At the End?" Allegra questioned as she dealt with new insight from her father's testimony.

"Yes, dear. When you come to your earthly end, it's about the redeeming power of the cross. It's also that promise of redemption that lifts you out of the darkness in life."

Calista raised her hands in praise. "Stand still and let the Lord perfect that which concerneth you. Psalms 138. You can feel the redeeming power in "Favor Found Me", my favorite of your songs."

"I love you, Boogie," Dewey addressed Calista by her family nickname. "Your insight is a precious gift."

As they processed Dewey's testimony, Regina experienced a deeper sense of belonging. She smiled at Dewey. Again, his special gift had ushered in a spirit of unity. And, yes, the prophet was right. It was time to discuss how they'd proceed in dealing with their children.

Tasnee said, "Daddy, you didn't join the BMA because of the restriction they would have put on you, right."

Regina braced herself, they all knew why Dewey never joined the BMA. Bishop Eddie Johnson revealed that his purpose went beyond denominations. Poor Tasnee had no idea how transparent her little schemes were.

"You all know I love the church of my salvation, but Johnson knew if I joined the Assembly, it would hinder many people caught up in denominationalism."

Tasnee opened her mouth to respond, but Dewey shut her down with a focused, hard-eye stare.

Regina gave him the look, he nodded and wrapped up. He seemed a little spent.

"Girls, I'm going to go and play for a while."

Everyone nodded. A chorus of "thank you Daddy" escorted Dewey to a conference room down the hall to the space he'd reserved for their rehearsals.

Regina stood before The Sisters Fellowship and decided not to push forward. "Ladies, let's stop for the day. You have about four hours before your rehearsal starts. Go shopping. Take a nap or hit the spa. Do something for yourselves collectively or individually. And as you go about your day reflect on your father's testimony and this question. If you had to crystalize your personal ministry and your ministry as a group into one word, what would that word be?"

Early on Wednesday morning, Regina reviewed the sheets of flip chart paper lining the walls of the conference room and sighed. Today was the last day for the retreat and her final chance to help the girls find their theme. One word to help them set a standard for their ministry.

As she looked into the expectant faces of Dewey's beautiful daughters, she took a deep breath. One of her mother's sayings rang in her ears. "Nothing beats a failure, but a try."

Dr. Regina Lawson ginned up her confidence and tried again. For the next two hours she repeated the instructions, reviewed the examples and reassured the girls they could come up with their theme. And again, the girls got stuck in the same hip-hope rut.

"I'm sorry," Allegra began, "but this hip-hope stuff is going to fade. I simply don't see sixty-year-old saints rapping on the mourners bench."

"But, Allegra," Tasnee jumped in. "You don't know. When we get that old, hip hop is all we'll know. My friends don't want to hear Daddy's old-style gospel, now. We need to be defined by something fresh."

"She's right. People have changed. The Lord is calling all kinds of people, not just the so-called church folks. We have got to modernize our sound, our approach," Bonita said. "We need to make music accessible for all God's people."

"It's a fad. It will pass," Allegra repeated her daily vote against hip-hope.

"Well, I want to try it. I've got people asking me to co-lab every day," Tasnee said.

Allegra sighed. "Tas, please go somewhere and sit down. And don't you dare enter into any collaborations with anybody. You can't put the family name out there like that."

Tasnee argued back, "I can do what I want. I'm of age."

Regina took a step back as the sisters went off on their tangent. Hip-hope had become an issue in every discussion. Time was running out, and they didn't have time to beat that tin drum this morning. She checked her watch. At noon she was leaving with Dewey for a taping at WSOL. There wasn't time to extend this work beyond today. And she didn't want to. Not for another minute.

"If you get into any legal issues, Daddy warned me not to help. Or he threatened to fire me. And I agree with him because we love you. Y'all don't understand there's so much more to this business than you see," Allegra blasted.

A frowning Calista said, "Allegra, let's remember she's the youngest."

Bonita looked up from her tablet. "Let's stop ganging up on baby sister. Maybe we should let her find her own way."

"Sisters, can we get back to the point," Jolee said. "This isn't getting us to where Dr. Regina is trying to take us. No matter what style of music we perform, this needs to be about our core. Who we profess to be. What's our bottom line? Our standard."

Calista put up her finger and waited until Jolee finished to add. "At the end of it all, we cannot sacrifice our unity."

"But we still get to follow our own paths, too," Tasnee said.

"That's right," Bonita chimed in. "Whatever we do individually, we stick together as sisters. We're family."

Regina picked up on the thread of hope from the spiritual leaders of the group. "Ladies, let's redo the exercise using the concepts of family, core, and unity. Take thirty minutes and see what you come up with."

Bonita hopped up to leave the room, like she had almost every time the session broke.

"Bo." Calista stopped her. "I need for you to stay and pray with me."

On Wednesday evening, Regina rejoiced in seeing Jolee refreshed and well rested enough to step into her role as the spokesperson for The Sisters Fellowship. Jolee stood before them in her full glory. Hair coiffured, full stage makeup and a beautifully tailored red pants suit. If medical school didn't work out, Jolee could definitely find work in the beauty and fashion industry. After three pretty rough days of discussion, squabbles, and revelation, the sisters had an answer.

"First, we want to thank the fabulous Dr. Regina Lawson for her patience and guidance as we've wrestled though this process," Jolee began. "After much prayer and some fighting, we've decided that sisterhood will be our guidepost. Everything we do now and in the future will be based upon sisterhood. All of our music, messages and actions will be guided by sisterhood. Our sisterhood," she motioned towards her sisters, "for the purpose of helping women see the benefits of working together instead of against other sisters. We chose this word to honor the powerful lesson our mothers taught us about what can happen when women work together. And, Dr. Lawson, sisterhood opens the door to our one word. Unity."

"Amen!" Dewey jumped up and shouted. "That's excellent. I love it and," he settled back into his chair, "it doesn't matter the style of music: gospel, classical, hip-hope as long as the message is consistent. That's what I've been trying to get you all to see. "Yes," he sang, "how beautiful it is for sisters to dwell together in unity."

Dewey stood with his daughters to applaud Regina's work.

She took in the praise while thanking God and her mother's wisdom. This was the moment she'd envisioned when putting together the agenda for this workshop. The successful conclusion Dewey foresaw. She looked into his eyes and mouthed a thank you as they savored the moment of triumph. Dewey and his know-it-all faith!

Allegra stepped forward and pulled a gift-wrapped package from under a table. "A small token of our appreciation. And before you open it, we wanted to make sure you have something to always remember us by. Although we are praying with Daddy that you will always be a part of our lives. After this week calling you Dr. Regina seems a little formal. So, we'd like to ask if we can call you Lady G. Lady, because we've noticed that Daddy calls you Lady. And G because you are a standards gang-sta!"

"Oh, of course," Regina agreed to the new name as she accepted their gift.

"We hope you like it."

"Oh," she exclaimed as she pulled out a framed painting of a choir of brown-skinned baby angels. "This is so beautiful. Thank you."

The girls clapped and sighed.

Regina teared up. More than the gift, the girls had given her a family name. Which was a significant milestone.

"So glad you like it," Jolee said. "I have a friend that's an artist, and it's not worth much today. But I believe that one day he will be famous as an artist or a surgeon."

"How did you know?"

"Daddy told us," Calista answered.

"I love this. Thank you, ladies. It's been a pleasure to work with you," she bubbled.

"Yeah, yeah, let's stop all of this talk and go eat." Dewey broke up their joy-fest. "Lady G is about to gush, then Calista will start, and the rest of you will follow. I don't have enough handkerchiefs. Lord, I am always outnumbered."

"And you love it," Allegra shouted.

Chapter Seventeen

As the sun is rising, the promise of a new song.
Go forth, in joy and sing the song of today.

Three weeks later, DW Thurman set out for Montgomery early. If his body had been treating him right, he would have driven straight to Regina last night. His spirit was willing, but his knees were weak. The doctors warned him not to put off his double knee replacement surgery for too much longer. The cannabis was losing its effectiveness, and Regina didn't support increasing his dosage. He'd have to make a choice soon. The girls were all sure Lady G would stand by him through his recovery. But, his pride didn't want her to see the weakness of his age.

"Even so," he whistled and sped down Interstate 24.

Today, would be a great day for the Earle Family. Victor Earle, Jr. was finally opening his business. And if the traffic stayed light, he and Lady G could have a little private party before the grand event.

"Ha-ha," Dewey hollered as he gloried over finding love in the September of his days.

For the past three weeks, while he traveled with The Sisters Fellowship, Regina had nested in Montgomery to help her son. Although it was generally accepted that Victor Earl, Jr. Esq., aka

Smith, didn't need any help. The success of the young man's business was not in doubt. Regina's oldest was the fine young man everyone praised. But, he'd prayed for him nonetheless.

As he merged onto Highway 85, Dewey bobbed his head and whistled along with the songs on Big Country AM. At his age, a new thing. A younger man might experience this kind of apprehensiveness when meeting a girl's parents. In a post-fifty romance, it was about meeting the ex.

"Now there's got to be a country song in this."

A tinge of apprehension chimed in his spirit as he thought about meeting Victor, Sr. today. Part of him wanted to dismiss Victor Earle by painting him as a fool. Wisdom warned him Earle, Sr. might prove a formidable adversary.

"I should thank the man. No, that's not the play," Dewey spoke aloud to his warring spirit. "Earle isn't my adversary. And he's the fool for letting Regina go." Dewey tapped on the steering wheel of his Maserati Spyder, while his better angels implored him not to be smug.

"My blessing, my blessing, my joy." He composed his own lyrics and sang along with an instrumental on the radio. His ability to recognize Regina's quality wasn't prophetic. It was the blessing of good sense that he'd found in his sixties.

Dewey looked forward to today, as much as any other member of the Lawson-Earle family. For comfort he'd wear khaki slacks and his favorite embroidered Cuban leisure shirts. White to keep cool in the Alabama sun that afternoon and a black shirt for this evening after the sun went down. He laughed; the girls called him Papi Chulo when he wore his favorite shirts. If his girls didn't have such a challenging schedule, they'd be in Montgomery today performing, too. It was time for the girls to spend some time with her boys.

"Come out, Montgomery," he prayed. Surely, a free DW

Thurman concert would bring out additional guests, and he prayed help Smith book out his place for the rest of the year.

∞

"Everything is more than in order. Why'd you drag me over here so early, woman?" Dewey teased as he stood beside the proud mother when they arrived at Smith's place several hours later. Later than the doting Regina wanted, but he was satisfied.

Regina glowed as she surveyed the yard. "I know, but I worry. Isn't this wonderful."

As expected, Smith had everything under control. Dewey stood back on his heels as he watched the young sista who owned the catering company running her team like a field general preparing to invade foreign territory. The chicken was prepped, hamburgers, and hot dogs were ready to be cooked on demand. The heavy-weight, grill-man looked like he knew what he was doing. And the fish, for later tonight, was still swimming. Before beginning his tour of the building, the grill-man offered Dewey two grilled breakfast biscuits.

"Thank you, my brother. It's no doubt we're in for some good eating, today!" Dewey sang after he wolfed down the warm, buttery biscuits.

With his father's assistance, Smith had purchased and improved a former neighborhood bank branch office in east Montgomery. The building was now a community space with private offices and a nice sized great room. Location perfect. The building was adjacent to an upper middle-class neighborhood where people could afford to rent out the space for family reunions, showers, and other social events.

Clever Smith had converted the former drive-thru into an extended patio and sodded the rest of the space to form a lush, green lawn. Perfect for outdoor events. He even had a rainbow-colored-bouncy-house-thing set-up for the little ones.

The place was already booked for three months with fraternity and sorority events. And a local caterer was pressing for a lease on the commercial kitchen. Another revenue stream. All of this, and an anticipated promotion at the Alabama Real Estate Commission. Victor Earle Jr. lived up to his billing.

Good music, good food, plenty of seating, and lots of help from his fraternity. A group of pledgees was falling all over themselves already to keep control of the trash, and the first guest hadn't arrived.

Dewey and Regina observed it all from a perch on the patio. "And," he nudged her, "Malik not doing too bad today, either."

Regina leaned over and gave him a peck on the cheek. His acceptance and understanding of Malik had been one of the keys to her heart. Malik was producing the concert today and would DJ at the after-party tonight.

By mid-morning, they were well into enjoying a nice event. In Malik's hands, the music production was on point. Without much lead time or assistance, Malik had Dewey's equipment in place and set up. Later today, he'd make Malik Earle an offer. But, only after he discussed the plan with the young man's father.

Regina groaned, then nudged him "Get ready to meet some of my former church members. They will all claim to love me and be your biggest fans." Another forfeiture of her divorce. Her membership at the church the Earle family helped found in the sixties. Dewey kissed her cheek and put on his stage smile. Today was part family reunion, part celebrity photo shoot, and all about meeting Victor Earle, Sr.

An hour later, in the midst of his meeting, greeting, eating, and selfie-taking, Dewey stopped and looked around. Victor Earle, Sr. had entered through the lawn gate, looking every bit the general counsel for Alabama's largest commercial real estate corporation. The man had a commanding presence and regal bearing. Dewey saw where the boys got their height and complexion. The Earles were what folks used to call high-yellow.

Victor Earle was also as gregarious as Regina had warned. Like any good politician, Earle shook every hand and kissed every baby in his path. He'd worked hard for his success and expected the reception he was getting. It might be up to an hour before he came face to face with Regina's ex-husband.

"Can I steal him away?" Regina asked as she pulled him away from some fans. They took two steps and she whispered. "That's Vic."

"I assumed as much. Where's his wife?"

"I'm sure she slid in after him. I've noticed that she doesn't care for Victor's glad-handing and greeting." Regina looked around the yard and pointed out Mandy Earle, standing by the lawn gate talking to Smith.

Dewey shook his head and looked up at the bright, blue, sun-streaked sky. *Thank you, Lord, for this foolish man.*

It took another forty minutes before Dewey was able to extend his right hand in fellowship to Victor Earle, Sr. After Regina smoothly handled the introductions, an uncomfortable awkward tension surrounded the two couples. Well, the three mature adults.

Instead of properly speaking, Mandy assessed Dewey, displayed a condescending smile and said, "I don't recognize him."

Dewey chuckled as Regina and Victor rolled their eyes. He'd encountered many Mandy Earles in his career. In her world, the fact she'd never heard of DW Thurman meant he couldn't be a world-renowned anything.

Victor's political savvy intervened. "Well, I can testify to having heard you sing every Sunday for over twenty years. And I assure you there were more than a few corporate dinners where a little of your music was snuck in by the hostess."

Dewey flashed his showman's smile. "I appreciate that. And let me congratulate you on raising two fine young men."

Victor swallowed hard. "I'm afraid the bulk of that compliment goes to Regina. She is a terrific mother. I'm real proud of the boys."

Regina glowed as she placed her hand on her chest. "Malik would love to hear you say that."

Victor groaned, "Not today, Regina."

When her back stiffened, Dewey's skill set kicked in. "I understand today is a day of celebration, for this is a great thing that Smith has done. Great things are coming for Malik, too, and I'd like to speak with you soon about him."

Victor bristled and slid his hands into the pockets of his slacks. "Sir, anything regarding Malik is between Regina and me."

Dewey mirrored Victor's actions. A trick he'd learned from a famous preacher. "I see us talking today."

The body mirroring didn't shake Earle's authoritative confidence. "I heard you claim vision to the future," Victor stated in a tone filled with disbelief.

Mandy giggled.

Regina drew in a sharp breath.

Dewey slipped his arm around her waist, and he pulled his lady close. Earle's incredulity didn't mean anything to him and couldn't raise his ire. Not today. And he'd been right not to dismiss the man as an outright fool. Victor's tone only confirmed that he was capable of solving his own problems.

Dewey shrugged. Of course, Victor Earle would have great confidence. But, DW Thurman had confidence too.

"With all due respect," he began. "I don't particularity believe in yours, mine, and ours."

Victor Earle reared back on his heels.

A motion Regina knew well, she turned and searched Dewey's face. "Maybe, this isn't the time."

He'd actually seen this moment in a vision he'd named fathers and sons. In his limited vision, he'd thought it was a premonition about meeting a potential son-in-law's father. "No, I'll say this now."

Three sets of eyes focused on Dewey in a way that didn't unnerve the veteran stage performer. "I want Malik to come to Atlanta. I've got enough work to keep him busy. And it's work he'll connect to."

Victor leaned forward. "Not necessary. Our family takes care of its own."

Dewey released his hold on Regina and took a step forward. "You're right, Earle. Family takes care of its own. And I'm prepared to get that boy started 'cause I won't keep a grown man in my house."

Victor looked quickly between Dewey and Regina. "You telling me you got plans to set up housekeeping with Regina? Don't you have enough women under what I understand are many roofs?"

Dewey had been deposed enough to recognize the attorney's questioning format. And he was determined not to get upset but... "My daughters." His voice went up an octave. "Absolutely. But," he modulated his tone, "this is Smith's day. We will conclude this conversation later." Dewey turned to Regina, "You're right, Lady. I'm sorry."

Mandy Earle blurted, "I say yes. I don't want Malik living with us."

Regina drew in a sharp breath.

Dewey shot her a warning glance. "Don't say a word," he whispered.

"Mandy, that's not for you to say." Victor shook his head with disapproval, then extended his right hand to Dewey. "You took me off guard. I didn't know anything about you becoming family. Let's get a couple of beers and sit down. Talk, man to man. I suddenly find myself interested in hearing what you have to say."

Mandy still chimed in her agreement, "Yes, let's discuss this."

Dewey shook his head *no*. "Brother to brother, ladies, please excuse us." He flashed Mandy his showman's smile. "Lady, come get me when Malik is ready for me to sing." Then closed his eyes and drew in a deep breath. "And Rena's here."

Victor's head turned sharply left, then right, before he landed a puzzled gaze upon Dewey.

"Oh, Lord." Regina sucked in a tense breath. "Thanks for the warning."

⚮

As she hurried through the crowd to get her sister, Regina gave thanks for Dewey's spiritual sight. Or was it an observation. His gifts usually spooked her, but today it was a blessing. As she searched for Rena, she assumed her role as Lawson-Earle peacekeeper. Anytime the Lawson and Earle families had come together since the divorce, there'd been tension. It took an act of grace to keep fireworks from setting off during Grandpa Earle's funeral two years ago.

Post-divorce the Earle family was still divided. Half of them were mad at Regina for letting their favorite son go. The rest were reeling from the purported insult to their mother by Victor marrying Mandy. And Rena maintained her anger with them all for the way they'd treated her for so many years.

⚮

Let the words of my mouth, Dewey prayed as he followed Victor Earle to an empty picnic table near the back of the yard. From that vantage point they could still observe the proceedings of the hour and maybe not be interrupted.

After they settled across from each other at the table, Dewey took a swig of the beer he picked up on their way to the table. Handling Victor wouldn't be any more difficult than managing a restless crowd.

"Let me start again. Malik, he does a halfway decent job behind the scenes for Regina. I've checked out your real estate website; his work is good there. And he's doing very well producing the entertainment for Smith today. The music hasn't missed a beat and he's already done an initial sound check for my performance. What I want to offer will allow him to set his projects up into a sustainable business."

Earle took a long draw from his beer and slammed the bottle down on the table. "I've heard you out, and we don't need your help."

Dewey drew in a sharp breath. So, Earle planned to be stubborn. Time to employ the persuasive skills of a hit song writer. "I'm sure you know the difference between want and need."

Victor took another draw from his bottle. "I do."

"I don't need to get married again." He paused. "But I want Regina."

Just like when he wrote a song, Dewey played with his words and tone to pull, then drop.

Victor frowned with a faraway look in his eyes. "What you want and need is of no consequence to me."

From the look in his eyes, it seemed like the thought of Regina moving on made Earle a touch nostalgic. The right place for the next lyric. That's how it was with people. As long as they are the ones moving on it was all good.

"Listen," Dewey leaned in, "I don't need an apprentice. But I want Regina, so I'm willing to do this for Malik."

"Thanks, but we'll figure it out." Victor slowly took another long drag from his bottle.

Dewey breathed, determined not to get angry with this proud man. As beads of sweat began to pool around Victor's forehead, he surmised that Earle would not be helped in this conversation by the sun beaming down on their heads. Most of the crowd had clustered under the patio for some cooling shade.

Dewey whipped off his cap, wiped his brow and decided not to finish his beer. It was too hot out here to drink, if he planned to bring this discussion to his intended close and sing later. "Let us reason together as brothers, talk this thing out."

Victor drained his bottle and slammed it on the table. "You ain't my brother."

Dewey nodded. Now that Victor was emotional, he had the upper hand. Earle didn't know that DW Thurman had handled far more complex conversations than this. The prophet had delivered messages in the midst of serious church and inter-denominational conflict. In Dewey's experience, it was usually the one with great success who became the godfather, the problem solver. Now this man was placed in the position of accepting an offering of help. There was no conflict here, if he was smart and let the Lord guide his tongue he could get at what they all wanted. The best for Malik.

"Then come let us reason together as men. And one day, if I'm blessed and Regina does marry me, I hope we can figure out how we work together for the sake of the young people involved." Dewey paused to let his words settle. "It is with all due respect that I offer my assistance. I've seen many young men like Malik with this Peter Pan thing. They want to hit it big without any connections, training, and sometimes without any real talent. I can give Malik the training he needs. Get him connected with some legitimate brokers in the music business, and make sure he knows how to manage in the boardroom with those lawyers."

Attorney Earle cracked a grin.

"Listen, I've even got enough gravitas left to give Malik some of that shine he's wanting."

Victor's head bobbled back and forth. "I'm going to always help my boys. Regina and I agree on that. But, I need for them to put some skin in the game. Like Smith. I didn't give him the money to buy this place. I gave him a loan."

Dewey nodded. "I agree. My offer doesn't come without a price. The first thing Malik is going to have to do when he gets to Atlanta is enroll at Morehouse."

Victor nodded his agreement and bobbled forward. "Our family values education and it is past time Malik earned his degree. You have my attention, sir. So, this starts in September?"

"No, immediately. He'll start with an internship under me and in the fall with a full class schedule. From what Malik tells me, it shouldn't take more than a year for him to piece together enough credits to earn a degree. With the credits he has and the production experience credit I believe Morehouse will grant him, it shouldn't take long for him to graduate. Malik may be ready to launch his own production company within two years."

Victor Earle's face went blank, his expression hard to read now that he was done trying to be a bully. That poker face of his was probably a great corporate asset.

"What do you want from me?"

"Nothing."

The pride of the accomplished man welled back up. "I can pay his tuition."

Dewey shook his head. "No need. He'll receive a family tuition waiver at Morehouse."

Victor sighed. "You two moving that quick?"

"No," Dewey moaned. "I've proposed and she's gracious enough to listen. But, I know she's not budging until Malik is settled."

Victor pulled out his smartphone and shot off a quick text. "I asked Mandy to bring us another round." He shook his head in disgust. "The only way to communicate with that generation. That girl has a law degree and no idea how annoying this is." He set his phone on the table. "Regina's a good girl," he drawled. "Never let my glass go dry. She took real good care of me."

Dewey didn't know if the man was intentionally trying to unsettle him or if he was waxing nostalgic over his loss. He cast a quick sideways glance in the direction where he last saw his lady. "My Regina is a great lady, and she does a good job taking care of herself."

"What's that supposed to mean?"

"Only that I thank God she is mine, and I am only hers."

With that the conversation went silent and Dewey offered a prayer of repentance for his shady remark.

"What," Earle paused, "what does Regina say?"

From what he knew Earle didn't usually care about his ex-wife's opinion.

Was this a tactic to keep from accepting the offer?

"Regina says yes. No. And sometimes maybe. Yes, to helping Malik as long as it leads to his earning a degree." Dewey frowned and took a draw from his now warm beer. "But mostly no to me."

They sat in silence until Mandy arrived with three ice cold bottles and sidled up next to her husband. Determined to become a part of this conversation, she opened the third beer.

Victor cooled his brow with the butt of his bottle, then raised a toast. "If Regina says so, thank you. Because I'm at my wits end with that boy. Don't know why he's not more like his brother."

Dewey bit his tongue to keep from saying what he really thought. Instead he raised his beer to his lips and enjoyed a spirit-cooling draw. "'Lik-a-be-al-rite."

"If Regina says so to what?" Mandy Earle cross-examined her husband.

Victor shrugged off her question, so Mandy twisted her blond locks and turned her attention to Dewey.

"Do you know Spike Lee?"

"Yes, I do."

Her eyes lit up, "Denzel's son?"

What did she do? Google Morehouse men?

Dewey rolled his eyes as the effects of the heat began to creep over him. He needed to get into some air conditioning soon or he wouldn't be fit to sing. He shook his head *no*. Even though he'd met the entire Washington family on several occasions.

Mandy continued with her list. "Did you know Martin Luther King?"

Dewey rose. "Dear child, I am not that old."

Chapter Eighteen

In awesome wonder about the way the Lord blesses,
I dare you now to take the next moments and think of his goodness to you.

"Now everyone knows why we are here and that this is not a religious service, but..." Dewey played a few bars of Bryon Cage's gospel hit, "I Will Bless the Lord." Those who knew the praise jam roared and cheered in anticipation. The audience didn't know it, but DW Thurman was already full after the successful conversation with Victor, Sr.

"Everything that hath breath will have to praise the Lord, and today we celebrate something praiseworthy. No matter what your beliefs, you ought to join in. Feel free to shout with a voice of triumph for this great victory."

Dewey signaled his drummer to kick the celebration concert into high gear. With a three-count, the combo burst into a joyous rendition of the tune. The multi-generational, multi-ethnic crowd—from lawyers to fast food workers, sang and swayed to the music. Doctors grooved with the unemployed, whites clapped in time with African-Americans. Everyone enjoyed the praise-jam, on one accord. Even the grill master raised his tongs in praise.

"Come on, y'all. This is a day of rejoicing." Dewey sang-spoke while the band played the tune through the bridge. He'd purposely chosen not to sing his music today, because this was not a DW Thurman concert. Today, he sang to thank the Lord for the fulfillment of the prophecy of sons.

The performance—his gift to Smith—had brought in the crowd. The entire lawn and patio was filled with the invited guests. Several of Smith's fraternity brothers were members of Montgomery PD and clearly experts on crowd control. Everything was decent and in order. He signaled for Malik to turn up the volume. A nice-sized crowd had also gathered on the other side of the fence, and he wanted to make sure they could hear good, too.

"Hallelujah," Dewey breathed as the song came to the end. During the thunderous applause, he thanked God for the gift he'd bestow on Malik later. When the applause died down and the people began to clamor for more, he used his skills to keep the crowd hyped, while he made them wait.

"I need the Lawson and Earle families to make their way to the stage. Come on and I mean all of you. Smith, where are you?" Dewey looked around for the man of the hour while the band played a little up-beat, spiritual ditty. "In the Baptist church they call this walking music. But today I feel like dancing. If you want to while the family's walking. Dance!"

His pianist slid next to him on the piano bench and picked up the second hand of the tune. They played together for a few bars before Dewey gave it over to his favorite grad student. His Morehouse band students had given him a positive report before the concert began. Malik was prepared and on time last night when they arrived. And as a side note, Malik took them all out to eat. Malik knew his hometown well, and they'd had some good food and good fun before Malik took them to their hotel.

As the family moved forward, Malik was instrumental in helping them all fall into place. He knew which members of the Earle family needed to be separated from his Aunt Rena. Another skill that would serve him well in the entertainment industry.

Dewey picked up the wireless mic and moved to join the family at center stage."

"Come here, Mr. Smith," he requested and the music stopped. "It took a few minutes for me to understand that Victor, Jr and Mr. Smith were the same person." He put his arm around the young man's shoulders. "I'm real proud to know you, sir. And you see these people?" Dewey stretched forth his hand to include the family and the crowd. "All assembled, because they are proud of you. To be young gifted, godly, and Black."

The crowd's pride burst forward with shouts and yells.

"Let everything that has breath." Dewey proclaimed. And the crescendo of vocal and musical praise increased. "Right now!"

He signaled to the drummer to bring the praise beat down to the level so he could give the crowd instruction.

"A celebration like this requires a dance. Watch now, if you don't know. I'm going to show you the Tarah. The version approved and agreed to by all the denominations." Dewey smiled at the three preachers sitting nearby. It almost took a papal summit to get the black churches to agree that this dance was an acceptable form of worship. "Well, everyone didn't agree, but…Whoo!"

DW's feet set off in several directions as he cut several dance steps. And few people called foul. He laughed. "Now that's not the Tarah. That was the DW's happy dance. Not approved for use in service. But y'all need to know, whew." He inhaled and wiped his brow. "I'm happy today! Glory! Glory!" DW Thurman hopped and shouted.

While the crowd laughed, he sought Regina's face and winked. "All right, parents, get over here with this amazing son and let's dance."

As Victor and Regina moved into place, Dewey demonstrated the required steps to the crowd. "Now in the end, kick your legs, as high as you possibly can. But don't you hurt yourself or nobody else. That would be out of order. Dancing and shouting is in order, because we are celebrating. Now let's get it!"

The music went forth and everyone danced with great joy. Except for Mandy Earle. The Lawson-Earle-Thurman clan laughed and praised and danced on one accord for several minutes. And when everyone was out of breath and began to retreat from the dance, the band played through. Then played a selection from the Fellowship's songbook, as Dewey moved into the background to rehydrate. It took two songs and some deep breathing before he felt able to sing again.

"Have you done enough?" His students teased when he signaled for them to end the set. His knees would make him pay for all that hopping around later. But it was so worth it to give God HIS glory and to bless Smith.

"Ladies and gentlemen, give it up for these Morehouse Men."

The crowd responded with a thunderous applause.

Dewey returned to the piano and played a warm tune to settle the crowd. He'd planned to sing Cage's "Majesty" and "Rain on this House" to end his set. But the Spirit led him to a song of conviction.

After the praise dance, Smith dutifully led his mother and grandmother to their lawn chairs in front of the stage. A skittish fraternity pledge had held their seats and made sure cold bottles of water were ready. Regina looked up at her oldest and smiled. Tall, strong, and proud, Smith stood sentry like beside his "best girls" as they cooled off. She took a long draw from her bottle and relaxed. After the first verse of a slow-moving praise song, she glanced up at Smith and froze. Instead of the easy grin she expected, she watched as a deep sadness and mourning crept over his countenance. Smith's proud, broad shoulders slumped.

No way.

She shook off her interpretation. *Maybe, he was touched by the power of the song.* Dewey was singing her soul happy, too. *No?* Smith was too much like his father. It wasn't typical for the Earle men to be slain in the spirit, but then again, she'd seen bishops weep under the Prophet's anointing.

Her smile clashed with the stormy eyes of her oldest. "What's wrong, son?"

Smith bowed his head and mumbled, "I just wanted you to be proud of me."

"Oh, Smith, we are so very proud of you. Always have been."

"You won't be soon. And Daddy will never be again." With sorrow-filled eyes, Smith strode away from her into his building.

Regina moved to follow, but Mother Earle reached for her arm. While she reassured Evelyn Earle that all was well, she worried. This business, like everything else Smith touched, would be successful. Hadn't there been enough commentary today for him to accept that? She'd reviewed his business plan and more importantly his father had. Regina sank into her lawn chair and let Dewey's anointing soothe her worried soul. She'd missed something with Smith.

Since about fourth grade, a specter had haunted her son. Smith had a crippling and destructive fear of failure. And to cover up any mistakes, he could be malicious and underhanded. When the boys were growing-up, Malik often suffered for his brother's anxiety.

"Mmmm." She wondered as she recalled something Malik told her a few weeks ago about Smith knowing someone or something she definitely wouldn't like.

It was hours before she saw either of her sons or Dewey. Vic and Mandy snuck away before the concert ended. Malik was busy producing the music. And Dewey's attentions were taken over by his fans. Sweet Dewey greeted every fan with his usual grace and signed everything from napkins to T-shirts. Regina searched the indoor and outdoor patio space several times as the afternoon waned for Smith. Once to say goodbye to his grandmother and again because his Aunt Rena wanted him. To occupy her mind, Regina stepped into a hostess role.

For the remainder of the afternoon, she gave tours, answered questions and made sure the party moved forward. It was after seven p.m. when she saw Smith again. But, then there was no talking to him. Smith was smashed and marching with his fraternity brothers.

"That chick thinks she's black man kryptonite. Leaning over to pass me a beer, trying her best to show me her boney chest."

Long after midnight, Regina laughed as she lay in Dewey's arms. Pillow talk was the best with Dewey. She loved the way he listened and teased, while they rested up for round two. "I'm going to pull out all her hair."

He grinned. "No need. I took care of Miss Mandy. All I did was sing your praises and Victor agreed. I know it's not a good night at their house tonight."

"Sometimes it's nice to hear you say what 'you know.' But, when was this?" She rolled over and resettled into the warmth of his embrace.

"Right before I sang," he answered with a smug grin. "Now, are you sure you agree with my plan and you're going to take your hand off. Let me do what needs to be done with Malik? 'Cause we both know it's not going to work if we're fighting about these grown children of ours. Like I told Vic, I don't believe in yours, mine and ours." Dewey gave her a sideways glance. "Um there aren't going to be any of ours. Right?"

She gave him a playful nudge. "You know I'm way past that."

"Still sexy." He stretched. "Lady, I'm too old to be in a constant dispute with my wife over the children. If we were raising children, that would be one thing, and don't you dare say Malik and Tasnee aren't grown."

"I don't want to fight about the children, either." Regina pulled at the brown diamond angel pendant she always wore. "Been there done that. Or rather been there, didn't do a good job at that. That's all I'm saying about Malik. I didn't do that great a job with him."

"Naw, you did fine. Ain't nothing wrong with Lik. He just need a little finishing. He's so much like me. I didn't want to go to college, so after high school, I toured with several revival choirs. But, I got tired after four years on the road, and Miss Minnie wouldn't let me come home and sit around. Mama made me enroll at Morehouse. I thought I was something for about two weeks until those classically trained music professors got in my stuff. Forming the Morehouse Ten was actually an assignment for me. A project designed to keep my restless butt in school. I didn't even get an 'A', but the project put me on firm foundation. I always knew I was supposed to be a traveling musician and Morehouse showed me how to get an education and travel. We worked that thing for seven years and I wound up with an MFA. This is why I understand Malik. I'm going to put him on the same type of assignment. He'll take some of the load off me and maybe he'll find the next new gospel superstar. But that won't be Tasnee."

"Thank you. But there's still Tasnee to think about."

"Not tonight."

Regina rolled over and stared up at the ceiling before closing her eyes to think. After a moment, she added. "Do you think it's all going to work out? We have seven children between us."

"As long as we stay on one accord. I know it's going to work out and I pray sooner rather than later. We need to go ahead and marry before it's everlasting too late. I'm not getting any younger." Dewey swung his legs over and sat on the side of the bed. He lowered his head and sighed. And the mood around them shifted.

Regina rolled over to lie behind him. "Are your knees bothering you? Do you need to smoke?"

She still didn't like it, but they'd arrived at a compromise about his smoking. As long as he kept it outside of the house, carried an Alabama cannabis card, and she didn't inadvertently catch a contact high.

Dewey looked down on her and nodded. "Yes, my knees are killing me. But, I've been popping those prescription pills. I'll take two more of those in a bit." He reached for her hand. "I'm so sorry, but I also have to share with you that trouble's brewing. Did you notice? I changed the final song in my set."

"Yes, I planned to ask you about that."

Dewey turned his soulful gaze on her and frowned. "Lady, it pains my soul, but I saw something in Smith today. A look I've seen many times over the years. A look of deep contrition that has always been followed by a revelation. This is where my observation and the second sight intersect. Whatever Smith is hiding, it's not good."

Regina's shoulders slumped. "I saw it too."

"You are observant," he said as a sad smile crept across his face. "Has he said anything to you?"

"No." Her voice trembled, "Apparently, I am no longer his secret-keeper. Dew, I'm actually glad you said something. I'm still struggling to understand your gifts, but tonight it's a comfort. There is something going on with Smith, and I'm not sure I can reach him."

"Come on, pray with me. For Smith and for all of our children."

Chapter Nineteen

Let this praise song
Fill your heart. Calm your mind. Soothe your soul.
Refreshed, Renewed, Redeemed.
Refreshed, Renewed, Redeemed.

On the first Saturday in September, Regina Lawson sat on the dais in the ballroom at the Bryant Conference Center at the University of Alabama, pushing another piece of banquet chicken around on a plate.

Happy Birthday to me.

She'd planned for Dewey to attend this event with her and celebrate her birthday at a cozy jazz club near campus. He'd refused. Joking that it might be her birthday, but he was on vacation. Then had the nerve to ask her to never again schedule anything the week before or after her birthday.

She put a fork full of banquet chicken in her mouth. As soon as this luncheon was over she and Rena had to hightail it back to Mobile. Dewey and John were on a deep sea fishing trip today, and they'd promised fresh fish for dinner. Mindful of her seat, Regina sat up straight, smiled and made small talk with the conference organizer sitting on her left.

"Dr. Lawson, do you have any connection with the University?"

"Yes, I have many fond memories of the two years my son spent here as a student."

The conversation flowed with the standard usual University administrator to parent questions. What did your son study? Did he have a good experience? When did he graduate?

"No to study or graduation." She frowned, "Malik went to more parties than classes."

Dr. Graham nodded. "If I had a nickel for every parent who told that story. If he ever wants to come back, you have my contact information. Now, if you're ready, Dr. Lawson, I'll step into my other role and start the program."

The Regional Director for the Sisters of Syrene moved to her place behind the table-top lectern. As the program formalities began, Regina looked to her left at the head table where her sister was holding court with the other regional leaders of the Sisters of Syrene. Rena had made some kind of horse trade with Dewey to come with her today. An agreement neither of them would let her in on. Nevertheless, she was glad her big sister was with her.

Forty minutes later, Dr. Regina Lawson glanced around the ballroom before rolling into the end of her address for the Sisters of Syrene young adult conference. No Malik to make funny faces to encourage her. She missed her old producer, but he'd improved her rider. Her new contract stipulated the organization provide a high quality video of her presentation. She took a deep breath and looked into the audience to reconnect with her friendly faces. She'd picked five friendly attendees out at the beginning of her speech. Faces of encouragement, to help her gauge the audience's attitude.

"You're looking for royalty to come in and sweep you off your feet. Looking for another person to improve your circumstances. I'm sorry, but it doesn't work this way. Gentlemen, are you looking for that African Queen to come in and move you out of your mother's basement? Did you finally get a date with a young lady that has it together and now you're running late because you had to wait for Mama to get home from work? So, you can use her car? No, you won't get a second chance with that queen. Because the young queen has a standard. But, next you'll meet Skipper. Skipper better known as Skip Her." Regina waved her hand in a move along motion. "Skipper got you giving her half of your child's support money, so she can get her hair and nails done. While your baby's mama is struggling to make the rent."

Amens flew around the room from the more seasoned women and some of the young mothers in the room.

"And my sisters I know you're praying for Prince Charming to take you away from your struggles. Sweep you off your feet and you don't even have a broom. You're not prepared. And I'm not talking about having your hair and nails done. Are you mentally prepared for the rigor of a lasting relationship? Prince Charming isn't looking for that *Real Housewives*-style-drama. Then yonder come Skippy riding."

The older folks laughed.

Most of the young people still hadn't caught the reference.

"Y'all don't know Skippy?" Regina threw her hands up in the air and turned her lips down in a rueful frown. "Maybe you know Skippy as the Destroyer. The one that roams the earth looking for whom he may devour. And you are easy game, because you don't have a standard. Skippy will ride into your life and take everything you *don't* have to give. Will leave you with baby number four. And you know he's never paid a dime of support for the child he left with your high school classmate." Regina took a step back and a sip of water while the crowd rumbled and roared.

"A standard will secure your future. Without a standard there is no bottom, no line that can't be crossed. Nothing a person won't say *no* to. No low is too low. We see it every evening on the six o'clock news. Something horrible happens and we sit back and wonder how a person gets themselves into such a mess. It's lack of a standard. Just going along with Skippy and them, because they never learned that it's okay to say *no*. You see the social media influencers got it twisted. They tell you all this standard talk will keep you from being young and having fun. That's Skippy's most retweeted lie. Didn't we party last night in peace? I hope you had a good time without worrying about a fight breaking out or the police coming to break up the dance."

When she referenced the dance party the conference arrangers hosted last night where only clean versions were played, over half the room smiled and applauded. Regina paused for a moment to let that sink in.

"And it's gotten into the church. No standard. Even the praise dancers be twerking."

The conference organizers and some of the preachers in the room stood and shouted.

"Young people, raise a standard in your life. Set your standard before the trials come. Because trials are coming. And your standard will help you make it through life's toughest challenges. Find those people in your community who are living a victorious life. You know the ones. The no-nonsense people. Spend time with people who have a standard. Then spend some time thinking about what *you* will not do. Now is the time to raise a standard in your life. And not just for your life, but for the lives of your family. And your children's children. I know it's hard to imagine, but if the Lord tarries, you'll find yourself in the September of your days. And the standard you set now will bear good or rotten fruit. Never forget Skippy is always out here looking for someone to prey upon. And when Skippy can tell by your walk, your talk and your dress that you don't have a standard, yonder come Skippy riding."

❦

"Whew, that was something," Rena said two hours later as they rushed away from the Bryant Conference Center. "Thank God the Tide is playing out of town or we'd be stuck here."

"Rena, they wouldn't have had the conference here if the team was in town." Regina spoke from her experience as a two-year Tide mom. The two years Malik spent in Tuscaloosa throwing away their money had been a lot of fun.

Regina rolled her shoulders to release the remaining speaker's energy from the event.

"I wish Dew had come with me. He would have enjoyed the program. And there's a cute little live jazz supper club. We could have celebrated my birthday and had a nice meal. All this driving back and forth doesn't seem necessary."

Rena merged on to State Route 69. "You could be grateful I agreed to come and thank me for saving you. Dewey don't want to go nowhere you and Victor used to hang out at."

Regina's head wobbled. "How do you claim to know so much about what Dewey wants?"

Rena smirked. "We talk."

"Um-hum, I noticed you two had quite a few little chest-chats this week." Regina chuckled.

Another mark in Dewey's favor, he and Rena were crazy about each other. "Then we could have gone to Storyville tonight for my birthday. Relaxed, had a nice meal, listened to the UA jazz students."

"Girl, you know I got some place to be tonight and I'm teaching Sunday School in the morning. Now, hush and rest up while I cover these miles."

Rena was in such a hurry to get home that they only made a quick stop for gas and sweet tea before racing out of T-town. Regina closed her eyes and exhaled. After a week of late nights with Dewey, she was a little tired.

⁘

A hundred miles later, Rena spoke out loud. "Gina, I am so proud of you. Your message on standards is tight. But it's right. That keep your heels, head and standards high poster has brought you a mighty long way."

Regina shifted in her seat. "Of course, you'd remember that poster. That mantra kept me out of a lot of trouble, and I guess it does inform my current work. I'm just speaking what Mama taught us, stirring in my experience and sprinkling in some of the stuff you put in my ear."

"Ha-ha, yonder come Skippy riding." Rena hooted. "I used to die laughing every time Mama said that. And Lord, when she used to say you can't hoot like an owl all night and expect to soar like an eagle the next day."

"Mama didn't say that. Lynn's father did."

They shared more laughs and remembrances as Rena exited onto Highway 43.

"Rena, slow down. This is a notorious county for speed traps. What's the hurry? I don't think Dewey and John are even back from their fishing trip. I sent a text a while ago and haven't heard back. My guess, they're still out of range. Wonder if they caught anything?"

"I know Dewey plans to catch something tonight," Rena teased.

Regina dismissed her sister's nonsense and watched the road for state troopers. "Sure, you don't want me to drive?"

"No ma'am. You drive like an old woman, and I told you I've got to get back."

"But, you didn't tell me why."

"Nun-ya. Just relax and enjoy the ride. If you want to do something, turn from this country music Dewey got you listening to and put on some of that hype-trap-trash, so I don't fall asleep at the wheel."

"You have to admit those country songs have great lyrics."

"Gurl, I've laughed, I've cried, and did a little boot-scoot-boogie in this seat. Now I can't wait to get home 'cause I feel like a woman."

Regina chuckled as she tuned the satellite radio to pick up WXBI out of Montgomery. "Let's see how long you can take this."

The sisters rode on for a while expressing outrage at the shocking lyrics and hard-driving beats. In between songs they discussed the music Rena's grandchildren were being exposed to by their parents.

"I keep telling John Junior and them that the first time I hear any of this filth coming out my grandbabies' mouths, I'm taking them to the woodshed. These babies don't have a chance with this filth ringing in their ears."

"I know." Regina nodded. "Bonita's still trying to pull her sisters into this hip-hope concept. She's convinced this music can be turned around to glorify God. But, I don't see it. From a spiritual or musical standpoint. I mean the girls can all sing, but only Tasnee can blow fast enough to match these beats."

"I'm not sure you're right. Our junior choir did that "Sixty-Six Books" song last Youth Day. And," Rena shrugged, "at least they know how many books are in the bible. I see some good in that. I just wished Young Iggy had rapped the books in order. Now that would cut down on the page-turning before Pastor reads the scripture. Maybe Malik can produce something for the girls. Isn't that why Dewey took him under his wing?"

"Girl, no, and I've warned Malik not to even bring that up. Dewey is certain that this hip-hope push is coming from Bonita's jailbird boyfriend. This is not a tree you want to climb with DW Thurman."

Two weeks after Smith's opening, Malik moved to Atlanta and Dewey had put him right to work. Between their travels and studio work, Regina found herself missing her man and her baby for most of the summer. And she had Malik to thank for Dewey's vacation week. Malik was in Philadelphia this weekend with The Sisters Fellowship instead of their father.

"Dewey's plan is working. Malik is working hard and excelling at every assignment," Regina crowed. "Dewey is pleased. Which makes me very happy."

"But you still won't marry him."

Regina took a sip of her sweet tea and focused on the white lines on the highway for a moment. This was the conversation she'd avoided last night by claiming the need to focus on today's presentation. She stretched her back a little in the seat. "I'm not ready to marry him."

"Gurrl, bye with all of that." Rena scoffed. "Mama would say you caught a big fish—reel 'em in."

As much as she loved Dewey, something in her spirit urged her to slow down. She hadn't been with him for a full year, yet. "Mama would also say, look before you leap."

"I don't get it. What else could you want from a man. He clearly adores you. And I know you didn't ask, but look at what's he's done for you." Rena took a sip from her biggie cup of tea. "A little birdie told me that you were looking at houses on the other side of the bay this week."

"What birdie?"

"A song bird."

"Hmmp, and he accuses me of telling you too much. We were on a wish drive. Don't act like you and John never took the scenic route to dream about those houses."

Rena shook a little in her seat. "Yeah, but *we'll* never come close to affording one."

"I have no intention of marrying or moving."

"You still haven't said a thing. I've never seen you happier and more fulfilled."

Regina sighed. "Being with Dewey is like a summer morning at the beach."

"I'm just glad you're over that he won't buy the cow if he can get the milk for free thing. Although that's how you got Vic." Rena reached for her cup and took another big gulp.

"I was twenty. Afraid if I got pregnant, I wouldn't finish college and Mama would kill me. But now I have no reason to buy a whole pig when all I want is a little sausage."

Rena spit sweet tea out of her mouth and screamed.

Regina whipped a wet nap out of her purse and handed it to her sister with a frown.

After wiping her mouth and the dashboard, Rena shot back. "Little sausage my eye. You know you're riding high on the hog with that one. Dewey turned you over and y'all done some other things you're not used to doing, too."

Regina covered her face with her hands to hide the blush of lust.

"Hold your head up, girl. It took you fifty-seven years to get a-dick-ed. Be happy. Enjoy it. And tell me why you're out here on this road talking nonsense."

"Whew." Regina waved her hand across her face to cool off from the hot flash of desire.

"So, what's the problem?" Rena asked. "He doesn't wants you for your money like that jack-leg preacher who tried to sidle up to you a few years ago."

Regina shifted in her seat. "No, of course not."

"Then what's bothering you, baby?"

"You know Dewey said there's trouble coming. And he's right. There is something wrong. Something I can't put my finger on—"

"Oh, so now you got the second sight." Rena mocked. "Then, tell me tonight's winning lottery numbers."

Regina rolled her eyes. The thought of growing older with Dewey assured and frightened her. Dewey was *Everything*. The best lover, *Ev-vaaa*. Not that she'd had many. But that spiritual, spooky side of him and the surety in his speech haunted her. Marrying him would add a mysticism to her life that she had no idea how to deal with. Dewey offered her more than she ever imagined for the price of her quiet September.

"Why marry when things are perfect? We don't need to marry to be together. They got that new L.A.T. thing now—living apart together. Our relationship works, even with the distance. I can stay in my house in Mobile. And he doesn't have to disrupt his life in Atlanta."

"You know that's not what Dew wants."

Regina frowned. Rena only saw the beautiful parts of her life with Dewey. Much like those who liked or criticized pictures posted on Gospel Gossip. Or those who saw them performing. They didn't know when Dewey shifted into his spiritual space, life wasn't pleasant. And she wasn't in a mental place where she wanted to worry about his mood shifts. Or if he'd gone 'round the bend or whatever else one did when married to a mystic.

It still haunted her how Dewey saw beyond the façade of the football player's wife they encountered in Birmingham. News of her death last month sent him into a three-day seclusion. That was followed by a week of dark moods, self-doubt, and lots of balled-up-paper on the floor. She was useless in the wake of his grief and almost drowned in his sorrow. Those days of mourning weakened his knees and shook the surety of his tone. The strain caused by his prophetic visions threatened to be her undoing. She simply didn't know how to take care of him or herself when he was in his prophetic state.

After closing her eyes for a second, Regina looked forward at the road and said, "I'm not going to give up my hard-won peace. Not even for Dewey."

"For all the good things you are, you can also be a stubborn ole bear," Rena said.

"You're right." She sighed. "I love every bright moment of life with Dewey. And I believe his word. Trouble is coming. I know my boys aren't perfect, but there's something going on with every one of the girls. Maybe... in a few years."

"Gurl, I hope you're not trying to wait till all those girls are settled. Or Smith and Malik for that matter. If that's the case, then let me tell you from experience as a mother of five, THAT will never happen."

Am I holding out on marrying him in the same way I'd held out on divorcing Vic?

Regina still hadn't figured out a role for herself in the girls' lives and felt helpless in the face of their troubles. Bonita had fallen deeper in love with her "pen-pal" as Dewey called him. No amount of advice or pleading could deter her. The relationship distanced Bonita from her father and sisters. Tasnee was moving in and out of the doghouse with everyone for oversharing on social media. Jolee was worried about her upcoming medical license exams. Calista was off in a deeply spiritual quest and barely eating or talking to anyone. And the burden of managing her sisters had Allegra acting like a proper witch with everyone.

Am I strategically planning to wait until the girls get settled?

"You still have no idea what the premonition Dewey had is all about?" Rena changed lanes and slowed down. "Are you sure, it's not Smith?"

After his grand opening, Smith's communications did improve. But he still kept his distance. He'd slyly send text and leave voice messages at odd hours to avoid any real-time conversation. She'd never say it, but she knew there was something disturbing him.

Rena broke into her thoughts. "I don't think this thing with Smith is nearly as bad as you are thinking. I'm going to agree with Vic—"

"Oh, let me take notes. You're agreeing with Vic. I'm shocked." Regina laughed.

"I'm just saying. We all know how Smith can catastrophize. If he's in a little hot water, Victor Earle, Jr. can work his way out. That man has a boat, life preserver, and he can swim. You two are just the same. You both want to have a perfect life with everything in its place. I remember how you were when you went through it with Victor. You never would have left Vic if you hadn't been confronted with the truth that your life wasn't perfect. That was a dark season and you came through; like Mama trained us to. If you keep living, there are going to be ups and downs. You might as well have someone to share the tough times with. Keep living and you will have another season of trouble with Dewey or without."

"You sound like Mama."

"Because in this she was right. You know me and John have been through it. But in the end, it all works out. Mama always said there is a pain that comes with loving. Isn't happiness with Dewey worth some of that loving pain?"

Chapter Twenty

Sing into the silence and wait until the Lord reveals a new song.

An hour later, Rena rolled into Mobile County and sped right past Regina's exit. "I'm going to stop by the mall and pick up a package. Something I need for tonight."

"You keep talking about what you're doing tonight but won't tell me what it is."

Rena smirked. "Stay out of married folks' business."

Ten minutes later, Regina grudgingly followed her sister into the anchor store at the mall. They walked straight to the Fashion Fair cosmetics counter where the consultant greeted Rena by name.

"Okay, what's really going on?" Regina demanded.

"Thought you might want to freshen up and fix your face while we're here. Make sure Dewey says 'whoo instead of ew' when you get home. I learned that one from your Mama." Rena winked at the consultant. "Just refresh us a little like we talked about. And I'll take a tube of Red Raisin lipstick, and don't forget that qualifies me for this month's free gift."

The consultant nodded and began to lay out her brushes and colors.

"Rena, I'm really ready to go home."

"And I'll take you as soon as John texts me. Now, would you just relax and enjoy this little cheap beauty treat. Remember how we used to come here for the free samples?"

The beauty consultant motioned for Regina to sit in a high bar chair next to her counter filled with the latest Fashion Fair cosmetics.

"Dr. Lawson, you don't mind if I add a little gold accent to your eyes? I think it will look gorgeous on you."

Regina closed her eyes and prayed she didn't look like a walking makeup counter when the over-made-up consultant finished with her.

∞

An hour later when Rena turned onto her street, Regina's jaw dropped. In addition to Dewey's Spyder, there were two other cars parked in her driveway and a caterer's truck in front of her house.

"Now, will you tell me what's going on."

"Hush, you're going to crease your make-up." Rena pulled into the driveway and parked behind Dewey. "Mr. Know-It-All said I couldn't keep a secret from you. When he asks, remember I didn't tell you a thing. Now listen, I know this is your house, but I have strict instructions to bring you round back. Dewey's been working on this all week. So, be gracious and don't fuss. And you look gorgeous."

Regina exhaled, adjusted her attitude and quietly followed.

"Oh, my God," she shouted when Rena opened the fence. Her backyard had been transformed into a romantic outdoor café. Strings of globe lights festooned the patio and several huge floral arrangements were strategically placed around the patio. No sign of her patio furniture or other backyard clutter.

A Queen Anne dining table and four high-back, purple cushioned chairs, sat in the center of the patio. A matching sideboard held the beverage service and several gift boxes. But, the perfect piéce de résistance. A piano had replaced the porch swing. The only things she recognized as her own was a pillow from her den on the piano bench.

"Happy Birthday! Relax and enjoy." Dewey greeted her with a kiss and a purple lady cocktail. "You look beautiful. Let's go take some pictures."

Dewey motioned towards a photo backdrop that she'd missed.

"This is so wonderful." She blushed. "Thank you."

"Happy Birthday, Dr. Lawson," the staff Dewey hired lined up to greet her. Just like she'd arrived for dinner at Downton Abbey.

"Okay, birthday girl first." The photographer posed and positioned Regina in the center of the photo backdrop and took a dozen photos. Then he invited Rena to join her. During the sisters' full photo-shoot, Dewey teased Rena about how well she responded to the paparazzi-style photo session.

Between sips of their signature cocktails, the small party took individual portraits, couples pictures and groups shots. The constant bursts of light from the camera reminded Regina of the last time she was assaulted by flashes. Thank God nothing negative had come out of the encounter they had in Dewey's garage months ago.

"Okay, that's enough for me," John said as he stepped away from the backdrop.

"Amen, brother," Dewey said and the men strolled towards the bar. "And enough of these pretty purple cocktails. Let's have some whiskey."

"I think I'm good on the pictures, too," Regina said.

"Okay, Dr. Lawson," the photographer acknowledged. "I'm going to change cameras and take a break. But just so you know, I'll be taking pictures all evening until you tell me to stop."

"I appreciate that."

"And," Dewey added, "he'll bring us an album in the morning, and you can decide which pictures, if any, you want to release on social media."

"That's fine, thank you for asking," Regina said.

A few pictures of DW Thurman's private life were de rigueur. And no matter how carefully she selected the photos for social media, there'd be blowback. Some social media troll would take exception to her birthday party, and she would not respond or react to any of the negative opinions.

After the photoshoot, they relaxed around the table and enjoyed more drinks and appetizers.

"My little sister was amazing. Her message is so timely and so many compliments. I had a hard time getting her out of there. I'm surprised she don't get the big head."

"I know what you mean. Her fans. I have the same problem." Dewey beamed. "I told you how effective she is."

"Yes, it's been a while since I heard her speak. Girl, you are good. I might even change some of my ways."

John laughed so hard he almost spit brown liquor. "Woman, I wish."

The evening flowed like the four of them had been friends for years. Regina leaned over and gave Dewey a big smooch. "This is the best birthday party ever. Thank you."

"I'm here to please. Now and later." He winked. Dewey stood to present the menu. "I bought it. So, I'm going to say I caught it. And ladies, we did go fishing, today. We just didn't catch anything edible."

On cue, the staff presented Regina with a colorful plate of grilled swordfish, calamari, and spinach on a bed of mashed fingerling potatoes. Dinner under a blanket of stars with a special sound recording. DW Thurman performing some of her favorite songs. His melodious voice paired as well with the meal as the wine.

"Oh, my God, Regina. Does he sing like that all the time?"

"Don't worry about that. Eat your fish." Regina winked at Dewey and melted a little more.

After dinner the chef presented the cake with a special flourish. Sparklers and DW Thurman singing the Stevie Wonder version of "Happy Birthday." The small white cake with a cascade of tiny frosting lilies joined fresh flowers on the plate. It reminded her of the top tier of a wedding cake.

"This is the prettiest cake I've ever seen." Regina smiled and posed for several photos with her cake.

"I hope it tastes as good as it looks," John said. "This is one of those cakes on that TV show Rena likes. I always wondered if those cakes tasted good or just looked pretty."

"Amen, brother. We're about to find out. I'm going to eat this tonight, and if it ain't right, I'll look for some pound cake at your house tomorrow," Dewey said when he joined them at the table.

After dessert, Regina opened her presents. An angel figurine from Africa from the boys, Rena and John gave her a book of poems. The girls gifted her a spa gift card. Bonita sent a handwritten letter, which she set aside to enjoy later. And with showmanship and flourish, Dewey presented a coat-sized box.

"This party was more than enough." Regina murmured as she pulled a dozen purple fabric swatches out of the box. "I don't get it?"

Dewey grinned. "Keep digging."

Under the fabric swatches, ribbons, and lace she found a lilac card. "I told you not to do this," she scolded Dewey.

They'd gone back and forth over the gown she needed to attend the gala celebration for WSOL next month. Regina grinned. This gift was the perfect excuse to get her to spend more time in Atlanta.

"What is it?" Rena asked.

"We can stop shopping. Dewey gifted me a designer in Atlanta to make my dress for the WSOL gala. Did you help him?"

"He asked if I knew anyone in Mobile. But, I couldn't think of anyone to recommend. You'd never wear anything the seamstresses I know make. I thought he gave up on that."

"When are you both going to learn that I am relentless," Dewey said. "Come, Lady, you can't have a party without dancing. Let's practice our Chicago-style stepping."

On cue, the dance music started.

"Dewey's been squawking all day 'bout that Chi-town stepping. But it ain't nuthin, but the Bop." John stood and reached out to his wife. "Come on, Rennie, let's show Dewey how we get down in the deep dirty south."

As a new stepper, Regina was two-left-feet while Rena and John waltzed around the patio like experienced step dancers.

"Man, where'd you learn to step like that?" Dewey asked.

"YouTube, my brother. We've been practicing all month. Just to show you up."

"Thank God for YouTube," Dewey shouted and spun Regina around until she waved her hands in surrender.

The twirling and spinning in the dance combined with the cocktails and wine with dinner. Woozy at the end of the second song, Regina waved Dewey off and she sat down. Instead of joining her at the table, he returned to the piano.

As she relaxed in her regal, high back chair, Dewey began to play. Lionel Richie's "Three Times A Lady" filling the patio with the song. She took a quick peek at Rena and John, slow-dragging and giggling like newlyweds, after over forty years of marriage. The love that flowed from Dewey's voice and instrument surrounded them all. Regina closed her eyes and reveled in the moment. As Dewey crooned, her imagination followed the lyrics to the end of a rainbow where he waited.

Being with Dewey wasn't a dream, vision or idea. And not a part of her plan. *Man plans, God laughs.* Until tonight she always thought the expression was negative, a warning against trying to control your destiny. But now God laughing was real and positive. She hadn't planned to care this deeply for Dewey. Didn't think she'd ever loved or was loved this completely. Being with Dewey was a double portion blessing and she didn't think she had the room to receive it.

The music stopped and Regina slowly returned to the patio. When she opened her eyes, her heart fluttered. Dewey moved towards her with the sofa pillow under his arm. They giggled like teenagers as he struggled to get down on one knee.

"Lady Regina, will you marry me?"

She looked down at her love and shook her head *no*. Then leaned forward to kiss his forehead. "This is quite a sweet setup. I love my birthday party, and I love you with an everlasting love."

"Was that finally a *yes*," Rena interrupted their moment.

"No," Dewey and Regina turned and replied in unison.

Dewey looked up and whispered, "I can't get up."

She kissed the top of his bald head, and they shared another laugh.

"John, can you help me, please. I can't get up."

"Absolutely, old man. Aren't you glad I suggested you use that pillow? 'Cause you might-of got your feelings hurt along with your knees."

"Thank you," Regina said as John helped her old man resettle into the chair next to hers. While Dewey rubbed his knees, she prayed his knee pain would pass, and he wouldn't need to smoke tonight.

"Baby, you must be crazy," Rena complained. "Dew does all this, and you still turn him down."

"Yeah, that's cold, sis," John said.

"Why y'all trippin'. I knew she wasn't going to say yes. I just wanted a public record." Dewey turned to the photographer. "You get a good shot of that."

"Yes, sir."

Regina shook her head at his antics and prayed the photographer was trustworthy. She knew Dewey would want to release some pictures from this evening, but it wouldn't be one with the Crown Prince of Gospel Music on his knees.

"Of course, she said *no*. How you going to propose and not bring that bling?" Rena complained because Dewey didn't have a ring.

Dewey rubbed his left knee and grinned. "I haven't found the right ring yet. When I do, she'll say yes."

"Because you know everything?" Regina teased.

"No, because you love me."

Regina nodded. "Facts."

"Dew, you absolutely spoil this girl," Rena said. "And owe me an apology. Did you see the look on her face when we walked in here this evening? I didn't tell her anything."

"I'll grant you full credit for that," Dewey said. "Thank you both for helping me pull this off. I couldn't have done it without you."

Regina yawned. "What a day. This has been the best birthday surprise. Thank you all."

Dewey learned over and kissed her cheek. "Fit for a queen, I hope?"

"Yes, sire," she whispered through a second yawn.

Dewey's head swiveled quickly to the right. "Y'all got to go. Now. Before Regina falls asleep on me. And well, that's not why I put all this together."

Rena and John passed a knowing glance.

Regina laughed as Dewey shooed their guests away.

Chapter Twenty-One

Precious is a love that grows in life's late afternoon.
Refuge from a long cold winter.

Happy with her life and all the goodness she'd found in Dewey, Regina now sang every day. Something she didn't remember doing until Rena reminded her that she used to sing all the time.

In the four weeks since her birthday, she'd spent every weekend in Atlanta. Getting fitted for her gown for the WSOL Gala and being treated like a queen by Dewey. At times it seemed as if she had two lives. Weekdays in Mobile, teaching and writing. Weekends fellowshipping with Minnie, the Mims family, and Malik. Dewey teased that she was using him as an excuse to check up on Malik. Last weekend she helped her youngest son set a standard to graduate from Morehouse.

The long night of prayer for Smith slowly faded from their discussions. She wouldn't mention it, but she thought Dewey had made a mistake. Everything was all right with Smith. Even if she still had a hard time getting him to call.

"You are a queen." Dewey beamed and circled his index finger commanding Regina to spin around again.

Regina's amethyst beaded-lace and chiffon gown sparkled as she took another twirl. A little more sparkle than she would have normally chosen, but the dress designer was right. Every bead and inch of the gown was perfect. She was even showing a little skin. Tonight, her gown rivaled the dresses walked by Hollywood royalty during the last Awards cycle.

With a flourish of his arm, the Crown Prince of Gospel Music bowed as low as he could. "Absolutely beautiful and I look forward to removing it later." He grinned. "After I pick up my award, I'll be wanting a reward."

This evening DW Thurman would accept the first Soul-Centered Network's Icon Award in a gala ceremony celebrating the network's inaugural broadcast. Regina flushed as she picked up her evening bag and followed Dewey to the door. Even with Dewey not leaving their suite for two days, they'd enjoyed the trip. Despite the swelling in his left knee, he'd been fresh, youthful and joyful. He finally admitted that the neglected care of his knees had exacted its toll. The energetic, boyish DW Thurman had to slow down.

Last night they solidified his plan to reduce his personal workload. First, he'd turn the management of the Fellowship over to Allegra, take a sabbatical from Morehouse and schedule the surgery. He promised to fully retire from touring if she'd marry him. Since he refused to use a cane for his red carpet entrance, Regina promised to stand very close to him all night.

An hour later, the Crown Prince of Gospel Music and the Standard Queen worked the red carpet at the Houston Convention Center. The media turnout for the event was more than she'd anticipated. They posed for Gospel-Gossip blog, Black Church News, BET, and the local national affiliate station.

"I feel like a movie star," she whispered as DW leaned on her for support. He nodded and answered another dozen of the same questions from bloggers and reporters. Then they moved into range of another hundred flashes. Then another. As they neared the end of the grand march a familiar voice called out.

"Well Come, Dr. Lawson."

Regina froze. The voice of the paparazzi photographer who caught her coming out of Dewey's condo so many months ago rang out above the others. She tugged at Dewey's hand and together they posed for several photographs for the young man who'd held true to his word. To express his gratitude, Dewey had thrown the young man several high-quality tips and recommended him for a few jobs.

"Thank you. And you still owe me that favor, Queen Regina."

"Getting you this gig wasn't enough?" Dewey teased.

"We'll see." The photographer took another series of shots. "Congratulations, again, DW."

The president of the SOL Network greeted them at the end of the red carpet walk. "Royalty is in the room," she said and escorted them through to the pre-dinner cocktail party. For the next hour Dewey was at the height of his charm—talking, laughing and reminiscing with station employees, local celebrities, church luminaries, and the waitstaff. He took pictures, signed programs, books and napkins. And blessed the young woman who brought him a glass of water he hadn't asked for with a hundred-dollar tip.

"Hurry up and put that in your pocket. And don't tell nobody."

"Thank you and praise the Lord. This will make a difference. The only reason I took this gig was to pay off a debt that's keeping me from getting a much-needed new car."

Regina passed him a knowing glance. *He always knows.*

"Let's go take our seat," she whispered after he rubbed his knee for the second time. His swollen knee would cut the evening short if he didn't sit soon. As they slowly moved through the ballroom, Regina mentally reviewed the program. Dinner served at eight, but the evening wouldn't end until well after midnight. After dinner, the awards ceremony, a little dancing that he would not partake in, and just before midnight a New Year's Eve style countdown to the network's launch. The performance of "Everlasting" Dewey taped over the summer would kick off the broadcast of a six-hour revival and prayer meeting featuring the best preaching, teaching and praying the Soul Centered Network could acquire.

An hour into the awards program celebrating the achievements of DW Thurman, Regina teared up. She was amazed at the recounting of his storied career and totally in awe that she was with him.

Dewey leaned over and whispered, "This is kinda overwhelming for me too."

"I'm so proud to be here with you." Overwhelmed with pride, Regina reached for his hand under the table as Yolanda Adams was introduced to sing "At The End."

The girls would have enjoyed this tribute to their father. But, Myra, Allegra and Bonita were in New York this weekend. On Monday morning, they'd settle the lawsuit against Young Iggy. And by Monday evening the family prayed, the law firm of Myra and Allegra would convince Bo to end her relationship. Calista had cancelled her ordination and was at odds with Dewey, so she didn't come. Jolee couldn't miss a minute of school, so they wouldn't see her until Thanksgiving break. And Tasnee declared she'd never sit through another program celebrating the life of DW Thurman. She found the testimonial events morbid. Ms. Minnie was dispatched to Chicago to help Deborah.

And Regina's evening bag buzzed. Again.

"Dewey, it's Malik. I'm going to step outside for a minute."

Regina left Houston three hours later on a chartered flight. Dewey refused to let her voice any concern about leaving. He only regretted not being able to leave the event and cancel his commitment to sing at the biggest Baptist Church in Houston on Sunday morning. During the flight, she replayed the call from Malik. Malik was short on details about the fight he and Smith had at their father's house earlier in the evening.

'Mommy, I know this is a big night for Dewey, but you should probably come home. Smith's been arrested and Mandy's pregnant.'

During the flight, she tried to contact Smith. But as usual. No answer. At the direction of a kind flight attendant, she put her phone away and tried to rest her brain.

As the plane taxied to the gate in Montgomery, she pulled out her phone. A text from Dewey and all the details on the Gospel-Gossip blog. The headline story read like a Tele-novella.

Prominent Montgomery attorneys fight over pregnant wife/stepmother/side-chick.

Amanda Earle, wife of Alabama real estate magnet, Victor Earle, Sr. announced that she was with child during a family dinner with her husband and stepsons this evening. Upon hearing the news, Victor Earle, Jr. Esq. turned over the table and Malik Earle announced—Jerry Springer-style—that he and Victor Jr. had known for months their stepmother had been stepping out on their daddy. At that point, a fight ensued between the Earle brothers. And stepmother/baby-mama/side-chick called the police

because she *feared* for her life and the life of her unborn
child. Who are the Earles? The family of Dewey
Thurman's lady, Dr. Regina Lawson Earle.

If the Earle family affair hadn't been connected to Dewey, it
might not have gone viral. Links and pictures were embedded
throughout the post. Standard professional headshots of Victor Sr.,
Victor Jr., and Mandy. Pictures from Smith's grand opening. And
photos of her and Dewey from tonight. Links to the official and
unofficial DW Thurman websites, The Sisters Fellowship, her
website, Smith's event space, and Earle Real Estate Holdings. And
every vile, ungodly, and hateful comment imaginable.

They attacked her as a mother.

> She's out giving advice and look at her own.
> Is not telling your father he's getting played an Earle family
> standard?

They disparaged Dewey and his daughters.

> He should have seen this coming.
> They need to follow the Jesus they sing about.
> BlessedAndHighlyFavored2 wrote: this is worse than the
> last gospel gossip scandal.

And embedded in the negative.

> May the Lord grant them all peace.
> SavedandSanctified wrote: They that sow in tears shall reap
> in joy. Psalm 126:5
> PK1974 posted: I'm praying for the entire family.

As soon as she deplaned, Regina reached out to her sons. No answer. Every mile or so as she was driven to her townhouse, she'd text or try to call. Neither answered and her Mom-worry-senses buzzed off the charts. Yes, it was in the middle of the night, but she needed them to at least acknowledge her. That would be enough to calm her fears. She had a million questions. But all she really needed tonight was to know they were both safe.

An hour after she arrived in Montgomery, Regina broke down and called Victor Sr. "I just need to know where my sons are," she blurted out when he answered.

Understandably, the man was angry. Regina held her breath through his vitriolic screed and felt a tinge of pity for Vic. There was no one to comfort him. He couldn't even run to his mother. Evelyn Earle would be quick with a "You reap what you sow."

When Vic stopped to catch his breath, she jumped in. "I just need to know they're safe."

Victor snorted. "Smith's line brothers bailed him out hours ago. And I believe Malik went back to Atlanta."

"Okay, that's all I needed to know. Goodbye."

She hung up the phone and as much as she wanted to, she didn't call Dewey. They shared a text after she landed, and she hoped he'd taken care of his knees and was asleep.

He saw this coming. Why didn't I believe him? Could I have stopped this? But how?

Dewey taught her that prophecy was often a word of warning. Instead of heeding the prophet's notice, she all but told Dewey he was wrong. She went to her knees and repented for her haughtiness in thinking the trouble would come from Dewey's children. Of course, she'd prayed for all of the children, since Dewey warned her trouble was coming. But offered a double-portion petition for Smith. She knew something was bothering him, a trouble she couldn't define.

The reliable Smith had become defensive, evasive and nowhere to be found. As hard as she tried, she'd only received a politician's response from her oldest son in the past month. She tried to write it off as Smith's anxiety over the success of his business.

When Dewey teased her about having a gift, she'd shrugged it off as a mother's intuition. For months she'd been stuck in confusion, between prophecy and observation. She and Dewey had a running conversation about her gift. According to Dewey, most things people assigned to observation were just common sense. Observations that came from a simple knowledge about the cycles of life. But most people didn't put those observations into action. He encouraged her to start trusting her spiritual gift.

"I should have tried harder."

A thousand times she thought about calling Victor. Now she regretted not keeping a clean line of communication open with her ex. At least now she knew why Smith wasn't talking to her. Her oldest son never could keep anything from her.

"A pain shared is a pain halved," she sang into the silence. "I have Dewey to share this trouble. And I better call Rena, soon."

After checking the time, she decided to wait a few hours. When she started to dial a few hours later, she drew in a weary breath.

Even at this early hour, Rena had a lot to say. "Baby, we were worried about the show business folk, and it's the Earle family that done showed out. That mess at Victor's house is trending all over the state. Twitter is aflutter. My notifications are out of control. Never in a trillion years would I have imagined this kind of reality TV drama in our life. You know I never liked that conniving witch, Mandy. And while I hate what you and the boys are going through, I don't have anything for Vic. What goes around comes around."

Regina held the phone and listened.

"I'll be there today to take care of you. And don't say nothing. If you'd told me Dewey wasn't with you, I'da been waiting at the airport last night. Say the word, and John and I will get on the road right now."

"No, please don't. I'm really okay. Tired, but okay. And you know what? I can't explain it, but I don't feel alone." She twisted her angel pendant around her index finger. "And I do need one thing. Can you bring my car? I think I'll be here until after I'm sure Smith is all right."

"Sure, we'll drive up in your car. Send me a text if you think of anything else you need from your house. Baby, try and get some rest. But, call me back if you need to talk before I get there."

"I will. I'm going to lay down now."

After hanging up, Regina wept. This horror was beyond her wildest imaginings. How had this happened in her normal family? Her mother would call this all "a shame before the living God."

How could Smith not tell his father about Mandy? Why did Malik join him in the deception? Could the arrest impact Smith's law license or job at the Real Estate Commission? A thousand questions with no answers raced through her mind. *Why didn't Malik stay in Montgomery? He knew I was on my way home.? And how did Mandy figure she could get away with this? Didn't she know Victor had a vasectomy before she married him?*

"Lord, why did Mandy call the police? She'd been with Victor long enough to know the danger. One of my boys could have been killed?"

Anger flared and the dark spirit that stalked her so many years ago when she considered murdering Victor returned. Instead of sleeping, she lay in bed shivering. At the height of his screed, Victor declared that he was done with both his sons. Of course, she knew he spoke out of his pain, but his words still seared her soul. Only God's grace could heal the split between her sons and their father. And take away her anger.

Groggy and jet lagged, Regina had difficulty pulling her thoughts together a few hours later when Dewey called.

"Lady, it's going to be all right."

"Is that a prophetic word, Dew."

"No, love. This is me talking. We will weather this storm."

"But the media attention. I'm afraid to check social media again. And I'm afraid not to."

"Don't check it. You don't need to read speculation and opinion, when you know the truth. The worst thing you can do is engage with the media. I promise this, too, will pass. How's Smith?"

Regina exhaled. "I haven't spoken to him, but his line brothers have been true to their bond. Thank God Cooper was on duty when they took Smith in. And despite saying he's through with Smith, Victor did call a judge last night. One of their frat brothers. Smith was in and out of custody before I landed. Cooper and Foster are with him."

"Foster's the reverend, right?"

"Yes, you met them both at Smith's opening."

"Good brothers. And have you heard from Lik?"

"Yes, he sent a text. He's alright. Said he went back to Atlanta to get his head together."

"Good, I left him a message to call me. I also reached out to Smith. I hate it when the children don't respond."

She nodded. "Dew, I'm so sorry I doubted you."

"Don't be. I'm praising the Lord that the boys are all right. And, I need to get going. The network is sending a car and an assistant to help me get around today. And later, I'll disconnect. Seek some guidance for us. Regina, it's going to be dark in the days to come, but there is the moonlight to guide us."

After she hung up, she experienced the pangs of missing Dewey. As much as she needed him, she wasn't alone or without his grace.

While she waited for Rena, Regina contented herself with DW Thurman's new song, "What So Ever."

⚬∞⚬

Armed with a pound cake and a carload full of groceries, Rena arrived and took over. Just like she had when they were little girls, Rena stood between the world and her baby sister. "I'm only answering the phone if it's Dew or the boys. Now you take a shower and get refreshed. I brought a nice roast for dinner."

Around two p.m., Smith's finally called. They didn't talk long because they agreed they needed to have an in-person conversation.

"Baby, your Aunt Rena is here and she brought a pound cake. Can we bring it by this evening?"

"Yes, and, Mommy, could you also bring a pan of spaghetti? Cooper and Foster were talking about it last night. They remember how you fed and helped us when we were pledging."

"Y'all remember all that interference I ran with Big Brother Earle-Almighty."

Smith emitted a sad chuckle.

"Give me a few hours. And, baby, I'll keep your Aunt Rena in check. We don't have to flesh it all out today. I just need to see your face. We'll really talk when you're ready."

⚬∞⚬

Late Monday afternoon, Regina turned on her laptop to try to get a little work done. The substitute taking her classes that week had a dozen questions, mostly about the curriculum. Before she began, she checked her social media feed. Things were slowing down, and the only member of the family who'd posted anything was Tasnee.

A simple thank you to one of her followers. Then, Tas responded to another supporter. And another, before immaturity got the best of her. Tasnee followed a negative thread that led to a downward spiral and a messy exchange. The barrage of negative comments that jumped from the thread twisted Regina's stomach into knots.

"Dewey will be furious and disappointed."

He was so careful with the family's image. This whole thing was a hell of a blow. Regina started typing; just one post to defend the Thurman family. Her family. Before she hit ENTER, she hesitated. Tasnee just proved any form of engagement was unwise. Having it out with strangers wasn't going to resolve anything. In that moment her spirit pulled away from the negative and dwelled on the refrain of "What So Ever."

"What-so-ever," she sang aloud as she went back to her email box and answered only the class-related questions from the substitute. "It is easy to get caught in the nasty new. Driven to distraction by input and information. Tempted to quit? To lash out? Tired? At the end of your rope? What so ever it is. Stay Faithful. What so ever."

"What's that you're singing," Rena yelled from the kitchen.

"Oh, sorry, didn't mean to be loud."

"No, baby. I'm happy to hear you sing."

Chapter Twenty-Two

Praising God for the moon.
That lesser light that guides us through the night.
The blessing of moonlight; where God works.

Four days later, Regina meditated on "What So Ever," as she waited in the conference room of Foster's south Montgomery church. After considering a dozen preachers, therapists and advisors, Rev. Foster was the only person everyone agreed upon to facilitate this discussion. For the next hour or so, the remnants of her once-nuclear family would try to find a way forward. Since Saturday night, Rev. Foster had worked with each member of the Lawson-Earle family.

Regina tried to steady herself by praying that her family wasn't beyond redemption. But, her nerves wouldn't settle. An unrepentant Malik sat on her left at the oval conference table, texting. Even after much prayer and long conversations, Malik was still a little defiant. As they waited for Victor, Sr. and Smith, Regina picked up the vibrations of gospel music. Dewey was playing and waiting in the church's small sanctuary.

Malik looked up from his phone. "Dewey's giving that old Hammond a workout."

Regina smiled. "He said he'd put that old organ through its paces."

The movement and sound created a protective bubble around her. She relaxed a bit in the assurance of his support.

When Victor Sr. entered, the air in the room took on an icy chill. "Regina. Malik."

Mother and son nodded as he chose a seat opposite them. While the three of them sat in silence, Regina pressed her foot into the floor. The vibrations from the organ continued to soothe her weary soul.

Minutes later Smith came in with Rev. Foster and took the open seat next to her.

"There is no right way to begin this," Rev. Foster began. "It's going to take time to heal the relationships shattered by lies of omission and commission. But there is one thing I can offer. We should begin this session with prayer."

Smith complained, "We never prayed together before."

Malik smirked.

Regina closed her eyes. Unable to look upon the trio that had been her entire life. All so deeply broken. Instead of speaking, she rested in the music streaming in from the floor.

"If we had, maybe we wouldn't find ourselves here. Go ahead, frat, and lead us," Victor, Sr. spoke as head of the family.

Rev. Foster nodded. "Thank you, Brother Earle. Before prayer, Dr. Lawson do you have anything you'd like to offer from your book of wisdom?"

Regina looked up and gave Rev. Foster a quick smile. "Thank you and yes. I'd like for us to keep one word in mind as we talk. Redemption. It's my only hope for this conversation, and I pray you can all agree."

Yesterday, her prayers led her to this word. Individually and as a family, they'd never make it without forgiveness and redemption. The prophet affirmed her observation. How did he know to start playing "At The End," in this moment?

With nods and groans, her fractured family agreed.

"Then, with our hearts and minds focused on redemption, let us pray." Rev Foster offered a short petition for the family that ended with "refresh, renew, redeem. Amen."

Victor Earle, Sr. charged into the space opened after the Amen. "Why is Thurman here? Regina, please go ask him to stop that infernal playing?"

She slipped off her shoes and pressed her bare feet into the floor to ground her soul to Dewey's music.

I've never felt as loved and supported as I do in this moment. And when he finds that ring, I'm saying yes.

She looked up and regarded her ex-husband for a second. "No."

Victor huffed. "I keep turning this over and over in my mind, and I just don't understand." He turned on his oldest son and spoke with the voice of corporate authority. "This is totally out of character for you. How could you do this to me?"

Smith's head swirled in an exorcist-style spin as fire rose in his eyes. "How could *you* cheat on my mother? You think we didn't feel her pain. Did you forget we lived with her worry when you couldn't be found? And the tears when she found out." Sparks of anger and defiance replaced the sorrow he carried when she saw him on Sunday.

"You are totally out of line," Victor Sr. spat out.

Smith fired back. "No, you were out of line when you let *her* break up our family."

Regina lifted her face and looked directly into her oldest son's eyes. Moved to tears, she reached for her oldest. She held Smith as she spoke, "Oh, no, baby. Our marriage had been an empty shell for years before the divorce."

As she held Smith, Victor cleared his throat.

She stopped breathing. *Please don't say anything to drive our fragile child over the edge.*

"Son," he said quietly.

She held Smith tighter.

"Your mother's right. Mandy didn't break up anything. I only married her because I needed someone to take care of me."

"I— didn't— plan." Smith began slowly in a broken and sorrowful tone. His trademark pride all but gone. "This never should have happened."

"Why didn't you tell me, son?" Victor demanded.

In his immaturity, Malik gloated. "I don't see why I'm here. I ain't done nothing but tell the truth."

There had always been some enmity between the brothers since Smith was the star child. Regina released Smith to lower Malik's attitude with a gaze. "We all need you to tell your truth today. That's why you're here. A grown man's truth about why you picked that moment to speak up. You knew about this for months, too. Why didn't you tell your father? You could have told me. Maybe things would be different if you had spoken that truth earlier. You might have saved us all this public trauma."

Malik stared at the floor as mute as a chastised child.

Victor rose and moved around the table to stand beside his youngest. "You got so much to say, son. Go ahead and speak your peace, now."

"I didn't think it would get outside the house like this. I'm so sorry." Malik bowed his head. "When she said she was pregnant, I just snapped. I mean I couldn't let her get away with that. Especially since me and Smith knew what she'd been doing. I know you are all mad at me."

Victor embraced his youngest. "Like your mother said, we're here for redemption. Please forgive *me* son. I beg all of you to forgive me. I am the root of all of this. We should have... No, I should have been more honest with you boys instead of trying to justify and cover up my actions.

We don't even need to talk further about what happened."

"Is that a healthy option," Rev. Foster queried.

"It's all that I can do right now to stay in this room. Boys, you've heard your Grandma Evelyn say this a thousand times, and I'll repeat it today. All we can do is keep on living."

"And your Grandmother Gladys would say pray for a better day," Regina added.

"But," Smith shook his head slowly, "look at what I've lost."

Several bookings for his event space had cancelled. He'd been suspended from the Real Estate Commission, and there was talk of a complaint against him before the Alabama Bar.

Only she knew that sorrow over his prospects was attempting to twist Smith's mind into believing his life might be over. Dewey and Regina prayed all night that Smith find some ray of hope.

"You haven't lost me, son." Regina reached for his hand as fresh tears crowded her eyes.

"I got you, bro." Malik moved over and stood behind his brother.

Victor returned to his seat "Son, you aren't on suspension because of what happened last week. That's retaliation against me. Jealously and envy have waited for years to bring me down a notch. You know there's people at the Commission who have been out to get me for years. And this is the reason we have a family business. Why I'm glad you have your own business."

Smith looked up at his father. "But, I've lost bookings."

"Son, we have a strong network." Victor extended his hand towards his estranged family. "We will work together for your success."

Regina smiled at the slight glimmer of hope in Smith's eyes.

"This is good," Rev. Foster said. "While it's going to take some time for you all to become whole again, let's praise God that we got through this first critical conversation. I'd like to suggest that this is a good place to stop. Unless anyone has a burning issue that needs to be addressed."

As much as she wanted to run out of this room and into Dewey's arms, one issue pulled at her soul. "I'm sorry, but I need to know. What about Mandy's baby?"

Smith spit out. "Don't worry about that. Mandy got rid of it."

Regina cringed as she took in the sting of death. "I've never liked that expression, and please never say that to me again."

This news added an old grief to her burden—Smith's deepest secret; the grandchild she'd never hold. At the time she agreed the abortion was the best action for Smith and the young lady. But was it pure selfishness that drove that decision so many years ago? So many of her friends had grandchildren born under less than ideal circumstances. She repented again for keeping the entire incident from Victor, to protect Smith's fragile ego. She chose not to share with her family that she'd spend the rest of her life working through this conundrum. Which sin was greater? Helping her son abort a baby conceived while he was in high school or keeping it from her husband.

"You sure, bro. *That* can't be trusted," Malik blurted out.

As the first tears ran down her cheek, Victor stood and reclaimed his corporate vice-president persona.

"It's true. I got a call about the medical insurance authorization since she's still legally my wife." Victor picked up his keys. "I will make myself available when you all are ready to talk again," he said before rushing out of the conference room.

In his wake, Malik asked, "Can I get a few minutes to talk to Smith?"

Regina's eyes misted. Her boys needed some time to repair their relationship, too. "Foster, if it's alright, I'll wait in the sanctuary with Dewey. I don't have a piano, and I suspect he's not done playing."

"Surely," Rev. Foster said. "I'm delighted DW Thurman is on our instrument, even though my Minister of Music is going to be salty, I didn't call him to come over. I'll walk out with you.

Before leaving the room, Regina turned to her oldest. "Smith, your Aunt Rena cooked before she left. Come have dinner with us if you can." Rena was headed home this afternoon, but she knew her sister wouldn't leave before preparing a full dinner and baking a pound cake for Dewey.

In the days that followed, peace abandoned the Earles. Regrets dogged every member of the family and threatened daily to derail their redemption. During the darkness, Dewey asked her to consider the moonlight and lean on his faith.

The weeks slowly passed. Weekly family counseling with Rev. Foster helped reduce the emotion. But, she couldn't see how the Lord would bring them back together. But, Dewey did. His vision of a time of peace with their children and grandchildren expanded to include their son's sons.

As the leaves browned, it seemed as if every one of the girls had issues. Jolee had barely passed her Med school exams. Calista declared herself a public theologian—whatever that meant. Bonita remained steadfast in her relationship and pushed harder for the hip-hope concept. The burdens of leading the Fellowship put a nasty edge on Allegra. Tasnee spent her days collaborating with her "Insta-gram fam" on a gospel drill song, which drove Dewey mad. And the boys both struggled.

Malik had conflicts with being what Dewey called his *umbrella man*, carrying clothing, getting food for musicians, supervising stage set-up and his academic course load. It took them all: Dewey, Regina, Rena, Victor and the girls to keep him on course.

Now that Smith had no secrets, she talked to him almost daily. As best she could, Regina tried to help her oldest son release the heavy burden of perfectionism. His guilt for his role in Victor's divorce kept Smith bound. Things got worse when Smith was forced to resign from the Real Estate Commission. Not for his work, but to atone for a sin of his father. The good ole boys at the Commission had been documenting for months that Smith spent his lunch hours at his event center. Then charged Victor Earle, Jr. with running a personal business on state time.

The fall passed in a blur as she struggled through teaching, writing, and traveling. It felt like she'd taken on two additional jobs. In October, she missed a second deadline and too many days of school. She was overbooked. Sick of traveling. Tired of not being with Dewey every day. And she still hadn't typed the two most important words on her manuscript: The End. Too drained to walk on the beach. The moonlight on her porch became the balm for her spirit.

Chapter Twenty-Three

Open the door to life and love
Open the door of your heart to his love
Open the door of your life to love one another
And watch joy rush in.

In spite of the drama, her speaking business thrived. Just like Mr. Know-It-All predicted. Invitations flooded in and her calendar was booked until the middle of next year. Had her message finally found its platform? Or was it the association with DW Thurman? Every invitation that seemed contingent upon DW Thurman showing up was turned down. Except for one.

Bishop Eddie Johnson personally asked her to submit a proposal to participate in the Gates Foundation's college tour. The proposed tour would stop at each of the sixteen Baptist Methodist Assembly (BMA) affiliated colleges and if accepted, Regina would deliver the keynote address at every stop. Before she could relax and enjoy a long Thanksgiving weekend, she had one more presentation.

Although she'd met everyone individually, Thanksgiving would be her first time with Dewey's family as a whole. She didn't know which event filled her with the most angst. Spending the holidays with Dewey's mother, ex-wives and daughters or meeting the Dean of the Baptist Methodist Assembly. Dewey strategically scheduled her meeting with the Gates Foundation, so he could write off their entire trip as a business expense.

Since she'd arrived in Chicago that morning, Dewey only stopped at their hotel long enough for her to change and drop off her luggage. He'd made lunch reservations at the famous Walnut Room. After lunch, they took a walking tour of State Street, which led them to the meeting at the Gates Foundation.

Dr. Regina Lawson took in a cleansing breath and looked down upon the bustling city from the fiftieth floor of a Chicago Loop high-rise office tower. Up here the noise and hustle of the city seemed to disappear. Quiet. But, the activity continued to flow. So many people and so much traffic. Orchestrated movements from pedestrians and drivers familiar with the symphony of the city. The bustling activity increased her anxiety about the meeting.

She turned away from the window and settled into the modern, warm décor of the Gates Foundation offices. After settling into a warm camel-colored leather office chair, Regina focused on the colorful paintings on the wall. The works by Faith Ringgold and Annie Lee soothed her soul. From what she'd read about the Gates family, these were the original, artist-signed pieces.

"Beautiful."

Regina took a deep breath and reached in her portfolio to review her paperwork. Somewhere in this suite of offices, Dewey was in his element. Signing autographs and taking pictures with the staff. She'd decided to skip the celebrity session in favor of a few quiet minutes to collect herself. This meeting was the final decision point for her and the Gates Foundation.

"Hey, you're ready. This is yours, if you want it," Dewey

whispered as he entered the room.

She looked up and winked. "Are you talking about the tour or you?"

"Both," he said with a twinkle in his eye and took the seat next to her. "I'm so glad you learned how to throw a joke at me. I'd kiss you, but Gates is right behind me."

Half an hour later as Regina neared the end of her presentation, she'd decided that the Rev. Doctor Finus Gates was pompous and pretentious. She hadn't missed his scowls, downward glances, and quickly scribbled notes during her presentation. The founder and president of the Gates Foundation appeared to be in his early forties, but his demeanor reminded her of a much older person. The hour she'd been granted to discuss how she might add value to the Foundation's college tour was waning and she wasn't sure.

"It is an old message," Rev. Gates began. "But you've packaged it in a way I believe the young people can receive it. Your words connote a choice. You speak of each person developing their own standard, not a one-standard fits all. Individualism and choice resonate with the young people. You have the credentials, a pleasing demeanor," he nodded, "and the Bishop of Atlanta speaks highly of you."

Regina exhaled. *Maybe it's going better than I thought.*

"Eh, I guess we'll have to thank Bishop Johnson for bringing Dr. Lawson to our attention." Rev. Gates chuckled, "He will never let us forget how we met you."

Dewey reached over and covered Regina's hand. "Did he tell you *who* brought Dr. Lawson to his attention?"

"Yes, yes." Finus Gates grinned. "We understand you made the introduction, and he also reminded us of the origin of "Everlasting.""

"Ha!" Dewey laughed.

"So," Rev. Gates shifted his attention, "Dr. Lawson, our goal is to try to keep them in school. Too many of our students aren't persisting to graduation, and we believe there is something in your work that might encourage them to set that standard for their lives. In addition, on each stop of the tour we will award scholarships to struggling BMA students to assist with that persistence."

Dewey asked, "Only BMA students?"

Rev. Gates cast him a sideways glance. "You know our tenets. We support our own. But if DW Thurman is offering, we'd be pleased to accept."

The BMA was a peculiar denomination, infamous for their practice of collective economics. To the extent possible, the Assembly kept their dollars circulating within their church. Twenty years ago, Regina wouldn't have been considered as a speaker for the church. And she suspected DW Thurman's relationship with the church was the only reason she had this opportunity.

Regina frowned. "I understand, but are all students welcome to attend the workshops?"

From the program overview, she knew there would be activities on the tour that were closed to non-member students. A condition she didn't particularly care for.

Rev. Gates lit up. "Oh, yes. Yes, our vision is that we fill the auditoriums at every stop. Our team is working with each school's administrative team to possibly make the tour a mandatory assignment. We planned so much good. In addition to your keynote, if you choose to join us, we are hosting career-focused workshops, an internship job fair, and some financial resources sessions. Open to all."

Regina nodded.

"But, our scholarships are for members only. But, we have uncovered another need. Which goes to DW's comment. Too many of our young people have real financial struggles. Many are already parents or caregivers. Their struggle is real. We'd like to offer some direct grants to help pay the rent, utility bills, transportation costs or put food on the table. We've been praying for a donor, and if DW Thurman wants to help, we'll happily accept his donation to fund the immediate assistance grants."

Dewey clapped in delight. "Lady, this tracks with the experiences you've shared with me."

Regina nodded. "Yes, I am pleased to hear this part of the plan. Please send me the details, and I will provide a donation from my family's company."

"Great. But that doesn't include me." Dewey frowned.

Dewey's charm prevailed and the Reverend Doctor Gates dropped his title and pretense.

Finus Gates laughed. "That reminds me. Please indulge me. My mother-in-law won't let me put my feet under her table again if I don't ask. Wedding bells for you two?"

"No, man." Dewey leaned back in his chair. "This woman still got me begging and praying. And I won't be mad if that answer makes it to Gospel Gossip dot com."

"Tsss..." Regina blew out and shook her head at Dewey's antics.

Finus Gates laughed again. "With your permission, I'll let my sister-in-law know. You'll be trending in an hour."

Regina sat quietly by as Dewey and Gates completed a lengthy mutual acquaintances exchange. Long after their allotted hour exhausted, they were laughing like old friends.

"May I step slightly out of line and ask if DW Thurman will be in attendance or following our tour?"

Dewey nodded. "Probably."

"Good, good." Rev Gates had a preacher habit of repeating his words. "May I ask if you'd be interested in a performance opportunity?"

Regina braced herself. She'd suspected an offer from the Gate

Foundation might be contingent on some appearance by the Crown Prince of Gospel Music. She frowned because she might have to turn down an offer that hadn't officially been extended.

"Perhaps." Dewey hedged.

Rev. Gates reached into his pocket and pulled out his phone to check a message, then said. "Let me know if this is out of line; I'd like to conduct a little personal business with you. Separate from the Foundation."

Dewey inclined his ear. "Interested."

"You see, Dewey, it's so hard for me to find gifts for my wife."

"'Cause I've heard you've given her everything under the sun."

Gates sighed. "Nothing but my burdens. I don't know if you're aware, but Cassandra is a classically-trained soprano. I'd like to find a way to get you to play for her. She's a fan, and she'll be thrilled at the idea of singing with you. And I'm thinking of a private affair. Just as a treat for our family."

"Then, that would be my pleasure. I understand your wife has a rare instrument that's only heard on special occasions."

Finus Gates nodded. "The voice of an angel."

"We're partial to angels." Dewey glanced at Regina and winked. "It would be a pleasure. No contract required. I'll call you to coordinate."

Finus Gates clapped in delight. "Only if you bill the Foundation for travel expenses for any stops you attend and accept my invitation to dine with us. And if you bring your clubs."

Dewey leaned forward. "Say less, man. Say less."

"And one last thing, Dewey. If your time permits, our annual open house is Saturday. If you two can please stop by? I'd love for you both to meet Cassandra. It's a casual affair. One of those things where the ladies talk upstairs and the men are banished to the basement. Where I have a golf simulator."

"Golf simulator?"

"PGA certified."

"I said, say less, man. Say less." Dewey mimicked Rev. Gate's style in accepting the invitation.

❦

Hours later, Regina stood on Deborah Bank's doorstep, with the wind whipping her scarf across her face. The famous Chicago Hawk welcomed her with an icy blast. Thanksgiving Eve in Chicago was a cold one, but it wasn't the cold that shook her. Even at her age, spending a holiday with a man's mother was a little daunting. And knowing both of Dewey's ex-wives were waiting beyond the ornate-carved wooden door delighted and frightened her. She'd spent time with them all individually and was Facebook friends with Deborah. But, she still approached the holiday with some anxiety.

"They already love you," Dewey whispered as the door opened.

"Welcome, Regina." Minnie Thurman, the not quite five-foot tall powerhouse behind her son's career, pulled the huge door open in welcome. "About time I lay eyes on you two again," she said and greeted Regina with a warm hug. She felt an immediate affinity with Dewey's mother when they first met, because they had something in common. They both adored Dewey.

In opposition to the weather, Minnie's welcome was Georgia sunshine and warm southern grace. They stepped into the cluttered family home and added their coats to the pile in the living room.

"Bo here?" Dewey asked.

"She just called; she's on her way. The rest of the girls are in the basement. Come on with me, Sister Regina. There's cooking to be done." Minnie took her hand and steered them beyond the living room. "Myra, Deb, Sister Regina's finally here."

Regina's knees locked at the kitchen's threshold. Dewey Thurman definitely had his type. They all looked so much alike, they could have been sisters. When she'd met them separately, she hadn't fully processed the resemblances. A few months ago, when someone asked which daughters were hers, she shrugged off the comment. Regina leaned back, hoping for Dewey's support. Nothing, but air behind her. Minnie Thurman placed a protective arm around her waist and pulled her into an ultra-modern stainless steel and smoky glass kitchen.

"Girl, come on. Dewey won't dare step foot in here." Myra, his first wife, chuckled. "I'll put him to work."

"Dew knows you're safe," Minnie said.

"That's right, Mama. We're grown folks and we know life's too short for any of that *Real Housewives*-style drama." Myra stepped away from a double-boiler she was nursing and hugged her. "Good to see you."

Deborah greeted her graciously from her perch at the table. Regina's heart went out to the frail woman barely sitting up in a padded kitchen chair. The divorce process had taken a toll on Deborah's physical appearance. Gaunt and terribly thin, but fighting to keep up appearances. This would be the last holiday for her in the house she grew up in.

Deborah smiled. "What are you going to cook, Sister Regina. We all work together here."

By some wondrous grace, these women were family. Sisters. Could she become their sister too? A member of Dewey's coven? Preparing Thanksgiving dinner with Dewey's ex-wives just didn't seem normal. *But then what is normal anymore?*

"My boys say I make killer mashed potatoes. If you have potatoes and PET Milk."

"Huh," Minnie said.

"Yes, warm PET Milk is my secret."

"Well, all right then. Learned something new today." Minnie clapped. "Here's an apron."

Deborah motioned toward a seat at the table.

"We always make sure Dewey has whatever time he needs with his girls," Myra offered.

Regina nodded in acknowledgment of the unsolicited advice.

"Dew tells me you make a good pot of greens, too," Minnie said as she supplied her with a peeler, potatoes, and a bowl.

Deborah frowned. "I pray they take the day off. I'm not up for it."

"Girlfriend, we're all praying for peace," Myra added.

"I know that's right," Minnie chimed in and the conversation flowed from there.

The cooking topics ranged from the weather for the weekend to current events. It was a great kitchen cooking party. Regina really liked these women. They might all look alike, but each of them had a different perspective and was special in her own way. Myra, stern and smart, yet approachable. Deborah undeniable sweet. And they were very respectful of each other and their relationship with Dewey. *Rena will never believe this.*

When the conversation turned to the ongoing arguments between Dewy and the girls, Regina rinsed potatoes and kept her mouth shut. Bonita was still "dating" the inmate. Tasnee's social media activity continued to cause them all grief. Jolee struggled this semester but had determined that she would not give up. Her sisters were calling her Zombie Jo because all she did was sleep this week. Calista's public theologian work didn't come with an income. But that didn't change her shopping habits. Allegra was lonely and doubtful she'd ever find real love. But the sharp tongue she'd inherited from his mother had caused some friction with her sisters. And there was still the ongoing conflict about the direction of the music.

Regina held her tongue; mum as the groom's mother at a wedding. The jury was still out on whether she helped or contributed to the confusion when she worked with the girls over the summer. And she wasn't about to share that this was one issue where she and Dewey disagreed. She'd prayed daily that he'd relax and let the girls add some spoken word to the new song he was working on. "Whatsoever," seemed like the perfect vehicle for a little hip-hope. But Dewey refused. In his vision, Rap, Hip-Hope, or Gospel Trap was not a part of the Fellowship's future. The ongoing argument was wreaking havoc on the sisters' unity.

"This thing with Bo has stirred up old, bad feelings," Deborah explained for Regina's benefit as the other mothers signified with nods. "Just when Reverend and Dewey seemed to come to terms," she sighed, "this thing ripped that all apart."

For a moment sadness sat in the room with them. The mood lingered as Regina took the potatoes off the burner. After she drained the potatoes, she mustered up the courage to ask the one question Dewey couldn't answer for her. She never even had coffee with Mandy. And here she was chatting and preparing the holiday meal with Dewey's ex-wives.

"How is it that you all were able to come together, spend holidays together, and work so closely together?"

Deborah leaned forward with a knowing smile on her face. "When you have a spiritually-gifted child and the only other woman you know with such a child is your husband's first wife, you work up the courage to ask the question."

Myra plopped down in the chair next to Deborah. "I didn't know how to answer her. So," she pointed at Minnie, "we went to the only woman we knew who had dealt with such a child."

Minnie took a seat at the table and began to frost a cake. "We decided years ago to band together for the girls." She glanced lovingly between her daughters-in-love. "All my girls. And look at the result. God's blest us. We're family. And The Sisters Fellowship is about to have their first number one gospel single." Minnie lifted the knife in praise. "That wouldn't have happened if we weren't on one accord."

"Yes." Deborah nodded. "Who knew the girls would have this kind of success?"

"Dewey." Mother Thurman raised the knife again to praise her son. "Dew knew."

Deborah shook her head. "I'll never comprehend it, and I've always been a little afraid of it. But now, I thank God for Dewey's gift. We had a real long talk last week and…" Deborah's voice trailed off a bit. "I believe everything will be alright."

The ladies fell silent for a moment. Divorce was never easy. But, if Dewey said she'd survive, Regina set herself in agreement with his word. She set the potatoes aside to cool and moved over to take the fourth seat at the table.

Minnie turned towards her and asked, "How do you feel about it, Sister Regina?"

❧

On Thanksgiving night as they were headed back to the Chicago Hyatt Regency, Regina pretended to be preoccupied with the scenery. The Chicago skyline was fabulous, but she'd seen it many times before.

The Thurman family's embrace had been more wonderful than she expected. Rena would never believe the warmth and fellowship. Cooking with Myra and Deb on Wednesday night reminded her of kitchen time with her mother and Rena. She hadn't enjoyed that sort of sisterhood with the Earle family.

Regina shivered and Dewey turned up the car's heater. But it wasn't lack of physical heat. The conversations about the prophetic gifts in the family left her unsettled. She'd done her best not to let her dis-ease affect the holiday. But, now looking up at the Chicago skyscrapers, she was—as the kids say—feeling some kind of way.

"It is lovely how focused everyone was on making Thanksgiving as happy a holiday as possible."

"That's what we do for the girls," Dewey responded.

Faith and foresight proved both a blessing and frightening gift tonight. Deborah's divorce was not yet finalized, but the church wanted her out of the parsonage. And she needed to find a job soon. After Thanksgiving dinner, Deborah shared the update from the church. She was under Episcopal order to vacate by the end of the year. And "of course" she was leaving Family Fellowship. Tasnee cried hysterically over the loss of her position in the church. The stillness in Bonita and Calista's reaction, juxtaposed with Tasnee's emotional outburst, unnerved Regina. They were both eerily silent before they went upstairs together to pray.

Dewey reached over for her hand. "Notwithstanding the talk we had with the girls, I'm happy. I'm so glad you spent the holiday with us. You know they all love you."

"Know? How am I supposed to know they love me," she snapped? She tried hard to never snap at Dewey, but tonight she was tired, overwhelmed and totally freaked out. Joining his wife-coven. Maybe? Belonging to a family of prophets?

Both Bonita and Calista had separately said eerie things to her this evening. Unnerving, prophetic things. Bonita spoke about the birth of new things in the family. And Calista shared a vision of grandchildren.

Coming from any of the other girls, the comments would have gone in one ear and out the other. Just harmless comments about the seasons of life. The girls were all old enough to have children. Since Bonita's boyfriend was in prison, Regina interpreted her comments as spiritual. And she didn't get the impression Calista was talking about any of her sisters. But it wasn't the comments as much as the surety in both their voices. They spoke with the same surety and authority Dewey carried. And given that Dewey had been dwelling with his vision about grandchildren for the past few weeks.

"How can you be so sure? How can you know?"

"Huh?" Dewey glanced over at her.

Happy he couldn't read her expression in the dark, Regina lowered her head. Maybe she was tired after a long day.

"Deb was a very able church administrator for many years, and she's looking for work in the non-profit sector. She has lots of friends, and there are many people that remember her father. This is how I know a job will open up for her soon, and her best friend is a realtor. I'm sure finding a house won't be an issue. And I also know you're going to marry me."

Since her birthday, he'd asked her to marry him every day. He even threatened to post his proposal in one of his morning praise songs if she didn't say yes soon. They had a running joke about her waiting for the ring. But tonight, she wasn't in a playful mood.

"Your knowing everything is annoying as hell."

Dewey's head swiveled around to look at her for a second, then quickly shifted back to the road. "Regina, I want you to say whatever is on your mind, but I need to ask you to hold it for a minute." He signaled and guided the car into the hotel's underground parking deck.

"Sure." She took a few deep breaths to calm her mind and let the man navigate the winding spiral path through the hotel's parking deck. She hated these big city lots that routed you through a concrete maze before dumping your car in a sea of underground vehicles. And God forbid you failed to park in one of the specific spots allotted for the hotel guests and had to deal with a big-city towing scheme. She relaxed a bit, comforted by the knowledge that Dewey listened and wanted her to speak her mind.

Once he opened the door to their suite, Regina plopped down on the sofa. It was a little late for vitriol, so she quietly let out. "I can't do it. I can't sit in the kitchen cooking with Deb and Myra, then have you bring in another woman and introduce her as number four."

Dewey sat beside her and exhaled. "Don't worry about that. I'm not going to marry anyone else. I didn't intend to marry you."

"Say what?"

He kissed her cheek softly, "For the past ten years I've doubted the vision. Then I met you. You know I had a vision that someday I'd have a son. And that the son would be a challenge. But five girls later, the prophesy became a mystery. Of course, I could father another child, but not outside of marriage. And like Abraham, when I am far too old to be having any more children, the good Lord gives me a double portion blessing of two sons. Because Smith definitely qualifies as a challenge. But the vision doesn't come to pass without you."

She shook her head. "That knowing thing. It's bothering me. And it's not just you. Sometimes talking to Calista and Bo is just creepy."

Dewey held her tightly. "Lady, I'm sorry. We don't mean to seem creepy. If the girls said anything, I'm sure it was meant in love, to bless you. With seven children between us, I'm sure my vision of grandchildren is more of an old man's dream. Regina, this gift does not control our lives. I don't know if you've changed your mind, but I hope you haven't. Because I love you and want to spend the September of my days beside you. Come on, Lady." He rose from the sofa. Then whispered a sing-song-y chant. "I know something you don't know."

Dewey's voice had ways of seducing her out of her doubts and moods. She grinned when he gave her a suggestive shrug and reached for her hand.

He led her into the sleeping room of their suite and dropped her hand after he opened the door and several balloons floated out to greet her.

"All for you."

Regina gloried at the site. Champagne, dozens of white roses, and what looked like a hundred white, gold, and clear balloons.

Dewey whistled his way across the room to the work desk.

Regina pushed past the balloons and followed. "All for me." She giggled and pushed away several balloons. At the desk, Dewey worked on a bottle of champagne.

"All for you."

"You shouldn't have done all of this. It's too much."

"I told you I had a surprise for you tonight." He opened a second bottle. "Because I know you've got to love me. To spend your holiday in this frozen land and with my crazy family."

Regina sat on one of the beds and took off her shoes. "I do. But this is too much." She stretched her arms out to include all the gifts in the room. Beyond the champagne, roses and balloons, there was a big gift box waiting for her on the second bed.

Dewey shrugged, smiled and popped the cork. As the wine bubbled up to his nose, he let out an endearing little, "Oop" as champagne flowed over his hands.

He moved toward her with a glass in one hand and a bottle in the other. Dewey sat next to her, nuzzled at her neck. And turned the bottle up to his lips.

Regina downed her glass and held it out for a refill. "Why do we have two beds?"

"There're some things we're going to do tonight, and I want a dry bed to sleep in."

He champagned and sang her out of her sweater, slacks, and cuddle duds. By the time they started on the second bottle, she was naked and giggling.

For the next few hours they spilled more than just champagne on the sheets. And just when, she thought they'd move to the dry bed, Dewey turned her over. He poured a bit of wine on her back and chased it down stream with his tongue. She floated through the bubbles, balloons, giggles, and kisses. He straddled her and slowly, softly licked, kissed and breathed his way back up to her neck. When he entered, he whispered, "Set a date for next year."

Regina woke up late the next day with a slight throbbing in her head. She rolled over and groaned. What a night. She pulled the sheets up closer to her neck. Thankful Dewey had the foresight to have a dry bed for them to sleep in.

After putting on the nightgown and robe she'd intended to wear last night, Regina sat at the edge of the bed. Still woozy from last night's champagne, she yawned, stretched and took a few deep breaths to clear her head. In the other room she heard Dewey moving around. She was going to have to start taking Zumba again to keep up with him. After thanking God for the wonder of loving Dewey, she slipped into the living room of their suite.

Shiny, silky, shirtless, he sat in an arm chair rapidly texting. The swirly, sparse, gray hairs on his chest stood out in sharp contrast to his vitality. Dewey's gray hairs were only a smoke signal. That man had plenty of white-hot fire within.

She flushed as memories of some of the things they did last night flashed into her mind. *Lord, Have Mercy.*

"Good morning." Dewey looked up from his phone. "I'm sorry, but we have a problem."

Regina sighed. As she reached up to touch her throbbing head, she poked herself in the eye. She waved her left hand in front of her face to discover a ring she didn't realize she was wearing.

"Aww, it's beautiful." She gawked at the diamond engagement ring Dewey must of slipped on her finger while she slept. "Dew, this is too much."

He dropped the phone on a side table and stood grinning. "You know you like it." As he moved towards her, a hint of sadness dimmed his smile. "Well, I hope you like it, and if you don't, we can take it back and get whatever you want. But it's not too much, for you, my love."

Regina studied the gleaming pear-shaped rock and exclaimed, "You know it's perfect!"

Dewey shrugged and moved over to the tray sitting on a side table and pulled a bottle of wine from an ice bucket. "Yeah, I know."

"More champagne," she asked?

"Hair of the dog. Mimosa?"

Regina grinned. "Yes, since we're celebrating." *Just a quick drink before heading to the shower.* "What's happened?"

"Well." He handed her a glass of freshly-squeezed orange juice and champagne. "I changed my scheduled morning praise song and instead posted something about how thankful and happy I am."

After all my heart was left ajar.
And love has entered.
A sweet refuge for the winter of my days.

"This is beautiful, thank you?" Regina relaxed on the sofa.

"Allegra saw it and tweeted back to ask if the praise song had anything to do with you. I thought it was a private message and tweeted back that you'd finally surrendered." He plopped down beside her. "It's gone viral. Hashtag MrsDWT3 is trending."

Regina took a sip of her breakfast, nodded slowly, then drained her glass. "In for a penny, in for a pound. I'll call the boys after I shower."

"Wait, listen to this…" He put his phone on speaker and they listened to several congratulatory messages from close friends and family. Myra and Minnie sent a joint congratulatory voice mail. The very sweet Deborah send a text. And there were messages from three of the five girls. Dewey surmised that Bo was probably somewhere praying. Regina bit her lip and hoped Volcano Tasnee wouldn't erupt today.

For the next two hours, Dewey's phone buzzed and dinged continuously. His publicist, agent, half of his friends and fans worldwide texted, emailed, posted, tweeted or Facebooked. When she turned on her phone, the mailbox overflowed with text messages and missed calls. Instead of going Black Friday shopping with the girls, she stayed behind to respond to her messages. When the phone rang and Rena's picture flashed on the screen, Dewey insisted on answering her sister's call.

And they'd have to wait to share the news with her boys. Neither responded to her call or text.

Chapter Twenty-Four

With the rising of the sun, anticipation?
In the Autumn of days, the promise of Spring?
Praise him at all times and in all seasons

It was after one pm on black Friday when Dewey and Regina arrived at Deborah's empty house. The *girls* were still out shopping. No problem getting in, Dewey knew the garage code. Rena would call it strange, for the ex-husband to have access to the house.

"Remember I used to live here."

Regina chuckled as she heated up Thanksgiving leftovers. Rena would definitely have some comments about this.

The only way to describe this situation is grace.

She worried as she fixed Dewey a plate. Was it right to bring their joy into the house after Deborah's announcement last night? From what she'd seen of the mini-mansion it would take a small army and a minor miracle to meet the deadline the church gave Deborah to vacate this house.

As they ate in silence, Regina pondered over a new concern. In the midst of their great happiness, Dewey couldn't settle. Since she'd started trusting her observation skills, she'd become more attuned to picking up on certain cues. She now knew when there was something swirling in Dewey's spirit. As they finished lunch, she prayed. Dewey never spoke much while he meditated or wrestled with the spirits. He'd tell her what he could. When he was ready. Outwardly, she presented a picture of calm. Internally, she worked to maintain a spirit of peace. Maybe she was ready to marry into this crazy, wonderful insightful family.

"It's uncharacteristic not to have heard from Bo yet. I'm going to shoot her another text. Matter of fact, I'm going to text Allegra. She'll get Bo to call us."

Allegra responded quickly. "Bo's not with us."

"It's time." Dewey blew his stack and vented about things coming to a head with Bonita.

For months, they'd all tried to encourage Bonita to end her relationship. But, she wouldn't budge. She was so sure she was right. Last week she'd begged her stepfather to invite Rev. Omni to join the staff at Family Fellowship as the prison outreach minister and received a firm and swift *no*.

Regina checked the time and fretted. It was almost two. The shoppers wouldn't stay out much longer. Maybe it was best if they weren't here when they returned.

After eating, Dewey fell deeper into his spooky-spiritual mood. Like a good shepherd, he wasn't content to have heard from family, friends and fans from all over the world. Four of his girls had checked in. But he hadn't heard from one.

She tried to restore his good humor with wedding talk. But, now he was highly irritated and close to needing a prayer closet.

He paced while she cleaned up the kitchen. Loving Dewey came with some challenges, drama, and pain, and she was ready to walk beside him. *A shared burden lightens the load.* She smiled, grateful to have her mother's wisdom to guide her today. And now that she'd said yes, he was obligated to schedule that knee surgery. She'd remind him of that later when he was ready to joke around.

The Thurman family was a true coterie. A unique group of individuals banded together for a common goal: the success of the girls. What a blessing to join such a clan. Last night they'd celebrated the joy of uniting. This morning they'd prayed for the unity and fellowship of their blended and extended family. A family that would be more like *Modern Family* than the *Brady Bunch*. And hopefully, not as dramatic as the dysfunctional family in her favorite reality TV show. They'd weathered the storm with her boys and while not yet whole, the Earles were healing.

Regina glanced over at her fiancé and tried to figure out how to get him to settle down.

"Dew, let's go watch the replay of Macy's parade," she suggested after she'd wiped down the counters. One of Dewey's many friends had scored a Broadway musical and the show-stopping tune was one of featured performances at Harold Square.

⚬∞⚬

Halfway through the replay of the parade, Bonita bounced in and plopped down on a sofa in the den.

"Hey, you two. Congratulations!" Bonita smiled. "And, I have an announcement too. I'm getting married on Sunday."

Regina's eyes widened and her head jerked to observe Dewey's reaction. No smile. No joy. The air around him stilled as he struggled to stand. The room seemed to darken as tension rose between father and daughter.

"I'll give you two some privacy." Regina stood in an attempt to sidestep the rising storm.

"No." Bo countered. "I want you to stay with us."

Slowly and soulfully, Dewey inhaled. "It's not going to work," he hissed.

Regina caught her breath. *Is he talking to me or Bo?*

Bonita shot darts at her dad with her eyes. "How do you know it's not going to work? I see myself married, Daddy. This is right, I know it."

Regina's eyes rolled around the tastefully decorated, ultra-cozy room. Only a skilled decorator could combine black leather furniture with indigo blue accents. And only two skilled communicators could come out of this conversation without major damage to their relationship.

Dewey's face creased into a deep, old man's scowl, and he folded his arms across his body. "Tell me more about this man who wants to marry my daughter. This *man* who knows I'm in town and hasn't made no attempt to ask me for your hand. Are you kidding me, Bo?"

Bonita lips tightened.

"What's his Christian name? How old is he? How's he going to support you? How many children does he have?" Dewey shotgunned his questions.

Bonita's eyes rolled around in her head. "Why are you asking me, Daddy. You already know?"

Out of the side of her eye, Regina noted Dewey's stormy posture and demeanor. She'd seen Dewey's anointing change the atmosphere in many spaces, but never in anger.

"I'm just asking common questions. You come in here and tell us you're getting married on Sunday. Who knew you were engaged?" He shook his head. "You know this ain't right?"

Bonita closed her eyes as her right foot began to shake. "Daddy, tell me what you know."

Dewey shook his head and spoke in an icy tone. "No. It's time for you to tell me."

Regina kept her focus on Dewey as he dug in.

Oh, my God, Bo and Calista both shared messages last night about grandchildren. Is Bo expecting? How did that happen? When he told me what he knew about Bo's relationship, he worried that Bo would never become a mother. This news changes everything.

"Why bother?" Bonita huffed into the thick silence as her hands clinched at her sides. "All my life you've seen all and known all. You've just been waiting for me to come to you?"

Regina braced herself as the conversation moved into prophet, spooky territory. Bonita seemed prepared for her father's ire. *Had she foreseen this conversation?* She sat silently in the rising battle between the diviners. It didn't require a gift of prophecy to know that there was something beneath the surface that neither father or daughter were ready to say.

Dewey rubbed his head and squeezed his eyes with his right hand. Then nodded in that all-knowing way, that often annoyed and unnerved her. "You haven't answered my questions."

All the joy drained from Bonita's face, and her hands fell open.

Regina didn't want to openly smile in the midst of this critical conversation, but her heart was filled with joy over the care Dewey exhibited for each of his girls. Dewey already knew the answers to all the questions he posed. She did too.

"Since you can't speak…" Dewey sat on the sofa and methodically revealed what he knew. Dewey had a complete dossier on Omari Moore. Street name: Omni the Avenger. Common story: poor boy growing up in the inner city, no father in the home, no high school diploma, gang affiliation. And before his incarceration at nineteen, Omari had fathered three children by two different girls. Sadly, his oldest son was also a convicted felon.

Regina recognized Dewey's technique of laying out the evidence from watching the lawyers in her family. The examination of the facts regarding Bo's intended were damning. What power did this Svengali have over Bonita? From what she'd read about women in prison relationships, the outlook wasn't positive.

Bonita looked up with full, round eyes. "Daddy, I love him."

"There's no way he can love you," Dewey shouted. "Not while bringing all that into your life. He's not even a free man."

"But he is free." Bonita's face lit up as she explained.

After serving twenty-three of a twenty-five year sentence, Omari Moore was paroled from the state prison on Tuesday afternoon. The terms of his release required a five-night stay at a half-way house.

"…for reintegration into society. He hasn't come to the house because he couldn't. This morning I leased a house for us, and I've been out shopping for furniture all day. He doesn't have anything in his home today, because I didn't fully believe in his vision. But I intend to have everything ready for him on Sunday."

Regina bowed her head and wiped the tears from her cheeks. The more Bonita shared, the deeper the pain that pierced her gut. She groaned as pain and joy collided like oil and water in her stomach.

Dewey glanced over at Regina clutching her stomach as she wept. He'd focused so much on his visions of the future, he failed to account for trouble on the journey. Was it fair to ask her to be here? To give up her hard-won peace for the turmoil in his life?

He rubbed his head, then returned his focus to Bonita. He'd banked on Omni's continued incarceration to pull his daughter away from the relationship. "I just don't see it, Bo. It's too much. How's he going to provide for you? What about his children and their mothers?"

Puffs of smoke seemed to emit from Bonita's flared nostrils. "Don't be a hypocrite Daddy; you have two ex-wives."

"Exactly. Ex-wives, not baby-mamas. And I provided for all of my children. What responsibility could this cat have taken for his children? I'm sure if he was a working, responsible man providing for his family twenty years ago, he wouldn't have been sent to prison. Real men don't roam the streets after midnight jacking cars and taking them on joyrides. Or robbing small business owners."

Bonita couldn't even raise her eyes to look at her father.

"Daddy, Omni's been exonerated based on judicial misconduct. And the judge who took so many of our men out of their homes and sentenced them to state-supported slavery will soon be behind bars himself." Bonita stood as she preached. "Praise be to God that the captives have been freed. Now Omni and his brothers convicted by a racist police force and a devil in a black robe have been redeemed and returned. Amen, he's able." Bonita lifted her hands in praise.

Dewey made direct eye contact with a wide-eyed Regina.

"Now is the season for restoration. We've weathered the storm and can begin our lives anew. Daddy, Omni's been called to pastor a church that his cousin oversees in the city. Bishop is signing him out of the transitional living facility on Sunday morning, and we are getting married at his first Sunday service. And Bishop's arranging a reception for us." Bonita beamed and pumped her uplifted hands. "God is good, and he did just what Omni said HE would."

Bonita's phone chimed. "It's Omni." She grinned and pulled her phone out to check a message. "He said the meeting at the church is going well, but everybody is asking if you're coming."

"Coming where?" Dewey plopped down on the sofa.

"Please, Daddy. We know it's just a storefront, but if you come on Sunday…"

"A storefront," Dewey scoffed, "is not a reliable income. And what church? What denomination? What Bishop in his right mind would call…"

"I know what you're thinking, Daddy, but don't say it. God has provided and we'll grow. Just like you grew Family Fellowship with a strong and vibrant music ministry. You've got to hear our flow, our lyrics and record us. When Omni spits and I sing through the bridge, the people are blessed. When we minister together in the chapel, it's transformational."

Dewey's stomach churned, and his head started swimming. How could his smart, perceptive daughter be so naive and gullible?

"I'm not recording nothing," he yelled. "Is he using you to get some kind of record deal through me? I see now. All of this hip-hope, hip-hop-beat-hype is his thing. Right? He's been the push behind this whole thing? I should have seen it months ago."

"Dewey," Regina uttered as she reached for his hand.

"Yes." Bo's shoulders slumped as she joined them on the sofa. "Daddy, it's a strong concept and a good idea."

"Bo, baby. I'm sorry, but nothing you've said is a good idea."

Bonita's whole body shook. "If you won't help us, we'll fund the demo ourselves. I've got savings. Our lawyers are filing suit against the state. Omni will be compensated. We'll have money."

Dewey spit out, "The lawyers will be compensated."

Bonita sidestepped her father's sarcasm. "God will bless and we'll get by."

"More like he'll get over on you. And by the way, Bo, where were you last night? Running in this house late for family dinner?"

"Not your business, Daddy. But, yes, I went to spend what little time I could with Omni," Bo said with stars in her eyes.

Dewey hopped up. "Oh, my Holy Father! Jesus! Bo, please don't even think about letting this man touch you." Dewey yelled as his fist went through the nearest wall. Regina raced to his side.

"Daddy, that's not for you to worry about that."

This was a side of her fiancé she hadn't seen. Dewey rattled. Well, the whole thing had her shook, too. She stared for a moment at the baseball-sized hole in the faux-stone-painted wall.

If anything in his hand is broken…

She ran to the kitchen for an ice pack.

Given the state of the relationship between Dewey and Deborah's husband and the church; that hole needed to get repaired before Monday. Years of managing properties with Victor had taught her a little about paint and drywall. As soon as someone could drive her to the hardware store, she'd get what she needed and repair the wall.

Less than a minute later, Dewey paused long enough to let her wrap his hand in a dish-towel ice pack. Then she sat with Bonita on the couch as Dewey marched around the room with an ice-wrapped hand.

Nothing Bonita said made any sense. Bo, who always seemed as clear and sure of herself as her father, had been completely conned. Nothing Dewey said about the harsh realities of dealing with an ex-convict and marrying under these circumstances resonated. Everything out of Bonita's mouth was fairytale hope.

When Regina looked up at Dewey on his next pass, he seemed to mumble something that sounded like help in her direction.

She closed her eyes tightly. What was her role in this situation? What could a future second stepmother say?

"You should talk to your mother," she whispered.

"That's all you've got." Father and daughter beat out in unison and perfect harmony.

She reached up and pulled at her hair. The accusation underlying their words stung. They wanted her guidance. She was the one running around the country giving advice to young women. But there was nothing in her presentations about this situation. In her wildest imaginings, she couldn't have made this scenario up. Surely these two prophets should have a word of wisdom, a vision, an observation. Something?

"Dewey, will you please sit down."

Dewey stopped in his tracks and regarded her with an icy stare. Then trained his gaze on his daughter.

"Bo, there is no way this is going to work. No! It will work. With you working yourself to death trying to support him and possibly his children. And God only knows what this church is going to require of you."

"Daddy, I'm ready. I've seen it. Omni and I are going to be fine."

Dewey exhaled in frustration and plopped down next to Regina on the sofa. Her vital, handsome, sexy, sixty-two-year old fiancé seemed to age ten years since the argument with Bonita began. She took his injured hand in hers. His breathing labored as she turned his hand over to examine it for swelling.

It was so out of character for him to have punched that wall. Dewey was always so careful with his hands; any injury or swelling would impact his ability to play. She caressed his now-cold palm and turned his hand over again for further inspection. Thankfully, his knuckles only showed a little redness from the impact.

She prayed that Myra would hold her tongue when the others arrived from the shopping trip. Everyone warned her Myra had a keen intellect and a razor-sharp whip of a tongue. And Minnie, she understood, could be worse under this kind of stress.

Dewey gave her a weak *thank you* before speaking in a weak, tired tone. "Bo, even with our gift, we cannot always see to the end of a personal matter. What you're seeing is God's will for you to be married. I see *you* married. But not to this man."

"Daddy, my vision is clear."

Dewey winced. "Hear me. I see you all in long, happy marriages, but that's the dream of a father. You just can't *see* clearly right now. I never could in my personal life. If I could, do you think I'd be twice-divorced? Let me tell you what I know as a man. An old man. Your father."

Bo exhaled and moved closer to her father.

"Dude hasn't even asked to meet me, man to man. In spite of his incarceration, if he had contacted me in any way I'da heard him out. Mail works two ways, you know. And I understand that you've provided phone privileges for him. For you, I would have taken his call. I would have listened. I would have visited him in prison, if he'd asked. This tells me more about his character than you are willing to see."

"That's just old fashioned." She huffed, as a deep frown of conviction crept across her face.

"No, Bo. Common decency has not gone out of style. This is someone wanting to be a part of our family. Asking for my beloved daughter's hand would not have been out of order. I'll agree our family is different, and this can't be easy, but he's not here." His voice went up an octave. "Not here to speak with me in person. Or meet your mother and sisters. And you know something's wrong, because you couldn't get him to come. What I'm saying doesn't have anything to do with his past. If this was any kind of real, reformed, decent, honest man he'd-of sat you down and demanded to be here. Do you think this is Lady G's ideal place to be?"

Regina sucked in her breath.

He pulled his hand from her embrace as his voice began to crescendo. "Do you think she wants to be here, in my ex-wife's house? Do you think it's easy for me to have my daughters live with Banks? You know I can't stand that man. No! But for my girls, for this family." Fully animated, Dewey pointed between himself and Regina. "We're here. Placing certain things aside for you girls." He drew in a deep breath. Then rose in fury.

"Get out of this relationship, and dear God, I pray you've been careful." He took a deep breath and raged on. "The rates of HIV among men in prison ain't nothing to play with. I hope you know that the infection rate among African-American women is still the fastest rising." He waved both of his hands in front of his face. "I don't need to know what you girls do, but I don't want to see you a-bunch-a baby mamas. And I damn sure don't want to see any of you infected with AIDS."

Bonita winced in pain. "Daddy, don't."

"Dewey, I don't think—"

"No! You can't see this," he yelled.

Dewey came to a dead stop and closed his eyes. The room stood still as he thought. After a moment, he drew in several audibly deep, long, breaths and nodded.

Regina prayed. *Lord, please send a word of revelation this moment.*

After a short pause, Dewey exhaled and repositioned his feet. "Get out of this, Bo."

"I won't."

Dewey's eyes flew open, and he stared down at his daughter with fire in his eyes. "Tell you what," he whispered in a soul-chilling tone. "Get out of this, or you're out of the Fellowship."

"Daddy!"

"That's it." His voice regained its color. "You get married. You're out. And ain't a darn thing you can do about it. You see none-a y'all read your contracts. I told you, each one of you, a thousand times, not to trust anyone in this business. Not even me. Told you all to get educated; to read the contract. And by the way, if you're out of the Fellowship, you got nothing more coming. No rights. No royalties. No claim to future profits. And don't think your mother is going to support you. You know how she is. Who do you think taught *me* entertainment law?"

Dewey looked down at Bonita before trudging toward the door with slumped shoulders. "Don't look at me like that, Bo. Your mother drew up your contact."

Regina stood. Should she follow him? She had something to say, now. But, she dared not interrupt Dewey's steely, cold rant. He'd delivered a word, but not from the Lord. He'd shared his reactions as a father and he'd struck a nerve. Poor Bonita sank deep into the sofa, sobbing. Being in the Fellowship meant the world to all the girls.

"Bonita, you'll always have a home with your Daddy. But, I can't have married women in my group. So, run tell your man that!" exploded out of Dewey's mouth.

Like a storm cloud over the bay, Dewey blew out of the room. And, finally, she knew exactly what to do. Regina sat and held Bo as she cried.

In-between sobs, Bonita prayed. Her vocalization came out slow, guttural and incomprehensible. No words, just soul-crushing moans. Every so often an actual word emitted from Bonita's lips. Words, Regina didn't attempt to decipher. Well it didn't matter, Bonita's feelings—words—were meant for God. It took a while, but once Bonita was emotionally spent, she clearly heard Rev. Bonita Thurman ask the Lord for clarity of sight.

All of their children had some level of turmoil in their lives. And at the moment, Bo's trouble seemed the most headed for destruction. As she sat there searching for words to minister to her, Rev. Bonita Thurman ministered to her. Every person in their extended and blended family needed the blessing of clear sight.

Chapter Twenty-Five

What does God do with broken pieces.
Refresh, renew, redeem. Praise the Lord for broken pieces.
Refresh, renew, redeem.

On Saturday afternoon between cycles of worrying and praying, Dewey couldn't settle. She'd never seen him this disturbed and worried about leaving him in the morning for her speaking engagement in Birmingham. As they sat together in the hotel suite, remnants of their earlier celebration seemed to mock them. The high floating balloons drifted and landed around them like picnic flies. The roses seemed to wilt more each hour in response to their grief.

"Bo's getting married tomorrow afternoon, and I can't stop it," Dewey mumbled over and over.

"I...I..." Regina wheezed, as her mind whirled. She found it difficult to pull her thoughts together. Dewey's despair and dark mood continued to spiral downward today. Last night they'd all tried and failed to persuade Bonita to slow down. To wait. No one could get Bo to see that marriage to Omni would be a disaster. Rev. Bonita Thurman vehemently declared her vision was clear.

Late last night, the soft-hearted Deborah broke ranks. Deb reminded the family that her fifteen-year marriage had begun under less-than-ideal circumstances. Dewey's blowup was so intense, Minnie assigned Regina to talk him through his disappointment. For Bonita, the sisters remembered their standard of sisterhood and unity. This afternoon the girls were spread out all over Chicagoland, trying to pull things together for Bonita's wedding.

"We talked about this all last night." Regina picked up the continuing dialogue. "Myra still disagrees, but she's out with Bo and Allegra looking for a wedding dress."

"Myra decided to hold her nose and tongue. I didn't," Dewey hissed.

"We agreed it would be a mistake for Bo to feel like she couldn't come back to us."

"True, because she will be back."

"Is that a prophetic word, Dew?"

"No, Love. This is Daddy talking. Ain't no way this can be right. We still haven't been able to meet this man. And I guess there's no time today with Bo and 'em running around trying to buy dresses and shoes. Poor Jolee is going to be up all night doing hair. I know she's assisting in love. But, everyone's hair and all the makeup? We can't keep sending Jo back to school exhausted." Dewey bowed his head; his sorrow deepened each hour. "I can't even go help Deb and Mama, because they know I'll go nuclear if Bo's rental house isn't up to standard."

Instead of shopping, Deb and Minnie were pulling together some furniture and household items to help Bonita set up housekeeping. A couple of friends from the church were bringing a truck to help this afternoon.

"Dewey, nobody wants you moving furniture with your hand in a bandage."

Regina's heart ached to see her vital, playful fiancé so frail. "So, what are we doing today? Did you want to drive out to Rev. Gates' open house?"

"No, no. I'm not fit to be around people. But, Finus did call when you were in the shower."

Regina tensed. "Does he know about Bonita?"

"Yes, news travels fast among the faithful. He's adding us to his personal prayer list. And he sends you his best personal regards and congratulations. And, my dear, those congratulations include your selection to join their tour. His office will send contracts next week, and please ask Allegra for the legal review."

Regina exhaled. "That's great."

"By the way, I meant to ask if you've heard from Lik?"

"Yes, he sent a text. The boys are having a fine time in Miami with their father. Golfing during the day. Clubbing again tonight. Smith's still getting his head together. Dew, I'm so sorry I doubted you."

"Don't be. I'm praising the Lord that the Earle boys are together. Lady, I'm so glad you're here with me. I knew," he paused, "not prophetically speaking, the day would come when I'd be all alone, because some things a girl can only get from her mother. The blessing of you came right on time."

"I'm feeling useless today, too. For the girls. And because the boys needed to be with their father this weekend. I'm so glad I'm not alone in this season."

"Lady," he flashed a small smile, "I am thankful, happy, and angry, all at the same time. Mad at myself for messing up my hand, so I can't play my way through. I am happy you are here, but I need to disconnect for a while. Seek some guidance and peace. Will you give me some time?"

"Of course, Dew." When she decided to marry him months ago, she accepted there would be times when Dewey wasn't available to her.

"Why don't you go to the hotel's spa or shopping? Maybe you can pick up some of those wedding magazines. And this evening after dinner, let's talk about our wedding. I'll listen to you go on about colors and flowers. Dresses and tablecloths. All that stuff."

"Okay." She smiled for the first time all day. "I think I will take a walk down the Mag Mile and buy a dozen wedding magazines. Thank you for the suggestion. I need to do something to take my mind off this mess, too."

⌘

With a planes-trains-and-automobiles day ahead of her, Regina flew to Birmingham on an eight a.m. flight Sunday morning. For a busy holiday weekend, the transport train from the terminal to the rental car desk was out of service. Thankfully, she made it to the Thanksgiving praise service in time to speak. She declined the invitation to stay for the fellowship dinner and raced to Mobile. She had strict instructions to bring her engagement ring to Rena.

After the full day speaking, a few hours of driving and showing off her ring, she was exhausted. At eight p.m., she slipped into bed. Instead of reviewing her lesson plans for the upcoming week, she let the TV watch her sleep.

Just until Dewey calls.

Regina startled. Dewey's ringtone. "Oh, Lord, two a.m. ." Middle-of-the-night phone calls always meant trouble. She gasped and reached for the phone. When Dewey didn't call this evening, she didn't worry. He had a lot going on today—the wedding, reception, and rushing to the airport to get everyone back in place. Bonita's wedding had thrown off every prearranged plan.

"Everyone's alive." Dewey blurted before cursing and spitting out his story. "Check this. Bo's marriage isn't legal."

She dropped the phone. "Lord, no."

Yesterday was only the sleet in Dewey's storm.

"Omni performed the rites his-self, without adhering to any legal requirements. And I wonder now if he knew what he was doing. The church was exactly what I thought. Fifty folding chairs and a portable keyboard. When that bishop invited me to play, I held up my bandaged hand. I didn't want to go to the reception, and at the same time, wasn't ready to leave my Bo. We only showed up at that welcome-home-slash-wedding-reception set up by Omni's cousin for Bo. Not knowing what would befall us."

Regina's eyes filled up. *Poor Bonita.*

"I'm going to tell you this in order because it's a lot. I didn't know that the reception was actually a fundraiser for the church. For a poor congregation, they had a nice crowd. Unbeknownst to Bonita, they'd promoted the event. Promising a performance by DW Thurman."

"Tell me you refused to sing."

"I wanted to but couldn't. Somehow Bo's credit card was on hold with the ticket broker as surety for the event. And when the people started getting restless, as mad as I was, I got on the keyboard."

"My God."

"It gets worse."

Regina sat up in bed. *What could be worse for dear Bonita?*

"It got a little rowdy, so I sang. But," the anger in his voice turned to sadness, "I would not sing "Everlasting." I just couldn't."

Regina's heart collapsed in her chest as she shared the depths of his sorrow. One of Dewey's highest dreams was to sing his song to each of his daughters on their wedding day. "My heart breaks for you."

Dewey took in a sharp breath. "Not done. I've told you about dinner. Lady, I can't believe how this con man got poor people to spend what they didn't have to come to a hundred-dollar-a-plate dinner. And, let me mention, dinner was not provided for our family. The *Bishop* didn't count on us needing to eat. So, I had to come out of my pocket for my mother, Myra, and the girls."

Regina's lungs contracted as the air rushed through her opened mouth.

"At Bo's request, I took Omni off to the side. I tried. I really did. Tried to create some peace for my Bo. Do you know," his voice went up an octave, "that ninja said not one word about how he loved and would provide for my daughter? Didn't apologize for the way he dishonored me, Myra, all of us. He just went on about the church game and how he'd be picking up a new truck in the morning—his plans for his 'cut' from the event." Dewey huffed. "That just added insult to injury. He had no plans to pay us for performing and no concern for any charges to Bo's credit. Called it all wedding and homecoming gifts. Didn't care that this isn't the way we run our business. Or that we will probably lose a booking behind this mess. It was all about Omni. And how—now that he was in the family," Dewey puffed, "he wants to get in the studio as soon as possible."

Regina gasped, but didn't interrupt.

"Before I could get a word in edgewise about my daughter, Lady, the building shook."

"No, Dewey. What else?"

"Regina, this man was already married."

"No," she shrieked.

"Omni had a prison wife he hadn't told about his release. She found out through Facebook. People posted pictures from the church service and the plugger about the reception. And sad thing is…she didn't come for him. She showed up and confronted Bo." Dewey's voice crumbled into a plaintive cry. "This woman burst into the place with a Glock and pointed it at my Bo."

"No, Lord."

"But God," he whispered. "I thank God Calista's truly a praying woman. Over all the shouting and running, Calista had the presence of mind to ask the woman if she had children. And in a moment of clarity, that woman stopped. Considered her children and that stayed her hand. I watched that gun fall to the floor in slow motion, like I was watching a movie. I'll never forget how long that gun spun around like it was choosing whether to hit my mother, daughter, or Myra. And glory be to God, it didn't go off. The police officer even called it a miracle. The gun jammed."

"Praise God!" Regina shouted. She hopped out of bed and began to pace. "Who called the police?"

"The Hall. Bunch of black people—and a gun. The Hall called with a quickness and the cops took the wrong one away. Omni was nowhere to be found when police arrived. But, that poor woman. She went to jail. And Myra's mouth almost got her arrested, too. Calista's praying for forgiveness, but I ain't got nothing for none of 'em. That woman who stuck a gun in my child's face. Or her husband." Dewey took a deep breath. "Bonita is devastated. We had to carry her out of there. All she's mumbled since this happened is that she should have seen this coming. Myra had to give her a sedative to get her through the airport. And the reason I didn't call earlier? Lady, the airport was a zoo and a mess. The busiest travel day of the year, and I needed an extra seat on an overbooked flight to Atlanta. Thank God some kind college student gave up his seat." Dewey stopped to catch his breath.

"Beyond being upset this thing is making Bo doubt her prophetic gift." He inhaled. "The gift doesn't operate clearly in our personal lives. Bo only saw half of the story. She knew she'd marry, but that's as far as her vision carried her. This is why we have to be careful who we share our visions with. Turns out she shared her vision early on in the prison ministry, and I think that's how Omni targeted her."

Tears streamed down Regina's face. It was too much to take in. Bo's trauma. Dewey's disappointment. Her heart clinched in her chest. This was far too much drama for one day, and she was too far away from her fiancé. She inhaled a sniffle. "Dew, where's Bo?"

"With Allegra. Couldn't stay with her mother. As you saw, Myra can be a little caustic when she's in pain. I intended to bring her home with me, but something in my spirit said *no*. Allegra will help her sister through this night."

Regina could feel Dewey's stress and agitation through the phone, which sometime aggravated his arthritis. "Why don't you light some up to help you calm down?"

"I-am-not-a-drug-addict," he hissed. "I take cannabis for my medical condition. Not when I'm angry." Dewey spit out. "And you ought to know that by now."

She shivered at his rebuke and held her breath while she waited for his next words.

Dewey drew a breath and his tone cooled. "I'm sorry, but I'm at the end. I can't sing or shout. Or take anymore. Lady, I really don't want to talk anymore. I just wish…" his voice trailed off, "I'd-a been able to come home to you."

"I'm real close to jumping in the car…"

"Don't. I need to rest my nerves, and my heart can't take worrying about you out on the road."

Regina wiped her tears away with the back of her hand. "Know that I am close in spirit. And," she lifted her voice an octave to add a ray of hopefulness to her tone, "I know from, "At the End," that when you come to the end. Pray."

"I'm so through. I can't," he whined. "Pray for us."

Good Lord. What prayer could help in this situation, and who was she to pray for God's prophet? What words could reach the emptiness in his spirit? Regina inhaled.

"Dear, Lord," she began, "first for the godly man at the head of our family."

Regina began to pray in a way she didn't think she was capable.

She petitioned the Lord for strength and clear vision. She praised God and thanked Him for the way He solved problems. And she thanked Him in advance for working things out in everyone's life. "Lord, grant Bo peace. Help her see the vision we all have for her life and happiness."

Like an intermittent windshield wiper, Dewey began to whisper, "Amen."

She prayed for protection against hoodrats and hoodlums for the girls. "And yeah, Lord, even for my sons—"

"Our sons." He interrupted. "Lord, for both of our boys."

Regina whipped her eyes and continued to pray. And when she reached the end of her words, Dewey mumbled "…refreshed, renewed, redeemed. Refreshed, renewed, redeemed." He chanted the refrain from "At The End" for several moments before saying. "Dear, Regina, in our family we do this. After prayer there is nothing else to say."

He held the phone line open while she processed his meaning.

Overnight, the news of Bo's drama made its way to all the social media outlets. By Monday morning, The Sisters Fellowship, MrsDWT3, and hashtag Step-Mama-Baby-Drama-Times-Two was trending. Social media gave no quarter and had no chill. In the case against the Lawson-Earle-Thurman family, Black Twitter remains undefeated. And Regina had to return a favor. The photographer who took those early morning pictures in Dewey's garage months ago sent her a direct message. "Calling in that favor. I need a photo from Bonita Thurman's *wedding*."

Weary from the late nights of crying and consoling, Regina poured herself a glass of wine and headed to the patio at two o'clock on Tuesday afternoon to enjoy a quiet afternoon.

"To the future."

Thank God Dewey agreed to slow down after they married. And more importantly, he promised to have his knee surgery ninety days after their wedding. His way of forcing her to set a date. It was overwhelming being engaged to DW Thurman. This week, she'd received a dozen requests for interviews, photographs, and comments. The mailbox on her phone was full and her email box was out of space. Working through the drama with their children had taken its toll. Dewey claimed he didn't see it, but her hair had grayed. And she needed to see a doctor soon about her blood pressure.

But, as of an hour ago, she was on sabbatical from the college with only one item on her agenda today. Driving to Montgomery for dinner.

"A pain shared is a pain halved." She finished her wine and closed her eye to imagine Dewey at peace, swinging beside her.

"Hmm." She exhaled, deeply relieved that the decision she made this morning was a reality. The quiet September she planned would have to wait. In truth, she never had the perfect, quiet, idyllic life she imagined. With today's issues and whatever trauma to follow, she and Dewey would get through it together.

When the phone rang, she opened her eyes only because it was Dewey's ringtone.

"Promise fulfilled." Dewey rushed the words as soon as she answered. "Allegra's going to handle the photo request and is drawing up a photo release. Bonita's wedding photo will appear on the WSOL's news feed. After that, we cannot control where else it will show up. But we can control what we do. No interviews consciously or unconsciously about Bo. And Tas claims to be on a self-imposed social media blackout for the next two weeks."

It took a moment to wrap her head around that notion.

Dewey was right. There was no way they could work out their individual and collective issues before a cyber audience. But, then again with the way Twitterverse worked, everything would most likely get paraded about in the public square.

"Lady, I'm missing you and need you. I'm torn between coming to Mobile and staying here."

"Then, I guess you don't know everything. I'm on sabbatical until next fall. I'm driving to Montgomery to have dinner with Smith this evening, and I'll be in Atlanta tomorrow by noon. I hope to give Myra and Allegra some relief and take care of you."

As December progressed every member of the Thurman-Lawson-Earle family suffered, publicly and privately. The nasty Twitter trolls and Facebook assassins tried every trick they knew to get a rise out of any member of the family. But, as a family they set a standard against anything sent to destroy their unity. Even Tasnee chilled out.

Chapter Twenty-Six

Sweet hour of prayer, sweet hour of prayer.
The secret place of peace and repair.
The height of truth is now revealed.
I sing with joy for now I'm healed.

Since she didn't have any daughters, Regina was used to being alone in the kitchen on Christmas Eve. Victor insisted on having the boys last year, so she'd spent the holidays alone. This year her little house by the sea overflowed with the blessing of family, just like she'd dreamed.

"Maybe what I called hopes and dreams were actual visions?"

Accepting her spiritual gifts came with a peace she still didn't fully understand.

"What so ever," she sang as she immersed her hands in a sink filled with cold, salty water. Swish, swish and the collard greens for Christmas had their first wash. The dirty water coursed down the drain and reminded her of how quickly things changed. The secret, double-life of some pastor in New York washed the Lawson-Thurman-Earle saga right off the front page of Gospel Gossip. Most of the sensationalism from the scandals had washed away. Things weren't fully resolved, but she knew a season of joy was on the way.

Her smile broadened as laughter from the patio reached her ears. The children were getting along famously, swapping stories about growing up. Dewey would be back from the grocery store soon and they'd join the young people and clean up any misrepresentation made about how they'd been raised.

"It is easy to get caught up in the nasty new. Driven to distraction by input and information. Tempted to quit? To lash out? Tired? At the end of your rope? What so ever it is. Stay Faithful. What so ever."

"I'm back," Dewey announced as he entered the house through the garage. "Love hearing you sing," he said and set a grocery bag on the island. Then yelled out the back door, "Malik, come help the old man get a box out of the car."

He moved over to the sink, wrapped his arms around Regina's waist and nibbled at her neck. "Why aren't those girls in here helping you? They know how to clean and cut."

She leaned into his love. "They offered, but I want to do this myself. I'm enjoying the time with my thoughts. I'm almost done. Only a few things left to do, and we should be in good shape for Christmas dinner."

Dewey moved over to the refrigerator and opened and closed the door twice. "You sure you don't need anything else."

"I think I'm good."

"I don't know. Seems like something's missing."

When his vision was unclear, Dewey tended to fret. But, she'd learned to be patient. *Whatever it is will be revealed.* She moved across the kitchen and embraced him. "Are you missing your mama?"

"We all are. But no," Dewey frowned a bit, "that's not what it is."

Another testament to the fellowship of Dewey's sister-wives. Myra, Deborah and Minnie were spending the holidays in Hawaii. The family trauma had drained Minnie's energy, so Myra planned the trip to help Mama Minnie recharge. Deborah tagged along for the fellowship and to celebrate her new house and job as a program coordinator at Moody Bible Institute.

Regina released him and moved back to the sink to finish washing the collards. This time the water ran clean through the rich green leaves. Green and clean was her hope for the holidays and the new year. Malik and Smith were repairing their relationship. Deborah's daughters were moving through the painful joy of their mother's life changes. Bonita was progressing through her heartbreak and Allegra had settled into her role as manager of The Sisters Fellowship.

"Clean and green. It is." Regina raised her hands in triumph as she settled on the theme and colors for her spring wedding.

The door slammed behind Malik as he hauled in a box from the car. "What else did you buy, old man?" Malik said as he pulled bottles out of their protective mesh sleeves. "Remy, Uncle Nearest, Royal Crown, red and white wine. Dewey's got the good stuff. This is going to be a Christmas par-t-a-y. And two bottles of champagne?"

Regina dropped the ten-pound sack of potatoes she'd just picked up and made a sharp turn. She prayed her youngest didn't catch the wanton look in her eyes.

"Take the champagne back to the car." Dewey barked his orders. "Then send Tasnee in here. Lady, what's brother John drink again?"

"Whatever you got with coke. He's never been a discriminating drinker." She glanced over at Dewey as he rearranged bottles on the rolling bar cart he'd brought home yesterday.

He stood back from his cart for a moment, then said, "I don't know. Something's missing."

Regina smirked, "I'm not sure that little wagon of yours can hold anything else and not fall apart."

"Don't you worry about that."

Tasnee slammed the door to announce her arrival. "What?"

"Baby, help Lady G peel those potatoes."

Tasnee's eyes grew larger as she considered the task. "Daddy, I just got my nails done."

Dewey picked up the peeler on the island and placed it in her freshly-manicured hands.

"Ugh," she complained.

"Lady, are you sure I got everything?"

Her eyebrows furrowed as she looked again at the overstocked bar trolley. "Looks okay."

"But?"

"Where's the Tanqueray?" She shook her head. "No. We don't need that. T-n-T was Vic's drink when we were coming up."

Dewey said, "Okay, then I'm-ma get some T when we go out for the pizza. And I wish I'd ordered more eggnog."

New family tradition. Dewey shared how the Thurmans always had pizza on Christmas Eve. Growing up, a pizza rose to the level of a Christmas present for Dewey and his deceased older brother. Mother Minnie would take a bus to the other side of Atlanta to pick up the Christmas Eve treat for her sons. The Thurmans also only ate, drank, and fellowshipped on Christmas Day.

She was in charge of the food and Dewey the beverages. She'd intended to sit and peel with Tasnee, but maybe Dewey need to talk. Regina wiped her hands on her apron before taking it off.

"Tas, why don't you do half of these, then pass the rest to your sister?"

"Which one?"

"You choose. I'm going to ride to the store with your dad."

⁓

Late Christmas morning Regina exhaled and relaxed on the patio with Dewey. So far, a lovely holiday. Santa Dewey had showered them all with too many presents. She had no idea where to put the three-foot angel statue he gave her. Dinner was at three, but she was already stuffed. Bonita and Calista had played chef for breakfast. She should have joined the girls for their walk on the beach to work off those Belgium waffles. Instead she sat on the patio sipping more calories. Spiked Christmas coffee, courtesy of bartender Dew.

"Dew, I've got to get up in a minute and finish dinner."

He looked up at the sound of a car engine. "Aw, relax, Regina. Dinner can wait another minute. I think I'll have a second cup. Want one?"

"Nope, if I drink anymore of your coffee, dinner's going be ruined. But, I'm happy to sit with you for a little while longer. The quiet is nice."

For the past three days with nine adults in residence, the house had been an absolute zoo. She prayed their children walked more than a mile.

Dewey turned his head as another car passed. Since they'd been sitting, he looked up expectantly every time he heard a car pass. It was almost as if he expected someone. But Rena's family wasn't due until after two.

"Yes, I'm enjoying the quiet. And you're wrong for putting the children out of the house."

"What?" She giggled like a schoolgirl. "The girls wanted to take a walk on the beach. The boys decided to join them. Besides, I sensed you needed some quiet time. Are you sure you don't have something on your heart or mind?"

"Um, not sure," he rubbed his head, "but nothing I want to speak on. Yet. And I can't play it through. If we're going to keep this house you're going to have to give up a room for me to have a piano."

"You know that's not possible."

As well as everything had come together for them, they had a few sticky points. Her haven—her little house by the ocean—didn't have space for his instruments. Hosting this holiday had proven that this house wasn't big enough for their blended family. She'd call a realtor early next year and start looking for that dream house across the bay.

Dewey took in a breath of fresh sea air. "I can't shake this feeling that something is about to happen."

Regina nodded. "I noticed."

"It's a Christmas miracle. You've accepted your gift of observation."

She had acknowledged and accepted the wisdom of observation that came with age. Along with the duty to speak up in love to try and prevent heartache and disaster for those she loved. Or anyone else who'd listen.

"Is it more trouble, Dew?"

"How can I say what I'm not clearly seeing? It's one of those things that can go either way."

Her light buzz faded as she attempted to decode his message. It would probably take the rest of her life to fully embrace the mystery of Dewey's gift. But it was getting a little easier, every day. Instead of questioning, she'd practice patience and wait it out. "I'm going to start dinner."

∾

For the most part, the family enjoyed a food and beverage-fueled Christmas day. Rena's family arrived at three and added more cheer. The highlight of the afternoon was watching the Soul-Centered Network's Thurman Family Christmas sing-a-long. Tasnee posted a couple of *approved* videos of their antics, which immediately trended. Everyone seemed to have a good time. Except for Dewey. He wasn't settled or sober.

As the afternoon wore on, every now and then, Dewey looked out the window. Calista and Bonita quietly took turns keeping watch with their father. The other girls just went on with their holiday. But,

Dewey's behavior made Rena nervous. Every time he went to the window, she asked, "Are you expecting someone?"

After the tenth time, Regina said, "Just let it go."

Allegra looked up from a book she was reading with Rena's grandbaby and winked. Bo took Aunt Rena aside to explain how best to deal with Dewey's state.

Praise the Lord.

After weeks of mourning, Bonita had begun to move forward. Bo's experience even helped Regina learn to live with the slightly spooky stuff. Other than spending some time in prayer earlier, Rev. Bonita seemed to enjoy the holiday. Another Christmas miracle. Their Bo was broken, but mending. Dewey had dedicated a special praise song to her last week.

What can God do with broken pieces?
Consider the mosaic of a stained-glass window.
Broken pieces turned into a masterpiece.
There's beauty in repair.

In their private devotions, Dewey and Regina praised the Lord for crafting a seven-panel stained glass window from the broken pieces of each of their children's lives. A masterpiece that would perpetually be under construction. And each time a little glass was broken, they'd experience the pain that comes with loving. But after the Master finished his handiwork, they'd glory in the beauty of the repair. Together.

Shortly after six, the Christmas cheer caught up with Dewey, and he began to nod. Regina was just about to nudge him when the doorbell rang. The sound pulled Dewey out of his stupor. He popped up and hurried with her to the front door.

"I just hoped to see the Angels."

Regina froze for a moment before turning her face into Dewey's shoulder. Her ex-husband was the last person she expected to show up on her doorstep today. After she took a few deep breaths, Dewey nudged her and she turned to face Victor.

"Please come in and behold your sons. And meet my daughters," Dewey shouted.

Regina caught a hitch in her heart as she beheld the Christmas miracle. "Merry Christmas, Vic. I'll call the boys."

Dewey extended his right hand and a huge welcoming smile, then embraced Victor with a one-armed-handshake bro-hug. "Welcome with one caveat," he slurred. "She's mine."

"I understand and thank you, sir."

Before calling the boys, Regina took a quick assessment of Victor. It seemed the man had lost some of his commanding presence. It took a measure of humility for her ex-husband to ring the bell, and she wondered how long he'd sat in front of the house before ringing. A wave of understanding washed over her and she exhaled. This was the visitor Dewey expected. And instead of trying to figure out how he knew what he knew, she decided to be graceful. She winked at Dewey, grateful that he'd prepared her for this moment.

"Allow me." Dewey flashed his showman's smile and he reached for Victor's jacket. "And if I may suggest, asking the boys to join you in the study. We got a fresh bottle of Tanqueray and, Lady," he turned to Regina, "will you warm the pots up. I'm sure Victor's hungry, and we got plenty."

When Victor cleared his throat to protest, Regina held up a warning finger and bobbed her head in agreement.

"Thank you, thank you both."

"Dad? Thought I heard your voice." Malik Earle raced into the foyer. Smith followed a few steps behind.

"Merry Christmas, Dad."

To give the Earle men some privacy, Dewey ambled back into the den to share the glad tidings with the girls. She backed away and hurried to the kitchen to catch Rena.

∞

"Oh, that's just too freaky," Rena exclaimed. "I don't believe it. How'd Dewey know Vic was coming here. Are you sure the boys didn't call their father?"

"No." Regina shook her head. "I can tell by looking at him that Vic barely knows what led him here today. He hasn't been near this house in years. And, Rena, please don't start anything. It took a lot for Victor to come here today. Let's keep the peace. It's Christmas."

"This ain't peace." Rena huffed. "Dewey got us all three sheets to the wind. Ain't nobody sober enough to start no mess."

"Then I'm grateful for the grace of the spirits. Dewey has redefined Christmas cheer. If this is how the Thurmans drink on Christmas," Regina inhaled, "I'm glad he's not working any more this year. I don't think Dew will be fit until the middle of January."

"Amen. Let me finish fixing this little plate for John. He needs to put some more food on his stomach. So I don't have to start arguing with him. We all know how he gets when he's full."

Regina winced. "Vic's talking to the boys in the study now. Can you come back and help me warm up the food after you take John his plate? And ask Allegra if she can get her father to go lay down somewhere."

∞

An hour later, Victor popped his head into the kitchen. "Merry Christmas, Rena. Dewey said you might have some greens left?"

"Merry Christmas, Victor. We sure do. And Regina put her foot in Mama's dressing recipe. We got it all warmed up and ready. Come sit down. I'll fix your plate and leave room for dessert. I saved you the last slice of pound cake. And Regina made a red velvet cake, too."

"Whew, y'all going to have to roll me out of here." Victor moved into the kitchen and accepted a holiday hug from his ex-sister-in-law.

Between bites of his overflowing Christmas dinner plate. Victor provided an update on his life. He was almost divorced and soon retired.

"Unbeknownst to me, the management committee began meeting on the golf course on Sunday mornings. Because they knew I'd be in church. Those good ole boys finally got that opening they'd been looking for. I finally got outplayed. They presented my resignation letter last week. I'm on vacation until the end of the year. After all those years. Out. No gold watch or celebration. Just like that." He snapped his fingers. "Remember how we used to talk about having a big party, and I would say it would be your party, too, because you were the secret to my success."

Regina nodded in remembrance.

"Regina worked as hard as you did to get into that C-suite." Rena signified.

Victor nodded. "You're right. I have come to understand and appreciate that."

Rena passed Regina a bit of side-eye, then said, "I'm so proud of my little sister. Dr. Lawson's crafted quite a career for herself. Speaking engagements all over the country, and a book coming out next year."

"Yes, I know," Victor agreed. "I'm proud of her, too. Mama said you're making a ton of money selling people the common sense that used to be free. And she's so happy for you. Regina, will you please send her an autographed book? I'll pay you for it. Matter of fact, send fifty signed copies to the real estate office. We'll put one in every unit."

"Okay, will do. But, Evelyn knows she's on the pre-release list. Some of that everyday wisdom comes from her."

"She didn't tell me all that. I'm glad you two never lost contact."

"Your mother wouldn't abide by that. You know what family means to her."

Victor looked down at his half-finished plate. "Now that I'm at this crossroad and have had a lot of time to think about it. I, too, realize the importance of family. I've made mistakes. Now here I am with nothing to do and no one to do it with."

"You don't believe that," Regina challenged. Even though his family had come down hard on him, there was forgiveness in the Earle family. Evelyn Earle wouldn't have that any other way either.

"I know. I'll always have family and the frat."

They sat silently while Victor finished his dinner. And just before the atmosphere turned stale. Rena suggested he look up Angela Wilson.

"Rena, you are a mess." Regina hooted. "Lord, Angela Wilson. Why'd you bring her up?"

"Because she always wanted Vic and," Rena pointed at Victor, "I recall your saying she was a fine-looking woman."

Victor looked up with a little shame in his eyes. "There is no way I could ever call Angela. Her life is a mess. Not, that I have any room to talk. Her oldest son is in and out of jail and her daughters are a bunch of baby mamas. She's constantly before the church board with some request to help her family through another self-imposed crisis. Besides, she's mad at me because we," he waved his index finger between himself and Regina, "turned her down for a rental house last year. Malik dodged a bullet there."

Regina joined in. "I remember Malik's senior year in high school. I worked double-time trying to keep Angela away from you and Malik away from Angela's daughter. That girl had her heart set on

Malik. I'm glad we went ahead and sent him to Tuscaloosa early. If he hadn't started at Alabama that summer, I think she might have got him."

Regina moved to the counter to cut Victor a piece of pound cake. The little blessing their mother taught them was still a family tradition. People always felt better when you told them you saved the last piece of cake for them.

Rena cried, "Praise the Lord and cut me a sliver of that cake, too."

Regina wiped her hands with a dish towel and sent up a silent praise. This was something she never expected to see again. Rena and Victor bantering across the kitchen table.

"Vic, would you like coffee with your cake. Or Dewey had some excellent eggnog shipped in from Chicago. You should try it. And there's a full bar in the den. I can go get you something."

"No, thank you. Just more water for me, please. And if it's all right, Dewey asked me to join him and John on the porch for some Christmas cheer. You don't mind if I stay, do you?"

"Of course not. We're just one big, happy family enjoying the holiday. But, don't let Dewey pour your drink. He has a heavy hand."

Chapter Twenty-Seven

Press on ever onwards look forward to light
Ever onward, upward towards a better day
Upward always ever is the praise song for today.

Regina stretched and yawned before she began sorting plates and glasses. Time to wash yet another load of dishes. Around nine everyone came through the kitchen for round two. Her kitchen was another mess, and she couldn't be happier. Between the meeting, eating, and greeting, it had been quite a holiday. There had also been a lot of drinking. Dewy had been three sheets to the wind since noon. He'd even garnered sufficient liquid courage to play horse at the park. The video Tasnee took of Dewey's antics on the basketball court was perfect for *America's Funniest Home Videos*.

Regina sighed and prayed. Hopefully, Dewey's knees would hold out until midnight. She was dog-tired and as soon as that tour bus pulled away, she was going to get into bed and not move for the next two days. She considered asking the boys to help, but they'd half do and she'd have to wash the holiday dishes a second time before storing them. Maybe she should have asked the girls to clean the kitchen, but in a way, they were first time guests. Best to let the sisters enjoy themselves today, since they were back to work tomorrow.

The Sisters Fellowship was leaving at midnight to travel to Baton Rouge. Another gift: Dewey was sending Smith and Malik on the Kwanzaa tour with them. The tour would stop for the balance of the week in Lake Charles to conduct a series of youth choir workshops. Then onto Houston to participate in a live watch-night-service on WSOL.

"May I help you with the dishes?"

Regina startled at the unfamiliar request. The Lord truly worked in mysterious ways. Victor Earle actually offering to help with the dishes?

"Sure, thanks. Can you get the plates rinsed and loaded?"

They worked in near silence for almost twenty minutes. The music of kitchen collaboration, complimented by a driving beat from the den. Tasnee and Malik were beat boxing. Everyone else freestyle rapping and in between songs, Dewey argued with them about their lyrics. She happily stayed in the kitchen to avoid Dewey's favorite friendly argument.

Regina worked around Victor, emptying and consolidating containers for the leftovers. When the trash can filled, she began to tie up the overflowing trash bag.

"I'll get that," he offered. "I should have helped you more."

"I appreciate your saying that."

While Victor took yet another bag of trash outside, Regina started the dishwasher.

Best Christmas ever.

Despite the social media headlines and the memes, they'd all endured. Grown stronger. Closer. As her mother would say, "Look at God."

Regina grinned. Their family was healing. The broken places were slowly being made whole. In time they'd emerge stronger. She definitely had to incorporate a piece of stained glass art into their new home, when she found it.

"Whatsoever," she sang.

"What's that?" Victor asked as he closed the back door.

"Oh, nothing. It's a new song Dewey and the girls are working on. And, I think Malik is going to produce a spoken word segment on the track."

"Wow, that's great." Victor sat at one of the high chairs around the kitchen island. "Regina, I can't tell you how mightily sorry I am about—"

"Don't. It's all right. And I don't want to rehash anything. We're just looking forward to the new year and what-so-ever happens we're going to trust in the Lord."

"Amen, but I'm still sorry for the hurt I caused."

Regina nodded and sat opposite him. They sat across the kitchen island and had an honest discussion about life, health, and the future.

Victor grimaced. "Christmas morning in an empty house with my bruised ego. I realized that I'd lost the one thing of real value in life. My family. Not the job I neglected you all for. Not the positions I held in the church, fraternity, or community. In all my getting, I failed to get understanding, and I lost my good wife and almost lost my sons." Victor took off his glasses and rubbed his eyes. "All I could think about was how badly I wanted to see my sons and those angels for Christmas. I'm glad you put them out this year. The guardians on the driveway were like a sign when I turned the corner. They gave me the courage to ring the bell."

Regina only nodded. She had no words and took no pleasure in her ex-husband's pain. "It took some work getting them out this year. And I think I finally agree with you. I may have too many."

In every room of the house, her angels joyfully heralded a new season for her family. Today, she added six more. Rena had blessed her with five brightly colored fabric angels decked out in colors and fabrics that reflected each girl's personality. And she had no idea what to do with the cherub statue Dewey gave her.

"Well, I enjoyed seeing them all. And meeting the new angels in your life."

"Yes, the girls are wonderful."

"You always wanted a daughter, and now you've got five."

Regina glowed. "I love them all. It's like that blessing so big there isn't room to receive it."

Victor cast his glance downward.

"I'm sure you'll find someone to share your life with."

"I don't know being twice-divorced."

"It's possible for a twice-divorced man to find someone. Ask Dewey."

"He's a great man. I've actually been listening to his music lately. For some reason, it felt familiar. I've found some solace in DW Thurman's songs. It's not just the music, but his lyrics. "At the End" really pulled me back from the edge. And now refreshed, renewed, redeemed is my daily prayer chant."

"If you are comfortable, it would bless Dewey to hear you say that."

Victor nodded. "Well, favor certainly found you. I can't get over how calm and confident you are now. You and the boys are doing great things. Dewey told me about the BMA college tour that you are doing in the Fall. That's awesome."

Things were in a good place for the boys, too. Malik was graduating in May, and Smith's network had stepped up their support for him. His hall was booked through to next December with fraternity meetings, weddings and church socials. And the caterer from his grand opening had just signed a three-year lease for the commercial kitchen. Things were going so well he'd decided to take a few years off from the law.

"I'll make sure to ask Malik how he wants to celebrate his

graduation. If you'll let me host that blessed event. And if you agree, I want to talk to Smith about taking over the business."

Regina froze, running Earle Holdings was Vic's retirement dream. For him to give it all over to Smith was a significant step. "I think that's an excellent idea."

"Of course, I'll want to stick around for the first month or so to transition. And I'm thinking about going on the fraternity's golf tour in February. I've made plans to keep busy in retirement. And some day if it's possible, maybe I'll look for a more mature woman to spend some time with."

"Angela will take your call," she teased.

Victor laughed. "No way. Not that I have any room to talk. But, I don't want or need any more drama in this life. You know that's trouble and Rena ain't right for bringing her up. When I'm ready. Maybe I'll meet someone who's been married before. A lady whose husband didn't appreciate her. Should I be ashamed to say I think I want someone that knows how to take care of a man?"

"No, I think that's fair."

"I want what I had," he nodded and paused, "but I know I can never have what I messed up."

Regina hoped her smile didn't look too much like a gloat. "Why don't you just let the Lord lead you? I definitely didn't see my life turning out like this. I never dreamed I'd remarry."

"And please believe me when I say I wish you every happiness. How heavy is that rock on your hand?"

Regina extended her hand and Victor reached across the expanse of the island to admire her engagement ring.

"Oh no! No, my brother. Hold up. I ain't going to have this. This ain't New Year's Eve. And ain't going to be no auld or lang syne, up in here," Dewey shouted.

Victor quickly released her hand and stood.

Regina laughed at the impish grin on Dewey's lips and reached out for him.

"That's something I didn't see. My Lady in the kitchen holding hands with another man." Dewey tsked and hobbled into the kitchen.

Victor Earle stood straight. "I was just congratulating the angel of this house on your engagement."

"Thank you," Dewey said. "She is an angel."

With that agreement, Dewey pulled out a stool. "Lady, I really don't need to put one more bite in my mouth, but can you give me a small sliver of that pound cake and a strong cup of coffee."

"Yes, Dew. Are you sure you're okay?"

"I got a few hours left. But as soon as we see that bus off, I'm done."

"I hear you. Vic, would you like coffee, too?"

"No, ma'am. But, if I'm welcome to stay awhile longer, I think I'd like to try some of that eggnog everybody's raving about. But just a little. I have overindulged."

Dewey laughed. "We all have, but I think it was in order. We've been through it in the last few months."

Regina poured their drinks and listened as Dewey and Victor chatted about Smith's future.

"Well, I hope to have a real estate transaction for Smith to close soon. And I'm never playing basketball with him again."

Victor laughed. "He's always been competitive."

"Yeah," Dewey grumbled. "I call it cheating."

"That, too." Victor affirmed and took a sip of eggnog. "Man, that's good."

As Dewey casually chatted with her ex-husband, Regina marveled at his grace. He's the only man she knew who would welcome an ex-husband as a brother. She hoped Victor experienced the same warmth today that she'd felt when Minnie welcomed her into Deborah's home. Because of Dewey's faith, they'd enjoy an extraordinary family in the future, and she couldn't wait for that tour bus to arrive so they could put every one of them out.

"I know I said it outside, but thank you again for taking Malik under your arm. He's made great progress at Morehouse. I reviewed his business plan and it's solid."

Dewey grinned. "Yes, he worked on that with our Allegra. But for the final test, I asked my first wife, Myra, to make sure it's airtight. She's a shark. She's represented me for years and has never lost a case on my behalf. I'll let you know what Myra says, then we can fight over who will be Malik's first investor."

Victor nodded. "I'll look forward to that debate."

As the three of them sat around the island talking, the house seemed to grow silent. "I don't know why they're resting up to get on a bus. These young people are a true mystery," Dewey said.

Regina smiled. "If I know the boys, they're trying to lay low so I don't call them in to sweep and mop this kitchen."

Victor and Dewey both looked around the spotless kitchen. The hum of the dishwasher carried the silence.

"Well, thank you again for the hospitality," Victor said. "It did my heart good to see the angels, old and new. But I missed one. Gina, where's the black angel?"

"They all black ain't they," Dewey cried. "I mean I questioned the features of some of them light-brites. But, don't tell me there's more. There's so many black angels watching over us in this whole house, Regina's got me kind-a, sort-a, freaked out. Everywhere I go, inside and out. Angels watching over me. And those two Nubian warrior, archangels guarding the driveway. Those brothers are something."

Victor and Regina exploded in laughter. Victor held his side as he caught his breath, then pushed out, "Where she at?"

"Ugh, I don't put her out anymore. You're the only one that could stand to look at that ole-ugly thing."

Dewey looked between them with a questioning gaze. "Let me in on the joke?"

Regina reached out for Dewey's hand and explained. "The black angel was given to the Earle family by a seemingly well-meaning white woman I met when the boys were playing club baseball."

"Dewey, you know the type." Victor took over the explanation. "Nice-white lady who assumed because I never showed up for games or practices that Regina was a single mom. So, she took us on as a charity project. Always trying to give the boys some handoffs. Or offering a ride to and from practice. Provided that Regina could bring the boys to her house. If you get my meaning."

"Yes." Dewey chuckled. "I get it."

"Anyway," Regina continued, "because she was 'nice' she felt she could question me about everything I had. From the car I drove to where my money came from, and the angel necklace I always wear. She didn't quite believe my diamond was real, because she'd never seen a brown one."

Victor picked up the story again. "After she learned that Regina liked black angels, she found this thing—something made in China for black folk, because we'll allegedly buy anything. This squat-ole, ugly, fat mammie-looking, black ceramic winged thing with huge blue eyes. And when I say black—I don't mean African-American. This thing is tar-baby black."

Regina twisted her lips. "I hated it. After sitting with me through two seasons of baseball and meeting our family, she thought that was an acceptable gift? I only brought it home to show Vic how ridiculous it was."

"And I insisted we keep it as a lesson to the boys about the soft bigotry of," Victor lifted his fingers in air quotes, "well-meaning white folks."

"I got to see this mess." Dewey grinned. "Do you still have it?"

She nodded slowly.

"Why don't you go find it while Vic and I take ourselves to the den. I need to put my legs up."

Christmas ended just as Dewey foresaw, in the quiet warmth of love and fellowship. Their unusual blended family laughing, singing Christmas carols, and fellowshipping in the den.

Chapter Twenty-Eight

There is Joy After

Regina Lawson twirled like a teenager in her first prom dress. Within the hour she'd marry her *everlasting love.* The mellow cream-colored lace gown fit beautifully. Thanks to Spanx and her talented dress designer in Atlanta. Despite the obvious age on her face and the streak of gray in her hair, she was as excited as any first-time bride. Giddy.

"Rena, I really appreciate your keeping up with the work on our house while we are away."

"No problem. Don't worry, and I won't call you unless it's something major."

Regina Lawson's vision for her dream house had evolved. The renovations on the nine-bedroom home she and Dewey purchased two months ago were over budget and behind schedule. DW Thurman required space for two pianos and a music production studio. Her new house slept twenty and had a chef's kitchen. She'd need every inch of that counter space to prep and serve meals for their brood.

"And please remember when the drapes come for the studio, don't accept them unless they are a real-regal-purple befitting the Crown

Prince of Gospel Music. If they aren't right, send them back. And I will deal with it when we get home."

The soundproofing for the studio and theatre curtains were her wedding gift to Dewey.

"I got you."

As of last month, DW Thurman was semi-retired with plans to record and produce videos from his new state-of-the-art home studio. She prayed her husband would quickly settle into his new creative spaces. There were still songs to be written and artists to mentor.

"And, don't you dare cook a thing in my new kitchen." Regina repeated an instruction she knew her sister wouldn't listen to.

"Come on, let me christen it for you?"

"Don't you dare. Dewey and I will christen every room in that house when we move in, and he's able."

Rena clapped her hands in joy. "I've created a monster."

Regina spun around in front of the mirror and grinned.

"You look beautiful," Rena said. "But, will you please sit and let me finish. Once I put this flower in your hair, that's it. You'll be ready."

The September bride princess sat in front of the full length mirror in the honeymoon suite of the Mobile Hilton. Her stylist Vernice finished dressing her hair half an hour ago and all she needed now was the finishing touch. Rena had insisted on placing the flower in her hair, since she'd chosen not to wear a veil. No mystery or anything hidden on either side. Both she and Dewy knew what they were getting.

"I feel like a June bride."

"Then let me give you some marriage advice from Mama, young lady."

"Can I stop you?"

Rena smoothed her hair back and tucked a magnolia into the

chignon bun. "Mama would be real proud to be here today. This flower is in her memory. And I want you to always keep a little money in a can for yourself."

"That's what she told me the first time." Regina laughed and paused for a moment to reflect. "I remember your marriage advice, too."

The sisters giggled as they flashed back to Regina's first wedding day when Rena suggested she get a little freaky on her wedding night.

"Same advice applies, but go easy. You don't want to spend your honeymoon in the ER." Rena patted her lovingly on the shoulders. "You're ready for the pictures. By the way, in case you missed it. Allegra's been chatting up that photographer the SOL network sent since last night."

"Oh, I saw it. Remember I have the gift of observation. Those two seem to have hit it off."

"I still don't understand why you insisted on hiring that rude young man."

Regina stood and twisted before the mirror until she could see the flower in her hair. "I like him. He does really good work, and he's proven to be trustworthy. He will know which photos to leak out on social media."

"Oh, he's the one who caught you creepin'. I'm so glad you listened to me and allowed yourself to fall in love with Dewey."

"No, Rena." She slowly moved her head so the flower would not shift out of place. "I didn't fall in love with Dewey. I walked into this love with a clear mind and Dewey opened my heart. For a heart left ajar, love is well come."

"Dewey's going to flip when you come down the aisle singing."

In a twist, Regina planned to surprise her fiancé by singing Natalie Cole's "This Will be an Everlasting Love" to him as she walked down the aisle.

"I can't wait to see the expression on his face." Regina admired herself again. "I'm ready."

"Okay, I'll let your photographer in and see you out there."

Regina Lawson drew in a deep breath in the last moments she'd have to herself today. Their plans were set. A month-long honeymoon cruise followed by four months in Atlanta for Dewey's knee surgery and recovery. While he rehabbed, she planned to finish her book and in September, they'd move into their dream house. And in the fullness of time, they'd sit on the porch swing surrounded by their grandchildren.

Epilogue

Forty years ago, I had a vision of being the bridegroom on a beach with his sons. After my first church wedding I doubted the vision. I was young and immature. When I married a second time in a hurry-up courthouse ceremony, I knew my actions had hindered what the Lord had planned for me. After five daughters, I put the prophecy of sons in the box with the beach wedding. I never understood why this vision never came to pass, yet never faded. Now I know. I was leaning on my own understanding.

Today, the Bridegroom waits on the beach with his sons.
Where I will sing and dance with my September Love.
Slow and relaxing on a Sunday afternoon.
Smooth and refreshing as a song from my youth.

The End

About the Author

In 2004 Regena made a pact with her nephew, "…if you give me a college degree, I'll write a book." Today, her nephew's college diploma graces the mantle of her suburban Chicago home, and she is the author of five contemporary women's fiction novels with Christian and romantic elements.

Except on Sunday — Can she love him; except on Sunday?
Believe In Me — In ninety days she'll have to choose between love and loyalty.
Love's Remnant — After all, love remains.
Grace Changes Everything — A misfit minister, a questioning chemist, and one simple truth.
The September Standard — Will she fall into a quiet season or spring forward with Joy?

Regena's novels explore the complex simplicity of falling in love—in these complicated days. Regena's honors include Debut Author of the Year, Shades of Romance Magazine and 2017 finalist, Illinois Soon to be Famous Author Project. Visit her at www.RegenaBryant.com or @Regena_Bryant on twitter.

CPSIA information can be obtained
at www.ICGtesting.com
Printed in the USA
BVHW070313301121
622779BV00007B/415

9 780990 578086